BLACK
BLOOD

BLACK BLOOD

JANE EDDIE

The Book Guild Ltd

First published in Great Britain in 2019 by
The Book Guild Ltd
9 Priory Business Park
Wistow Road, Kibworth
Leicestershire, LE8 0RX
Freephone: 0800 999 2982
www.bookguild.co.uk
Email: info@bookguild.co.uk
Twitter: @bookguild

Typeset in 12pt Adobe Jenson Pro

Printed and bound in the UK by TJ International, Padstow, Cornwall

ISBN 978 1913208 066

British Library Cataloguing in Publication Data.
A catalogue record for this book is available from the British Library.

To everyone who helped and believed in me.

Chapter One

Christmas Day

She struggled to open her eyes, to shake off that groggy feeling, that moment between sleep and waking where reality is conflicted. But this was more than just waking from a bad dream. She tried to pull herself free from whatever was holding her in this trance-like state. It was like swimming in molasses, pulling free only to be dragged back under. Where was she? Her surroundings did not feel familiar. She could hear voices, soft, whispering, but could not make out what was being said or to whom the voices belonged. Wherever she was, she knew she was in danger; it was instinctive, even though she couldn't recall what that danger was. She felt paralysed, trapped between consciousness and subconsciousness. She knew she had to shake herself out of this and she had to do it soon.

Her eyelids fluttered and for a few brief seconds she could make out nothing more than bright white lights. She could hear the hypnotic, rhythmical bleep of a machine. *Was that a life support monitor?* It sounded clinical, like every bleep was an acknowledgement of life continuing, of blood continuing to pump around her body. *But that was a good thing, surely.* She was alive, even though she was torn between two parallel universes.

She continued to battle the forces of subconsciousness, the fingers of darkness clawing at her body to keep her in their world. But she was strong, and she knew she could fight them. After all, she had been fighting for the past few years. And she had a secret to tell, but who could she trust?

Chapter Two

Three months earlier

D anni closed the flat door behind her, pulled the collar of her coat up, tightened the purple wool scarf around her neck and pulled her matching bobble hat down over her ears. The temperature was dropping and she could see her breath in the cold morning air. The grey granite of the buildings, married with the grey skies, made the day seem more depressing than normal. She stuffed her hands in her pockets, dropped her head into the wind and started to make her way down Esslemont Avenue. The leaves had fallen from the trees and the pavement was slippery with a covering of frost, the tell-tale signs that winter was fast approaching. Rows of satellite dishes clung to the sides of the buildings she walked past, pointing to the sky as though they were drawing the winter towards them.

Danni made her way to the office where she worked as a legal assistant. She had been a promising trainee corporate lawyer before she was forced to flee her life in London, a life that had seemed perfect to others looking in, and one that had once also seemed perfect to Danni. That was before he started to hit her. To control her. To make her feel worthless and ugly. She had escaped from Mark just over a year ago, but he was a detective inspector with the Metropolitan Police and she was sure he was still looking for her. After all, he was one of those detectives that always got his man and never gave up on a case. That had been one of the things she used to love about him, his persistence and determination. She had found it endearing. But to him, Danni was now just another case to close. Permanently. He had told her what he would do to her if she tried to leave him and she didn't doubt that he meant every word he said. But for now, she felt she was safe.

She had moved to Aberdeen, the other end of the country, and had kept a low profile. She closed her Facebook account, wanting to remain off the radar. She had managed to secure a job working for one of the oil majors, but the downturn had seen her moved sideways and then downwards if she wanted to keep working. Now she was barely holding on to a job as a legal assistant, although glorified dogsbody seemed a more appropriate title, as the legal work was practically non-existent. She was not unattractive, with shoulder-length mousy-brown hair and entrancing green eyes. Her pale complexion and freckles across her cheeks gave her an elfin appearance and made her look younger than her thirty-something years. She was single, but that was through choice. She was not ready to enter into another relationship. She didn't trust herself to make the right choice after Mark.

Since moving to Aberdeen, her job was continually at risk, with redundancies prevalent throughout the city on an almost daily basis as the industry continued in turmoil. If no-one saw the oil price crash of 2014 coming, then they certainly could not have predicted what was to happen several years later. The industry had failed to learn from the lessons of the past. Yet again, it gleefully stuck its fingers in its ears and sang, "La-la-la, I can't hear you!" The production cuts by OPEC, driven by Saudi Arabia and emulated by Russia, drove the price of oil back to a point where oil companies started spending like there was no tomorrow, and acting like the price would continue to increase. How short were their memories? Their greed drove them to extract the black blood that ran through the very veins of the earth at any cost, sucking the life not just from the planet but from those who worked in the industry too.

It was difficult to put a figure on it, but the media suggested that around 150,000 had lost their jobs during the previous downturn, with only a fraction of those being re-employed. Many left, vowing never to return. Those who had remained in employment were made to feel fortunate that they had jobs and were now doing the work of at least two people, with the added stress that that piled upon them. And, whilst pay had begun to creep up, they were now working for a fraction of the salaries they had enjoyed during the heyday. Danni was one of the lucky ones, or unlucky, depending on how you viewed it. She had a job.

The fall-out from Brexit had seen sanctions lifted on Russia by the British government. The UK's oil and gas trade was worth £73 billion a year, but the inability to negotiate constructive trade agreements with the European Union had led to discussions with Russia, who were only too willing to help. They bought up oil licences from the UK majors who were desperate to get out in favour of more economic projects, even though their stock response to any redundancies announced was 'their continued commitment to the North Sea'. Nobody believed this, and it was only a matter of time until they sold out. The only question was who to and at what cost? Aberdeen, once known as the Granite City, had now been nicknamed Little Moscow. Polish accents had once been common in the city, but since Brexit most of the Europeans had returned to their homeland and been replaced by the Russians.

Since the Russians took over the company Danni worked for, she had gradually been side-lined from any actual legal work and spent most of her time in the file room. She didn't mind, it kept her away from the office politics and the daily grind; plus she could plug in her headphones and listen to the local radio station through her mobile, which helped to pass the time. The station played mainly '80s music, but that was all right, she had grown up listening to that and the heavy, repetitive *doof, doof, doof* of today's music did nothing for her.

Danni had once enjoyed her work, well, as much as anyone actually enjoys work. She felt that she had a purpose in life. There had been a positive energy when you walked through the door. That had now been replaced by a dark cloud that had held its position over all those that worked in the city. The mood was now sombre and one of desperation. Desperation to get out, to find a better way to live, but where else was there to go? Since this latest downturn in the industry, Aberdeen had become desolate. Once the oil capital of Europe, the city's grey granite buildings now reflected and spawned the overwhelming feeling of depression.

The oil crash not only affected those working in the industry but all those across the city. Once thriving restaurants, clubs and bars, hosting Aberdeen's oil workers and their no-expense-spared lifestyles, they had now closed their doors for the last time. Every week another hostelry shut up shop, unable to break-even, never mind turn a profit. It was somewhat ironic. Churches that had lost their flocks had been sold and turned into pubs and nightclubs where the flocks had returned, albeit of a different nature, and worshipped a different God, with the familiar evils of greed, gluttony, pride and lust. But now the tables had turned again and the buildings, once hosts to mindless spending and pleasure, were now a refuge for the increasing number of the jobless, homeless and desperate of Aberdeen. Those queuing to get in were no longer there to have a good time, but perversely to get hand-outs from the foodbanks and charities that had been set up within the once-hallowed walls. Union Street was fast becoming a ghost town.

She made her way down past the Grammar school where mothers were already dropping off their children on their way to work. The stay-at-home wives who had done well living off their husbands' excessive salaries had been seen round town driving their Chelsea tractors. But nowadays it was a different story, as they could no longer afford their extravagant lifestyles; their Audi Q5s and Porsche Cayennes were returned to the respective dealers, the cars left on the forecourt and keys posted back through the letterbox in the dead of night to avoid the walk of shame into the showroom to return them. Those same stay-at-home wives were now frantically looking for work as their husbands' pay cheques had decreased, or disappeared, and they were now driving second-hand Vauxhalls and Fords, with the unlucky ones having to rely on Shanks's pony. The Grammar, being a state-run secondary school, had seen pupil numbers rise over the past year as parents had to pull their children from the private schools, like Robert Gordon's and Albyn, no longer able to afford the fees. Every penny was now a prisoner. The Grammar was the next best thing, being rated the second-best state school in Aberdeen behind Cults Academy. But Cults Academy's halo had slipped in the past following the fatal stabbing of a pupil on the premises. Unfortunately, this had been a sign of things to come.

Danni waited for the green man at the traffic lights and crossed Skene Street on to Rose Street, then turned left down Huntly Street and onwards to Union Street. She walked past the boarded-up shop fronts and beauty salons. Those shops that could afford to had moved into the empty units in one of Aberdeen's previously booming shopping centres, St Nicholas, Bon-Accord, Trinity Centre and Union Square. This had been the only way to avoid the continuing circle of smashed windows and raided stock, with their round-the-clock security guards and CCTV. The vacated main street shops were replaced by charity shops, pawnbrokers and bookies. Ramsdens and the Money Shop had opened up down the street from the jewellery shops of Jamieson and Carries, and Goldsmiths. They were doing a roaring trade paying peanuts for the expensive jewellery that had been showered on wives and girlfriends during the good times. Bookies positioned themselves next door, hoping to relieve the patrons of their slim takings and any remaining self-respect. Gambling their pawn money in the hope of just one big win to get them by.

Danni walked past the queues of people that snaked down Union Street waiting for the foodbanks to open. If they didn't get there early then they would get nothing, as supplies continued to dwindle. The homeless spilled out of the long since vacated buildings to take up their places in the doorways, although there was no point in begging, as the majority of those passing had no change to spare. The graffiti-littered streets were patrolled by vigilantes following an increase in violent crime. The sick smell of desperation lingering in the air had blanketed the entire city. Aberdeen had once been an affluent area but now thousands were on the streets or living hand to mouth.

As she left Union Street, walking to work on a warm summer's day, she would have been met by the putrid fragrance of fish as Market Street met Commercial Quay. But it was October and the grey skies were filled with the smell of winter and diesel from the vessels tied up side by side in the harbour waiting for that elusive contract to take them back out to sea. Scores of other vessels waited just offshore outside the harbour walls as their owners couldn't afford to pay the harbour dues. On any given day you could walk down the esplanade, along the beach front and watch the hypnotic bobbing up and down of the boats as they danced in time to the rise and fall of their fortunes and the waves. It didn't matter what time of year it was, there was always the shrill sound of the seagulls fighting over takeaway cartons that had been pulled out of bins or just thrown on the streets. They were vermin, flying rats, and the city was plagued with them.

Danni crossed the busy intersection at Guild Street and continued down Market Street. Her office was down by the harbour in the old Salvesen Tower building on Blaikies Quay. The office block had been built in the 1960s and was a typical concrete construction of that time and a blot on the landscape in comparison to the granite structures of nearby Union and Market Streets. There were several such buildings around the city, but the most notable of them all had been the old Aberdeen City Council building of St Nicholas House. It had dominated the skyline and towered over Provost Skene's House and Marischal College, one of Aberdeen's most iconic buildings, like an ugly ogre waiting to squash anyone that got in its way. Thankfully, that monstrosity had been demolished several years ago, but not without a great deal of controversy, replaced by less imposing, glass-sided buildings, with fake granite façades and a modern civic square. A new hotel – how many had questioned whether Aberdeen needed another hotel – offices, shops, cafes and restaurants which had once been thriving, now lay empty, abandoned, deserted by those who had supported its creation whilst Marischal College continued to be guarded by Robert the Bruce and his trusty steed.

Marischal Square had been developed as a focal point for the city, for its residents to enjoy and gather together. However, there was no gathering now except for the Protest Against Poverty rallies, which were quickly dispersed by Aberdeen's finest. Police Scotland might have moved their control centres to the Central Belt, but with their North East Divisional Headquarters just around the corner on Queen Street, they were always quick on the scene. Following the spate of terrorist attacks in London and Manchester and across Europe, there were now more bobbies on the beat and, with the exception of London, Aberdeen probably had the highest number per capita. But that was only because it was not just the UK government that was paying for them. Funding was now propped up by the Russians who had moved into the area, and some would say that control was now also in their hands. It was obvious to anyone who looked closely enough that several high-ranking officials were in the coat pockets of the Russians, and easily swayed to turn a blind eye when required.

Danni entered the main door of the office block and placed her hand on the biometric scanner that had been installed when the Russians moved in. The pad turned green and the glass door in front of her slid open. Security had been tightened, not only in relation to the recent string of terror attacks but also due to the latest oil price collapse. Offices had been ransacked all over town by disgruntled ex-employees who had given their all, only to be cast aside like useless broken toys that a child no longer wants to play with. Looting was rife in the city, with laptops and phones changing hands for money and drugs in the seedy bars that had bucked the trend and remained open. There were several of them around the harbour area, kept in business mainly by the supply boat crews who drunk their wages waiting for their next offshore trip.

She made her way to the lifts and pressed the up button. The lift doors opened and she stepped in. She placed her thumb on the control panel scanner and pushed the number ten button. An electronic voice announced 'Tenth floor, going up'. Her desk was on the eighth floor, but she didn't spend much time at it these days, so she might as well head straight up to the file room. The new management of the Russian firm Moskaneft wanted a summary of all the contracts and agreements that had been placed under the previous regime. So far, she had been working through the files for over a month and had barely scratched the surface. She had a long, thankless task ahead of her.

Danni walked along the corridor of the tenth floor to the file room at the far end. This was the management suite and had been refurbished following the takeover. No signs of recession in this part of the office. The dark brown carpet tiles had been replaced by a new bright blue carpet in line with the company's colour scheme. Pantone 286 C, to be exact. The company logo was derived from the colours of the Russian flag. The blue said to represent loyalty, white for generosity and the remaining colour of the tri-colour being red for courage.

Loyalty? *верность, преданность*. Well that was a joke. Once upon a time, loyalty was something that was earned, not forced upon you. Now loyalty was expected if you wanted to keep your job, a prerequisite to keep your name off the blacklist, and there was always a blacklist. But loyalty nowadays was given in a different form. It was a devotion to money only, as that was the key driver, so you could say in a roundabout way that loyalty was now proclaimed to whoever was the paymaster.

As she walked past the boardroom, she noticed several of the senior managers were already hunkered down in a pow-wow. A couple of the original board members had been retained as part of the takeover but the majority were now Russians who had moved over from Moskaneft's head office in Moscow. The managing director had apparently left the company two weeks ago with the company citing 'personal reasons' for his departure. Everyone knew that meant he had been pushed rather than jumped. Danni had never had any dealings with him, and why would he want to speak to the plebs, anyway? He had been brought in by the previous owners as a hatchet man to get rid of the deadwood and turn the company around, which he had done. They had come out of the previous crash with cash in the bank and were turning a small profit, which a lot of other companies were struggling to do. In fact, there were a lot fewer companies around now, especially the service companies. Danni had heard on the BBC and Sky News reports that an unprecedented number had filed for bankruptcy in the last few years. People turned up for work as normal one morning to be confronted by padlocked gates and a notice telling them the office was permanently closed and they should contact the administrators. PWC and KPMG had never been so busy.

Danni used her pass to enter the file room. She was privileged; not everyone was allowed access to this room. The reason she was given was that of confidentiality, as all the contracts, commercial and legal agreements were held there. However, Danni suspected it was more to do with the room being next door to the boardroom in the management suite and they wanted to keep the workers away from them as much as possible. They didn't want any unnecessary earwigging into their future plans. No need to let the workforce know what was actually going on. Keep them in the dark like mushrooms; feed them with shit.

Danni did sometimes overhear things, but then, who was she going to tell? She pretty much kept herself to herself. Her friend Mel – the only real friend she had in the company who she would have chatted with – was let go in the last round of redundancies. Mel had been forced to move down to Edinburgh to find work as there was nothing available in Aberdeen and she couldn't afford the rent on her flat. Surprisingly, it was actually cheaper to rent in Scotland's capital than it was in Aberdeen. She still kept in contact with her, but the friendship had already started to dwindle. She felt guilty. *What did they call it? Survivor's guilt?* She had kept her job while others probably more qualified than her had lost theirs. But then, she was paid peanuts, and the company could save more money by removing those on higher salaries.

Danni wasn't much for socialising. She didn't really have any friends, only some acquaintances and work colleagues. She preferred it that way. Anyway, she needed to keep a low profile as she didn't want her ex, Mark, getting wind of where she was. It had taken a lot of planning and courage to get away from him and she was scared he was still looking for her. She had left pretty much with only the clothes she was wearing. She had managed to take a few personal items with her but only those she could fit in a small holdall: some old photos and jewellery that had been handed down through the family. She hadn't even been in contact with her family since her escape other than to send them a short note to say she was leaving him and not to worry. She had posted it from London before she left so as not to give any indication as to where she would be. She had no idea where she would end up at the time of posting it.

Danni had been squirrelling away money for over a year before she left, enough to get her away and to start a new life without Mark. It had been difficult as he had controlled her every move. She had managed to get her hands on a pay as you go phone and set up a bank account that he knew nothing about. She was sure he was keeping tabs on her through the iPhone he had given her for Christmas. He seemed to know her every move, where she had been, who she had been speaking to. She had no life. She had stopped seeing her friends because of his jealousy. At first, she found it endearing that he wanted to spend so much time with her, but he became more and more possessive, asking her to stay at home with him rather than go out and see her friends. He slagged off her friends and manipulated her into thinking and feeling that she was worthless and only he could love her. Who else would want to be with a pathetic, snivelling, ugly bitch who belonged on the spinster's shelf? She had eventually lost contact with all her friends. And as Mark was a police detective, she couldn't turn to the police for help. She was truly on her own.

By the time she woke up and smelled the coffee it was too late. It was literally the slap in the face that she needed. The first time he hit her it came so out of the blue that she felt sure she must have provoked him. He said it was her fault, that she drove him to it, he didn't want to do it, but she just kept goading him. But as the beatings became more frequent and more vicious, she knew she had to get out or die trying.

Chapter Three

The room was dusky and dark with a musty smell of long-forgotten documents that had been filed many years ago with no intention of ever being retrieved. Cardboard boxes marked with long since passed destruction dates were piled high on shelves that were never designed to hold such a weight. Under the flickering artificial white light from the fluorescent tubes overhead, Danni pulled the next box from the shelf, blew off the dust and started documenting its contents. Her new employers wanted a summary of every contract in there, including an option for how they could get out of it without incurring any financial penalties. Danni had her assumptions that they were going to terminate all the existing contracts and bring in their own people to do the work. More Russians were likely to be descending on Aberdeen soon. The supermarkets had already replaced the foods on the 'Polish' aisle with Russian delights. Bottles of Medovukha, jars of pickled herrings, cucumbers and mushrooms, smoked sausage, *piroshki*, *blini*, everything you need to make *borsch*,

Russian caviar and vodka, supposedly superior to that of its Polish cousins.

As Danni pulled the next file from the box, she heard voices in the boardroom. She moved closer to the internal door that led directly to it. Her eavesdropping had given her the heads up in the past, and what she was about to hear was not to her liking. She was right, they were going to bring in more of their comrades, but not through the normal channels. The voices had distinctive Russian accents.

"We will cut the workforce by a further 100. They will be replaced by our colleagues from Moscow. We will call it… restructuring. I need a list of everyone who could potentially be a threat to our plans. Dmitry, you have reviewed the personnel files and have been monitoring the workforce; you know who we need to remove."

Danni backed away and snuck out of the file room down the back staircase to the eighth floor where her desk was situated. She didn't want anyone to know what she had heard, or indeed, that she had heard anything. She switched on her computer, and in the short time it had taken her to get back to her desk, an email had already been issued from corporate communications, announcing a townhall meeting within an hour. They were not hanging around. All personnel were to attend, and it was non-negotiable. Any pre-arranged meetings were to be rescheduled to ensure attendance. *Here we go again,* Danni thought to herself. *Who would stay and who would go? That was the million-dollar question, or should that be million-rouble?*

She made her way to the breakout area to make a coffee. Coffee was a staple part of her diet considering all the extra hours she had been working. Strong and black was how she liked it. Double shot espresso was her usual, but since they had removed all the coffee making machines as part of the cutbacks, she would have to do with two spoons of instant and a kettle of boiling water. Two colleagues entered the room.

"Did you see that email? I'll bet you anything that's more redundancies," said the girl. Danni thought her name was Rebecca, or Becky; she was one of the finance girls who sat along the corridor. Becky was young, early twenties, with straight, long blonde hair and deep brown eyes. She spent more time playing with her hair and flirting with her male colleagues than she did working. Danni bit her lip and turned to look out the window so they wouldn't see any reaction on her face. It had started to rain; it was that wet, sleety rain, the kind that soaked you to the skin within seconds. The weather reflected the inherent mood in the office.

"Yeah, I'd bet my house on it if I still had one!" replied Tony. Tony Black was one of the medics. He was due to check in for his trip offshore tomorrow and had been in the office for a meeting with the company doctor before travelling. He was around five foot ten with short blond hair that was spiked on top, dark brown eyes and a cheeky schoolboy grin. He had a bit of the Brad Pitts about him. Danni had met him before on a couple of occasions. The first time was when she had been called in to an emergency response exercise. She was part of the ER team as one of the administrators who kept records of the incident. On the last exercise she had to liaise with Tony to determine who was offshore and where they had evacuated everyone to. He had also been the instructor on the first aid course Danni had attended in the office. Tony had taken a bit of shine to her and had asked her out for a drink afterwards, but she thought he wanted to practise his mouth to mouth on her, so she had declined. He had been persistent, though, keeping in touch even after the brush-off, dropping her a cheeky email on occasion during his offshore trips. Danni had an inkling that he was actually married and was just chancing his arm. He wouldn't be the first offshore worker to have a 'girlfriend' in the city. As part of her ER duties, she was also trained to deal with phone calls from relatives in the event of an emergency. One of the scenarios that was always played out was when both the wife and the girlfriend called about the same person. She wasn't sure, but Danni suspected it was more common than she would care to acknowledge.

"What do you think Danni, you think we are for the chop?" asked Tony.

"What would I know about it?" replied Danni, a bit too defensively. "I'm just the hired help, I don't know what they are planning." She turned to leave before she gave away that she did know more than she was letting on.

Tony shrugged his shoulders and turned to Becky. "Was it something I said?"

They both laughed as Danni walked past.

"Just ignore her," said Becky. "She is so up herself, thinks she's better than the rest of us." Danni heard the comment. That couldn't have been any further from the truth. She just didn't want to get involved, couldn't get involved.

"Well we had better head down to the conference room and find out our fate," said Becky. "Are you coming?"

"I'll be down in a minute," said Tony. He left the breakout area and headed along the corridor towards Danni's desk.

"Hey sexy, what's got your knickers in a twist?" asked Tony.

"Nothing," replied Danni.

"Oh, come on, Becky's OK once you get to know her."

"If you like that sort of thing."

"Are you coming downstairs? Come on, I'll escort you. You never know, it might be the last time I get to see you."

Danni couldn't help but fall for his boyish charm. "Chance would be a fine thing!"

He put his arm through hers and dragged her along the corridor.

They entered the conference room, already packed to the gunnels by the remainder of the workforce. Whispered tones of rumour and speculation echoed around the room. Danni knew what was coming but she didn't realise it was going to be quite so brutal. The meeting only lasted five minutes. Despite the company's recent big oil find, these were difficult times, efficiency cuts had to be made to keep the company economic. The cost of production had crept up, cost cuts were inevitable, blah, blah, blah. She had heard it all before, several times, but this time there was a twist. As everyone left the room, they would be handed an envelope. In it was either your P45 or a letter confirming your job title and salary. If you received your P45 you would have one hour to clear your desk and would then be escorted from the office with no need to work any notice period. It was a fifty-fifty chance of staying or going. Russian roulette of a different sort. You either got the bullet or you dodged it. Everyone was still a casualty, just to varying degrees.

The Russians moved to the door of the conference room while the workers were made to line up in alphabetical order, reminiscent of being back in primary school. The envelopes were forced into their outstretched hands, taken grudgingly, the recipients not wanting to touch them for fear of what was waiting inside.

Danni waited towards the end of the queue, her last name being Ross. She could hear the weeping and wailing coming from the corridor from those who had already learned their fate. The cries of despair and anger became more evident as she moved up the line. She took the envelope and, clutching it to her chest unopened, she pushed her way through the bodies littering the hall. Grown men were on their knees in tears as the final blow had been struck, the mercy stroke.

Danni couldn't stand to listen to the chaos, so she walked quickly, almost ran, to the back stairwell, taking the steps two at a time up to the tenth floor and accessed the file room. She knew she would have peace and quiet in there to digest whatever was waiting for her and to contemplate her destiny. She looked at the envelope, scared to open it. What would she do if she had no job? She was barely making ends meet as it was and had no family she could turn to. Well, that wasn't strictly true, she knew they would be more than happy to help and support her, but they didn't know where she was, or what predicament she now found herself in. As much as she wanted to contact them, longed to hear her mother's voice, she couldn't risk it in case Mark was watching them, listening in to their calls. She was sure he had tapped her phone before she left, so it was entirely plausible that he had bugged her parents' house the last time they had visited. Would he still be looking for her after all this time? He would have been furious that she had slipped through his fingers, livid that she had the nerve to outsmart him long enough to escape his clutches. She wondered who had bared the brunt of his wrath in the aftermath.

She turned the envelope over and over in her hands, heart beating faster, palpitations beginning, her hands starting to shake. *Damn it, just open it*, she thought to herself, and pushed a finger into the corner of the envelope and began to pry the seal open, finally ripping at it. She pulled out the letter and started reading.

"Dear Ms Ross, Moskaneft hereby confirms your continued employment as an Administrative Assistant. Your salary will be reduced by ten per cent commencing from 1st December."

Short and to the point. Great, be thankful you still have a job, she thought to herself. But what sort of job? Her 'legal' status has been removed and her salary reduced accordingly. Danni had been subjected to previous pay cuts so would now be working for half what she had earned two years ago. She hoped her landlord would be understanding, as she was going to have to try to negotiate a reduction in her rent. She had been in that flat for almost a year through a private let. She paid monthly in cash to avoid any electronic paper trail. It was a convenient arrangement for both her and her landlord. She didn't care if he was paying tax on her rent payments. She thought she had been a good tenant, never complaining and keeping the place tidy. She knew the housing market was bad with so many people defaulting on their mortgages. For sale and for lease signs were ten a penny all over the city. She just hoped he was more worried about keeping some money coming in rather than risking the flat sitting empty and the problems associated with that. Many flats had squatters moving in and, with possession being nine-tenths of the law, it was difficult to evict them. The council and the police were not interested as there was nowhere to move these people to. She would have to play on his fears.

She hid in the file room for the remainder of the day, only leaving briefly to feed her caffeine craving, not wanting to have to face the aftermath of today's announcement. She didn't even go out to get lunch. At the back of five she thought it would be safe to head back to her desk and pick up her bag. She wondered how many would not be returning tomorrow.

"Ah, you made it, you're still here." She recognised Tony's voice without having to look up.

"Looks like you survived too, then?" she replied.

"Some of us survivors are heading downstairs to the Quarterdeck for a drink, are you coming?"

"No, thanks, I'm not in the mood to celebrate, or commiserate, or whatever it is you are doing."

"Ah, come on misery guts, just one, what harm can it do?"

"No thanks, I just want to go home."

"Come on, my offshore trip has been delayed a couple of days, and I'm gagging for a pint."

"Tony, give it a rest, I'm going home, OK?"

"Aw, but I want to celebrate with my favourite legal assistant."

"You mean admin assistant."

"Ouch." Tony made a gesture like he had just been burned. "I'm guessing they cut your pay too, then."

"Just a bit, but I'll survive."

"Well in that case, you have to let me buy you a drink."

"Well if it shuts you up, OK then. But only one."

Chapter Four

Danni woke up, her head thumping, tongue stuck to the roof of her mouth. *What happened last night?* She looked at the clock, the fluorescent green digits screaming it was 6:45am and her alarm was set to go off in fifteen minutes. As she pulled the covers over her head, she heard a noise coming from the kitchen. She leaped to her feet and instinctively reached for the top drawer of her bedside cabinet. She pulled the drawer open, keeping her eyes firmly on the bedroom door, her heart drumming in her ears, her right hand searching frantically for the handgun. Before she could pull it from the drawer the door opened. Danni froze as Tony walked in with two mugs of coffee.

"Hey, sleepyhead, what's up? You look like you've seen a ghost," said Tony.

Danni's heart was in her mouth and she was unable to speak, waiting for her breath to return.

"What's wrong? You look terrified." Tony laid the mugs down on the dressing table and walked towards Danni. He tried to put his arms around her to comfort her, but she pushed him away.

"What are you doing here?" she demanded.

"Well, I thought I was a bit more memorable than that," laughed Tony.

"Why, what happened last night? We didn't… did we?"

"No, we didn't. Call me picky, but I prefer my conquests to be with it, not comatose."

Danni looked down and realised she was still wearing the same clothes from yesterday.

"You were out of it, totally rubber. You were fairly putting them back."

"But I was only drinking orange juice."

"Yeah, if you say so! More like vodka with a splash of orange."

"No, I asked for just orange."

"And you trusted that lot not to lace your drink? Well, more fool you."

"I hadn't eaten all day."

"No wonder you were legless after the fourth," joked Tony. "You really don't remember leaving?"

"How did I get home?"

"I ordered a taxi at 9pm, but you were barely capable of walking, so I thought I'd better see you home. It took us a while to figure out where you lived. One of the girls from accounts said she thought it was the top end of Esslemont Avenue but didn't know what number. I left you sitting on the pavement while I tried your key in different doors until I found the right building, then had to buzz one of your neighbours to find out which flat it was. If your flat had been any further down the street I would probably have been arrested for burglary! I had to practically carry you up the stairs. You only just made it to the bathroom before you spewed everywhere! Don't worry, I cleaned it up – you're welcome!"

"Oh God, I'm so sorry, I'm mortified." Danni dropped her head, embarrassed, and started to blush, pink flushing her cheeks and red blotches appearing on her neck.

"I remember going down to the bar, and I remember John starting to pick a fight with that guy from accounts, the dark haired one, I don't know his name. Then I don't remember anything after that."

"Aye, you were pretty wasted! I was worried you were going to choke on your own puke, so I got you through to the bedroom, took your remaining shoe off – as you managed to lose one coming up the stairs – and put you in the recovery position. I slept on the floor beside you, so I could keep an eye on you."

Danni looked down and saw a plastic basin on the floor. A pillow and blanket were folded up and sitting on the chair beside the bedroom window.

"I guess I should say thanks. I honestly thought I was drinking OJ. I haven't drunk alcohol for over a year."

"Why, are you a recovering alchi or something?"

"No! I just needed to keep a clear head. It's a long story, one I don't have time for right now." The reality was she didn't want to get into the conversation with him, or anyone else come to think of it. She wanted that part of her life to stay firmly in her past.

"Look at the time, I need to get ready for work." Danni pushed past Tony, taking a mug of coffee out of his hand and gulping down a few mouthfuls before heading to the bathroom for a shower.

"Don't suppose I can join you?" joked Tony.

Danni slid the bathroom lock into place. "Don't even think about it."

*

Danni shared the taxi that Tony booked through the app on his phone. The taxi firms were all struggling to make a profit with the downturn and a couple of the larger ones had set up apps to make it easier to book and hopefully keep some trade. Several firms had seen their profits disappear and had sold out, and you could still pick up a private hire if you wanted to take the risk, ex-oil workers trying to make ends meet by doing the knowledge and renting out their vehicles. She would normally have walked and could have done with the fresh air given how hungover she felt, but she couldn't face it this morning, especially as the sleet had started.

Tony asked the taxi driver to stop just outside the Tivoli Theatre, which was just across the road from the Jury's Inn Hotel in Union Square where Tony was supposed to have stayed last night. It was just around the corner from the office.

"Better get changed before I come in, don't want everyone thinking I've been a dirty stop out. Plus, the company has paid for breakfast, so I might as well get my money's worth." Tony patted his stomach and ran towards the hotel door, the sleet now turning heavier.

The car pulled out into the rush hour traffic and signalled to turn right down Market Street. Danni looked out the window at the early morning commuters struggling to keep their umbrellas from turning inside out. It only took a couple of minutes to get to the office but during that time Danni started berating herself about how she had got in such a state last night. She couldn't remember the last time she had had a drink. She used to enjoy a social glass of wine with her friends when she stayed down in London. After work they would frequent one of the rooftop bars along the Southbank, sitting outside enjoying the spectacular view across the River Thames towards St Paul's Cathedral to the east, the London Eye and Big Ben to the west.

How she longed to go back to those days. The days before Mark, before he turned her life upside down. He had been in one of those bars the night they met. She was at the bar waiting to be served, her turn to get the round in. He was pushing back from the bar, through the crowd, carrying two pints. He tripped and spilled one of them down her dress. She was furious to start with, but when she looked up and saw those big brown puppy dog eyes she quickly melted. He was tall, over six foot, with a tanned complexion and designer stubble on his chiselled chin. She could tell he worked out. He was so apologetic. After Danni had dried herself off as best she could under the hand drier in the ladies, he and his buddies from the local police station had joined them. He bought them a bottle of champagne to say sorry, which she thought was a bit flash on his police salary. But, apart from having her dress stick to her and smelling like a brewery, she had enjoyed the evening. They had talked and laughed all evening; it felt like she had known him for years. Mark had shared a taxi back to her flat with two of her friends. He had been a true gentleman and helped her out of the taxi, not looking for an invite for coffee but asking if he could see her again. She gave him her number. *What the hell*, she thought, *there are a lot of creeps out there and he's a police detective, I feel safe with him.* How wrong could she have been?

"Miss, we are here," said the taxi driver. Danni looked up and saw they were indeed stopped outside Salvesen Tower. She snapped out of her daydream, climbed out of the car and dashed to the front door, not bothering to try to fight with an umbrella for all the distance. Still, she was soaked by the time she got inside. She went through the daily rigmarole of placing her hand on the biometric scanner to access the main building and the scanner to operate the lift. She had a sudden panic. What if her fingerprints were on file somewhere with her details? What if Mark could get access to them? Did he have a record of them that he could run through his police computer? Surely if he did then he would have found her by now; the scanners had been in place for a few months. Danni had changed her name through deed poll when she fled his clutches, but fingerprints could not be changed. She had been born Louise Margaret Roberts and had gone through school and university known as Lou. But from now on she would be known as Danielle Ross. Danni. Still, she would need to keep her wits about her, not let her guard down like she had done last night.

She headed up to her desk but stopped off in the ladies toilets to try to dry herself off with the hand dryer. She was only outside for a matter of seconds, but her hair and trousers were both soaked. She tied her hair back with a hairband that she found in the bottom of her handbag and went into one of the cubicles. The main door of the toilet opened, and she heard two people walk in.

"God, I feel rough, I don't know how I'm going to make it through today."

"Me too! Everyone was fair knocking them back last night."

She recognised one of the voices as being Becky, the girl Tony had been speaking to the day before in the coffee area. She had secretly hoped that Becky had received a different letter yesterday and would not be coming back in the office. She didn't know whom the other voice belonged to.

"I'd be surprised if John shows his face today after starting that fight with Bill."

"Ha ha, that was hilarious, I bet he never expected to be floored by little Bill. Serves him right, he's always been a bit of a dick, he had it coming."

"But did you see that girl from legal, what's her name, Debbie? She left with Tony, she was mortal, she had to be carried out."

"Oh, you mean Danni, yeah she's a stuck-up bitch," said Becky. "I don't know what Tony's doing with the likes of her. She's a total ice-queen, I think she's frigid. Anyway, she's clearly punching above her weight. I thought he was interested in me, but I'm not going near him if he's been with the likes of her. Obviously, he has strange taste in women."

"Yeah, if they are legless then he's clearly interested," laughed the other girl. "Come on, I need to get some caffeine before the boss gets in, and no amount of make-up is gonna cover up this hangover!"

Danni waited till she heard them leave before coming out of her cubicle. She knew Becky didn't like her, even though she had barely said two words to the girl. Now she knew why, she clearly had a crush on Tony and was pissed off that he was paying more attention to her. Not that she wanted any of that attention and she had made that clear on umpteen occasions.

She left the toilet and headed to her desk. She dropped off her coat and bag and switched on her computer to check her emails. Nothing that couldn't wait till she'd had another coffee. She headed to the coffee point, but just as she entered, she realised that Becky was still in there, flirting with another guy. Becky saw her; it was too late to turn around and leave.

"Hi Danni, how's the hangover? You were putting them back last night! I saw you leave with Tony; he's not appeared yet, what have you done with him?" Becky laughed, but it was a sneering laugh and when Danni looked at her it was clear that her resting bitch face was out in full force. She clearly hadn't realised that Danni had been in the toilets earlier.

"I haven't done anything with Tony," Danni retorted, "and I'd thank you to keep your nose out of my business."

"Hey, all I'm saying is there's no smoke without fire, am I right, Gregor?"

"Keep me out of this," replied Gregor and he backed off towards the fridge to get the milk.

Danni stormed out of the coffee area, pushing past Becky, causing her to spill her coffee.

"Hey, watch it!" Becky shouted.

"Well get out of my way and keep out of my way," declared Danni over her shoulder as she marched back to her desk.

Who the hell did she think she was? Danni wished Becky would drop dead.

Chapter Five

Offshore on the North Platform

"Are we all clear how this is gyan doon then?"

"Are you sure you want to go through with this, mate?"

"I'm a ticking time-bomb, pal, the Big C is gyan te get me one wye or anither and since them Russian bastards have taken awa oor medical insurance, I've nae got the cash to ging private. I winna last long enough if I hiv to wait on the NHS."

"But what about Jeannie and the boys; have you thought about how they will cope?"

"It's Jeannie and the boys I'm thinking o'. This wye she gets a pay oot fae the company through the death in service insurance, an' as they'll get 'i blame she should get some hush money ana. Otherwise she gets nowt. The boys' future will be secured and they'll hae a roof oor their heids, as the hoose will be paid aff and them fuckers at the bank can do 'een. Believe me, lads, I've thought aboot nithing else since I seen the doc."

"But what if they find out?"

"Fae's gyan to tell em? I hiv nae telt onyone else aboot this, hiv you, lads?"

"No of course I haven't."

"Nor me."

"Fine. So, this stays atween us, and Jeannie will see yis all right. She kens this is gyan to happen. We said oor goodbyes afore I got on the chopper. She kens it's the only wye. You'll get your cut fan they pay oot. We hiv te do it this trip afore onyone else finds oot aboot my condition as I winna get offshore again."

"Tonight, the drill crew change out. They've just finished the 8-1/2" section so we'll be moving a lot of kit around the deck for them. That will be the best time to do it."

"Tonight it is, then."

Chapter Six

Danni woke suddenly from a disturbing dream. She was clammy with sweat, but she couldn't quite remember why she was scared. She had been running. Running from someone or something and there was a high-pitched alarm going off. No, wait, it wasn't an alarm; it was her mobile phone. Who was calling her at this hour? She switched on her bedside light. It wasn't her own mobile, but the company issued phone. She quickly answered it.

"Yes?"

"Danni, this is System Operations. There has been an incident on one of the platforms; we need you in the office."

"Oh no, what's happened?"

"We'll give you more details when you get to the office. Please arrange for a taxi to collect you on the company account. How long will you be?"

"I'll be ten minutes from when the car arrives."

"Good, thanks, get here as quick as you can."

Danni pressed the end call button and threw back the duvet. She looked at the clock – 4am. The flat was freezing as the heating was not set to come on for another two hours. She opened the taxi app on her company phone and saw that a car was five minutes away. She pressed the button to book it. She switched on the main light and opened the wardrobe doors. Grabbing a pair of jeans, a T-shirt and a dark blue hooded top, she got dressed. She felt under the bed for her trainers and pulled them on over the socks she had been wearing in bed, quickly tying the laces. She went to the bathroom and splashed some water on her face, wiping it dry on the towel that was hanging over the radiator, still damp from the shower she took the night before. She brushed back her hair and tied it up in a pony tail. No time to put on any make-up, she grabbed her winter coat from its hook in the lobby, wrapped a scarf round her neck and pulled a woollen hat over her head. She went to the bedroom window and looked down to see a car pull up under the orange glow of the streetlight. She grabbed her handbag, stuffed both her phones inside and left the flat, pulling the door closed tight behind her. She felt her way down the stairs, using the light from her mobile to guide the way. The landing light had been out for several weeks now and she had sent several messages to the landlord asking for it to be fixed. He owned all the flats in this block and nobody else was going to fix it. She made a mental note to call him later and complain yet again. The cold air hit her when she opened the external door. "Bloody hell, it's Baltic," she said out loud as she shuddered against the cold. She could see her breath.

"Car for Moskaneft?" asked the taxi driver.

"Yes, heading to the office, please," replied Danni.

"Bunch of slave drivers, are they?" asked the driver.

"What? Oh, yeah, something like that," said Danni. She was aware they were not supposed to talk to anyone about an ongoing incident. Confidentiality and all that.

The car sped down Esslemont Avenue, turning left onto Skene Street. The traffic lights turned to green as the driver signalled right onto Rosemount Viaduct. Danni looked out the window towards His Majesty's Theatre, which was all lit up in the dark of the night. It would soon be panto season, *oh no it isn't, oh yes it is.* Danni felt like she was living in a panto these days; it certainly didn't feel like real life. The car veered right onto Union Terrace, it was too dark to make out the gardens down below, a hunting ground for the homeless. The quickest way to the office would be to turn down Union Street but the junction was blocked by police cars, their blue lights flashing and sirens wailing. Danni could see someone being manhandled into the back of a transit van. The police had their guns drawn, which was becoming a more common sight. *A burglary, a murder?* It would be reported along with all the other crimes on the news later that morning. They continued straight ahead, past the side entrance to the Trinity Centre, guarded by private security guards, and followed the road round to the left behind the centre and past the turn-off for the road to nowhere and onto Guild Street. The traffic lights changed to red as they approached. As the car came to a stop, Danni looked across the harbour towards the office building and could see several lights were on. The lights all worked from sensors so that meant there were others already in the office. The traffic lights changed, and the driver steered down Market Street and round onto Commercial Quay and Regent Road. The car pulled up and Danni got out, thanking the driver.

"Don't let them work you too hard," he joked.

"I won't." Danni dismissed him as she hastily made for the main door.

Danni headed straight to the conference room on the seventh floor, which doubled as the emergency response room. As she walked through the door, she was greeted with hushed tones and sullen faces. She knew something bad had happened.

"Thanks for coming so quickly, Danni." She looked round to see Mike, who was one of the incident controllers. He had been on the last exercise she had taken part in.

"No problem, so what's going on?" replied Danni.

"Afraid we've had a fatality on the North Platform. The investigation has just begun but looks like a container has fallen from the crane and crushed one of the deck crew."

"Shit," said Danni. "Who was it?" She was aware that Tony had travelled offshore yesterday afternoon, although it was unlikely he would have been out on the deck.

"It was Douglas Henderson. The boys knew him as Dougie. The police are on their way to inform his family as we speak."

"Right, what do you need me to do?"

"I need you to contact offshore and get a report from the medic. It's Tony Black who's onboard at the moment. Find out what he knows. I spoke to him briefly; he should have finished writing up his initial statement by now. We have more police heading to the airport and we are arranging for a helicopter to take them out as soon as possible to begin their investigation. This is the last bloody thing we need right now! The Russians are going to go apeshit."

Danni headed to one of the spare desks that had been set up. Several others were already manning phones, taking notes and making necessary arrangements. She opened the ER manual and found the phone number for the medic's office on the North Platform. She took a deep breath before pressing the numbers that would connect her with Tony. He was the last person she wanted to speak to after what had happened the other night.

Tony answered after the second ring. "North medic."

"Hi Tony, it's me, Danni."

"I knew you couldn't keep away from me," joked Tony, "but I didn't expect to hear from you so soon!"

"Yeah, yeah, very funny," said Danni. "This is a serious matter."

"Sorry," quipped Tony, "just trying to make light of a bad situation, but you're obviously not in that sort of mood."

Danni dismissed him and carried on with her task at hand. "I need your initial report of the incident. Can you email it through to me as soon as it's ready? And just to let you know, the police are on their way. I presume you've secured the area and accounted for all personnel onboard as per procedure ER-002."

"Right, so it's like that then is it?" retorted Tony. "Aye aye, Captain, all present and correct!"

"Tony, quit it, this is serious, it's not a time for your childish behaviour."

"Oh, someone got out of the wrong side of bed!"

"Tony!"

"OK, OK, I'll be serious. I'll get the formal report through to you shortly, but here's a quick summary for now. An incident occurred at approximately 3:15am. There is one fatality: a member of the deck crew, crushed by a container which was being moved by the starboard crane. It appears that one of the slings has snapped, causing the container to break free and fall approximately ten feet onto the deck below. Two other deck crew were present but were uninjured, however they are clearly in shock."

"OK, get the report written up and get it through to me ASAP."

"Danni."

"What?"

"Look, between you and me, something doesn't feel right with this."

"Why is that?"

"Well, for starters, lifts like these are supposed to be done during daylight hours, and when I asked, I was told they were under time pressure to get things in place for the drill crew to start in the morning. Apparently, they've been told that all areas offshore need to be more efficient."

"What's the problem?"

"I'm no expert, but I think the sling was deliberately damaged."

"But wouldn't they have checked them before the lift?"

"Well, they should have, but I'm getting conflicting stories as to who checked what. I hope I'm wrong, but I get the feeling there is more to this than meets the eye."

Danni turned her back on the rest of the room and looked out the window but was met with her own image staring back at her, reflecting against the darkness outside. A darkness that was unlikely to lift today.

"What, you think this was done on purpose?"

"I'm not saying that, but I heard stories through the grapevine that some of the accidents that have been reported on other platforms recently have not exactly been accidents."

"So, what are you saying?"

"Look, I don't want to say too much at the moment, but the word on the street is that some of these might have been suicide pacts. The guys have planned to help one of their own commit suicide by making it look like an accident so they can get life insurance pay-outs for the families."

"You can't be serious?"

"Hey, desperate times lead to desperate measures. After yesterday's announcement, it's not just you guys in the office that are affected, there will be more pay-offs offshore too.

Some of these guys are already below the breadline. They are living off hand-outs and foodbanks just to survive."

"But if the company finds out about this?"

"Unlikely, it's easy to blame the companies and difficult for them to prove otherwise with the shortcuts on safety and spending cuts. But this needs to stay between you and me for now. Look, I shouldn't have said anything to you. This conversation never happened, OK?"

"Shit, Tony, what the fuck did you have to tell me this for?" Danni slammed down the phone.

"Everything OK, Danni?" It was Mike, the incident controller.

Danni suddenly became aware that most of the people who were in the room had stopped what they were doing and were looking at her.

"Yes thanks, Mike. Erm, sorry, just a problem with the comms link in getting the report through and I know you need it urgently."

Danni knew that she had gone red with embarrassment, and hung her head, not wanting to make eye contact with anyone. She started to panic wondering what they had heard, playing over the conversation in her head, what she had actually said to Tony. Would they be able to figure out what they had been discussing? She didn't think she had said anything that could implicate her. They had all gone back to whatever they were doing so hopefully she was in the clear.

Danni walked over to the coffee pot and poured the remainder into a cup. *Great, a half cup of lukewarm stewed coffee. Why do these flasks never stay warm for long?* She grabbed the flasks and headed out of the room. "Just going to fill these up," she said to Mike.

"Good idea," he replied, "we are going to need plenty of caffeine to keep us going today."

Danni couldn't stop thinking about what Tony had said. *That gave a new meaning to the term assisted suicide. Was that a thing? Was that really going on offshore?* She thought back to the recent offshore incidents that had been on the news. There did seem to have been an increase in the past year or two, and the oil companies were getting the blame for cutting costs and compromising safety, but were people really that desperate that they would take their own lives to get money for their families? That, along with all the terrorism and racist attacks, what was the country coming to? *What sort of world are we living in now?* Every week there seemed to be a minute's silence being held for one atrocity or another. The news was full of doom and gloom, so she rarely wanted to turn on the TV when she got home at night. She preferred to listen to the local radio station, but even their news bulletins were depressing. Calls for donations to the foodbanks who were struggling to keep up with the demand for their services. *Please donate non-perishable items.* The Red Cross asking for clothing. A spate of break-ins in the area, muggings and robberies on the rise. *Was there any good news to report?*

Danni filled the coffee flasks and returned to the incident room. There seemed to be an increase in activity and an air of anxiety. She placed the flasks back on the table and returned to her post with a full, steaming hot cup of coffee this time.

"What's happened, have I missed something?" she asked Mike.

"I've just received a call from head office. The Russians are sending in their own team. As soon as they arrive, they will be taking over the investigation and we are to hand everything over to them."

"But that's crazy!" replied Danni. "They don't know the guys offshore or anything about the platform."

"I know," he said. "Between you and me this sounds like a cover up. I'm not one for conspiracy theories but... do you get where I'm going with this?"

Assisted suicide, conspiracy theories, what the hell was going on?!

The Russians arrived just after 8am, suited and booted, impeccably dressed as always with matching grey woollen overcoats. It was clear they had not been dragged out of their beds at 4am. Danni had seen some of them in the office before but there were several she did not recognise. The conversations were mainly in Russian, so she didn't have a clue what they were saying. She had thought about studying the language when they took over the company but had struggled to grasp the basic principles and had given up almost as quickly as she had started.

True to their word, they quickly took control of the incident room, speaking with each of the team members, and seizing all of the documents and reports that had been printed so far. The leader of the group, Aleksandr, stood at the front and whistled to get everyone's attention. "Moskaneft appreciates your assistance, but you are no longer required; we will take it from here. Please leave all documentation in the room. This is an ongoing incident and all aspects remain confidential. You are not to discuss this with anyone. You may return to your normal duties."

The team shuffled their way out of the room, looking puzzled, shaking heads and shrugging shoulders. *You may return to your normal duties,* thought Danni. *No recognition that most of us have been in here for four hours already. They certainly expected to get their money's worth.* Danni returned upstairs to her desk and switched on her computer, then made her way to the break out area. 8am and it was still dark outside. She was going to need a serious amount of coffee to get through the rest of the day. She heard footsteps approaching behind her and looked round to see Becky and one of her colleagues come in. *Great*, she thought, *this is just what I need.*

"Hey Danni, rocking the homeless look," laughed Becky. "I didn't realise it was dress like a down and out day." Her colleague looked at Danni and sniggered.

"I was called out in the middle of the night," sniped Danni.

"Why, what's so important that they need the help of an admin assistant at that time?" sneered Becky. "I know you were in the incident room, what's going on? It's all hush hush, top secret."

"I can't discuss it."

"There's no need to be so high and mighty about it. God, you really think you are something, don't you?"

"I'm not being high and mighty; I've been told we can't discuss it."

"Come on," she said to her colleague, "we're not going to get anything out of the ice queen here, might have guessed she would be like that."

Becky's colleague turned her nose up and sneered as Becky shoved Danni out of the way on her way past. *What have I ever done to her?* thought Danni. She was getting really pissed off with Becky's attitude towards her. Becky was the one that thought she was something and was only bothered because she wasn't in on what was going on and wasn't the centre of attention. She didn't have gossip to spread and her nose was out of joint. She needed taking down a peg or two and Danni felt up to the challenge.

Chapter Seven

Danni's day did not get any better. When she returned to her desk her boss shouted her over to his office. He was the company legal manager and loved to strut around like he owned the place. He was short and overweight with a decidedly large beer belly that was fighting to be free of his shirt, the buttons straining hard to keep the flab under wraps. His black, greasy hair was styled in a comb over to disguise his balding head, but no-one was fooled by the attempted cover up.

"Shut the door, Danni," he said.

"What's up?" she asked.

"The reports you have been writing up on the contracts."

"Yes, is there a problem with them?"

He leaned over towards her; the smell of stale sweat made Danni want to gag.

"The problem is you are taking too long. They want the process sped up; you are going to have to work late this week to get caught up."

"You've got to be joking!"

"Do I look like I'm joking?" His tone sounded like he was deadly serious. "Starting tonight you're going to have to work overtime to get through the files."

"But I've been up since 4am. I was called out for the incident on the North Platform."

"No excuses, Danni, just get it done." He turned his back on her, looking to his computer screen and started typing. Danni stood there, not believing what she had just heard.

"Get going, I want a draft report on my desk by the end of the month."

"But that's impossible!" exclaimed Danni.

"It's not up for debate, Danni. And I suggest you spend the rest of the day in the file room as the Russians won't want to see you looking like you've been dragged through a hedge backwards." It was true, the Russians had a strict dress code. You were to be dressed smartly at all times in the office and although females were allowed to wear trousers in the winter, it was expected that skirts were worn through the spring and summer. Also, shoes should have a heel of at least one inch. Completely sexist in this day and age, but it was written into the employee terms and conditions. They would not be happy to see Danni in her jeans and trainers. Danni didn't have many outfits. Her Dolce & Gabbana and Stella McCartney designer suits along with her Louboutin and Jimmy Choo shoes had been abandoned in London when she fled. She wondered what Mark had done with them. *Probably set fire to the lot, knowing him.*

"Are you still here?" her boss shouted.

Danni turned and opened the door, pulling it closed hard enough to make the door frame rattle in a show of annoyance. *The bastards!* She had already been working extra hours to get through the files and now they wanted more. *What the fuck did they want? Blood?*

She shuffled off down the hall to the back stairwell and swiped her pass against the pad to open the fire door. Taking the steps two at a time, she hurried upstairs to the tenth floor and into the file room, not wanting to be seen by any of the Russians. She sat down on the one chair that was in the room, a broken desk chair that had one arm and a rip in the material on the back support. It had been left here when the refurbishment on the management suite had been undertaken. The wheels squeaked when it moved. It should have been chucked in the skip, but the handyman must have missed it and it had been stuck in here out of sight.

Danni contemplated the task at hand, she had no idea how she was going to get through all the boxes and files in the timeline she had been set. *Start at the beginning,* she heard her mother's voice in her head, and it brought a smile to her face; albeit a sad smile as she missed her deeply. She wondered what she was up to, if her new husband was taking care of her. She had only met Steve a couple of times when they had visited London and once when she and Mark had headed out to visit them. Steve was also in the oil industry and had an elusive expat status in the Middle East, meaning her mother was well provided for and was living a privileged lifestyle not available to many in this day and age. Steve had plenty of money, as he had sold his company to one of the big service providers, Halliburton, who had been buying up a lot of competitors to increase their market share. Steve had been kept on to run the Middle East base. He didn't really need to work but wasn't quite ready to retire. The last time they had visited London her mother had told her of the parties at the country club. Steve's role was in business development. He was always wining and dining prospective clients and her mother had to go along, of course! That, along with her tireless charity work. *How the other half lived!* Danni wondered what her mother would think of her current lifestyle, living hand to mouth and always watching over her shoulder in case Mark was still looking for her.

She manhandled the next box of files from the shelf and dropped it down on the table, which was also a reject that had been hidden from view. A cloud of dust rose from the box and Danni sneezed. She blew the rest of the dust from the lid and opened it, removing the first file and starting to document its contents. A commercial agreement between Shell and a company that no longer existed. One who had sold out to Danni's previous employer who in turn had sold out to the Russians she currently worked for. Platforms had changed hands several times over the years and many of the original operators were no longer in business, either going bankrupt or selling out to naïve independent companies who would soon find out that the oil, that black blood that was sorely coveted was not so freely flowing. *What was that saying? All that glitters ain't gold.* There was a reason the majors were selling on their platforms. They were unable to turn a profit with their high overhead costs. The cost of drilling the wells to produce the black nectar had increased significantly and the fields they were discovering were much smaller. Not delivering so much bang for their buck. Even with the cost efficiency drives following the last downturn, these ageing monstrosities were not getting any younger and most were already well past their anticipated life expectancy. The cost to keep them maintained was no longer viable and was money the owners would not get back. A number of operators had been forced to start abandoning platforms, an inevitable cash drain that could not be avoided unless you were able to find some mug to buy them before they reached an uneconomical status.

The Russians had bought out Danni's employer last year, buying all four platforms as a job lot, and the liabilities that went with them. But they were on to a sure thing. They had done their homework and knew there were undiscovered fields that could be drilled and tied back to two of them. Danni had found out that the drones that had been flying around the North Sea were not surveillance drones in the normal sense of the word. The Russians had developed technology to map the oil reserves from the air, without having to use the normal subsurface techniques, and their results had been of a much greater accuracy. The ability to pin-point exactly where to drill for the last remaining oil veins was astounding. Every well that they had drilled, since they took over, had been a gusher. Their only problem was having to buy all four platforms, when all they needed was access to two of them. The other two were a financial drain that they would prefer to be rid of. But nobody was going to buy them, as if the Russians didn't want them then nothing was there to be found. But paying to abandon these platforms was not currently on their agenda. That was money down the drain and the Russians expected a return on every rouble that was spent. Or they had to find another way of doing things to save spending the money in the first place.

Danni had seen first-hand that they did not like to fritter away cold hard cash. Every penny was a prisoner and had to be accounted for. There were rumours that a couple of managers had been fired for not keeping within their budgets, and those who did had their budgets slashed as there was obviously too much sand-bagging in them. Cash was definitely king. But the oil price was falling again, hence the latest round of redundancies a few days ago, even though there were not enough people to do the work that was required. *Why let a little problem like that get in the way of their profits?!*

Chapter Eight

Danni's whole life had revolved around work over the last few weeks, not that she had much of a life to speak of. She had been working all the hours God sent. Her time at the gym had been replaced by lifting boxes in the file room. Any other exercise consisted of running to and from the office in the bitter cold and wet. It was dark when she left the flat and dark when she returned. She spent all day in a room with no windows. She was sure she was suffering from SAD. Maybe she should get one of those lights to help with that. She could take it into the office as no-one ever came into the file room, then at least she could pretend she was getting some daylight. She couldn't even remember the last time she did see daylight, never mind the sun. She wondered how the Russians coped with it, as it didn't seem to bother them. They were used to limited daylight, and to the freezing temperatures.

Why was it so cold in the North East? She was sure it must be colder in Moscow than it was here, but there couldn't be much in it. They didn't have cold like this in London, and if they did then everything came to a standstill and everyone stayed at home. It wasn't the temperature so much that was the issue, it was the biting, ice-cold wind that came straight off the North Sea, probably blowing all the way from Russia. It cut through you like a knife and chilled you to the bone. That coupled with the persistent drizzle and sleet that soaked you in seconds. The AccuWeather app on her phone told her the temperature outside was two degrees but the real-feel temperature was minus five. *Were Aberdonians born with an extra layer of skin? Maybe that was why they were addicted to butteries, all that fat. They needed to stock up to keep out the cold in the winter.* That was where she had been going wrong! Why had she moved to this grey, wet, godforsaken city?

Danni was totally fed up of being stuck in this room. She was starting to feel claustrophobic, like the walls were closing in on her. Here, alone, with no-one to talk to all day; not that she was that interested in what most of her colleagues had to say, but some adult conversation would be welcome. She spent most of the day plugged into her phone, listening to the local radio station. The music helped her pass the time. It was mostly '80s music they played, which reminded her of her childhood. It was what was played in the house by her mother. She couldn't argue with their logic, '80s music was definitely in a class of its own. That and swing music were her passion. Frank Sinatra, Dean Martin, Sammy Davis Jr, the Rat Pack. She loved all that and had several albums downloaded onto her phone. She also had old DVDs of the Rat Pack that she had bought second-hand through eBay or from Amazon. The TV was crap nowadays with all that reality rubbish, so she preferred to watch old films. She had a quite a collection of them.

"That was Madonna and *Like a Prayer*, and now with the time at 5pm, it's over to Martin in the news room."

"Thanks, Claire. A body has been found in the woodland at Countesswells on the western fringe of Aberdeen, between Cults and Westhill. The area is popular with dog walkers and runners. Anyone who has been there in the last few days is asked to contact Police Scotland on 101 if they have seen anything suspicious."

Another body, thought Danni. She felt sorry for the poor dog walker whose dog had sniffed it out, or run off and then stumbled across it. Bodies being found seemed to be a daily occurrence now, what with burglaries gone wrong, fights breaking out amongst the homeless and those queuing at the foodbanks. There was not enough food to go around and desperation was leading people literally to fight for their lives. But a body in the woods was different, that was either suicide or it had been dumped there as someone attempted to cover their tracks.

The woods were opposite the new housing development that had seen its fair share of problems. It had been given planning permission when the Aberdeen Western Peripheral Route had been approved. Danni had a vague recollection of it, as it made the news down south. The row over the AWPR had run on for years and it was rumoured that the leader of the anti-AWPR protest campaign had been forced to flee the country when the road was finally given the go-ahead after receiving death threats. The land near Countesswells was close to the route and had been reclassified. The initial developer, like many others in the area, had been suffering money problems and surprise, surprise, a Russian firm had stepped in to save the day. Well, that is what had been reported on the news, but the more likely scenario was that the Russians had taken over rather than bought out the company. There had been several industrial-related accidents on the site and the development had been on and off for years. The oil price not only affected those working in oil but had also had a major effect on the housing market. If people were worried about losing their jobs, they were not going to burden themselves with huge mortgages and solicitor's fees. Countesswells had been advertised as the possibility to 'live in the heart of a new community with its own identity, in tranquil western woodland a mere five minutes from the heart of the city'. It was also convenient for Westhill, where many of the oil companies were based, having moved out of the city to find cheaper business rates.

Danni had heard the adverts on the radio, offering hassle-free part-exchanges, free carpeting and curtains, your choice of kitchen and bathroom designs. Anything to attract people to move out there. The plan had included for schools and shops and thriving businesses, but until they could entice people to move out there and the development started to take in some money it was unlikely any of these would happen. Danni had not been out there, but she had seen pictures of it on the TV adverts. Lots of buildings in various states of construction but no real sign of life. With the exception of a few houses that had been sold early on before the latest oil price crash, the new community looked eerie, deserted, like a ghost town. You couldn't have paid her enough money to move out there. It looked like something out of a war zone. With all the rubble and piles of bricks and building materials lying around, it was difficult to tell whether the buildings were going up or coming down.

"Also in the news, three more oil service companies have announced job losses. The continued downturn..." Danni pulled the earphones out of her ears and dropped her phone on to the table. She didn't want to hear any more of this. There was never any good news, only death and depression. She needed to get out of here for a while and was in desperate need of a coffee. She had been in the office since 6am.

She made her way back down to the eighth floor so she could check her emails at the same time. She didn't like using the coffee area on the tenth floor, even though it was the only floor that had a proper coffee machine. It was monopolised by the Russians and she didn't want to fraternise with them, not that they would actually acknowledge her existence. She was like a ghost up there, in and out and nobody noticed or paid any attention to her. She might as well have been wearing an invisibility cloak.

She placed three spoons of the dark brown granules into a mug to make it strong enough to taste vaguely like coffee and to give her the caffeine hit she so badly craved. The kettle clicked as it came to a boil and she poured the hot water over the coffee, stirring vigorously. She threw the spoon into the sink and stood there, mug in hand, smelling the rancid aroma of instant coffee and looking out the window. It was midday and barely light. The cars travelling up and down Market Street had their lights on and their window wipers were swishing back and fore. The forecast was for the rain to continue all day. "Great, I'm really looking forward to going back out in that," she said out loud.

"You talking to your imaginary friend again?" laughed Becky.

Oh, brilliant. Danni hadn't heard her approach. The one person she wanted to avoid more than the Russians. She wished she had just stayed up on the tenth floor. Danni didn't rise to her quip and continued staring out the window.

"Haven't see you about for a few weeks, thought they had maybe got rid of you or something, or maybe that was just my wishful thinking," continued Becky.

"What is your problem?" asked Danni. "What have I ever done to you?"

"Oh, touched a nerve, have I?" retorted Becky.

Danni turned and walked out of the break area, she wasn't in the mood for Becky and her snide comments.

"Go fuck yourself," she replied and headed off back to her desk.

Becky rushed after her. "Yeah, who the hell do you think you are speaking to?" she shouted.

"A small-minded little slut who's not happy unless she's causing trouble and making people's lives a misery," stated Danni.

"No love, it's only you that I like to make miserable," she laughed. "Anyway, as much as I'd love to stop and chat, have you heard from Tony? He should have been back onshore by now."

Ah, now we're getting somewhere, thought Danni. Becky was jealous of her relationship with Tony. Not that she had a relationship. She barely knew the guy, but it was obvious the green-eyed monster had well and truly risen. Danni should have realised that if any man was paying attention to someone else other than Becky then she would be envious. She wasn't happy unless she was the centre of attention.

"Why would I have heard from Tony?" replied Danni.

"Well, you were pretty cosy when he was last onshore."

"There is nothing going on between us, you know."

"Yeah, right, whatever."

"Why are you so interested, anyway?"

"I'm not!"

"Yeah, sounds like it."

Becky screwed up her top lip and sneered at Danni before she turned and walked back towards her desk.

What was all that about? thought Danni. At least she now knew the reason for Becky's attitude towards her. Not that she could do anything about it. Anyway, it had been Tony that had been doing all the running, trying to strike up a friendship with her. It's not like she had been encouraging him. She wasn't even interested in him. She hadn't had a relationship since she had left Mark and she wasn't looking to start one anytime soon.

Danni walked back to her desk and grabbed her coat and bag. She had had enough for one day. As depressing as the weather was outside, it was less depressing than staying here any longer. She headed home, stopping in past Marks and Spencer's food hall on the way to pick up a ready meal for one. She was not in the mood for cooking tonight.

Chapter Nine

Danni felt like her head had only just hit the pillow when her radio alarm blared into life. "It's six o'clock and time to head over to Alistair in the newsroom."

"Thanks, Martin. The body found in woods near Countesswells yesterday has been identified as that of missing prominent oil manager, David Gordon. Gordon had been reported missing by his wife two days ago. Enquiries are currently ongoing into the cause of his death. Police are treating the incident as unexplained. There has been another terrorist attack in London overnight…"

Danni sat bolt upright in bed, had she heard that right? *The ex-CEO of Moskaneft had been found dead? That can't be right, surely?* There had been loads of rumours going around the office the day it was announced he was leaving for 'personal reasons'. Some believed he had pissed off the Russians one too many times by not following orders. Others of a more dramatic nature reckoned he had been literally taken out by the Russians and now, for someone like that to be found dead, it was going to raise many more questions than it answered. She switched on the bedside light, got out of bed and went through to the kitchen to switch on the coffee maker before jumping in the shower. *Work is going to be interesting today!* She would need to avoid Becky at all costs. She would be in her element with all that gossip to spread!

Danni reached the office by 6:45am and the management suite level was already lit up against the black of the early morning sky, meaning she wasn't the only one who had come in early. There were security guards outside to guide everyone into the building, past the reporters and TV camera crews who were already setting up camp. As she scurried through the crowd there were shouts of, "What do you think happened to Mr Gordon?"; "When did you last see him alive?"; "Why did Mr Gordon leave Moskaneft?"; "Is there any progress on the investigation into the death offshore?" Danni kept her head down with her scarf up over her face and was ushered into the office by the guards. They were big lads, and spoke with Russian accents, obviously hired in by the company.

As she passed through the security scanners there were additional guards on the reception desk making a log of names and checking passes. They looked inside her bag and she was swiped with a metal detector too.

"Apologies for this, Miss," said one of the security guards as he handed back her pass. "Extra security will be in place until further notice." He then waved her through towards the lifts. She did not ask him any questions as he did not look like he wanted to answer them. She could see why he had been chosen to guard the office as he was not someone that you would want to mess with. He must have been six foot four at least and built like the proverbial brick shithouse, dressed in a dark blue suit that didn't look like it had come off the rails at Marks and Spencer. He had a shaved head and piercing blue eyes that had an evil look with a scar down his left cheek. Danni thought he looked like a *James Bond* villain. As she made her way past the front desk, she half expected to see a white cat curled up on the chair behind the desk. What she did notice was that the handset of the main reception phone had been lifted off its cradle. No doubt it had been ringing off the hook with all those reporters wanting to be the first to get an exclusive interview, but she doubted that anyone was going to get past Ernst Stavro Blofeld.

Danni pushed the button for the lift and when it arrived the doors opened to reveal yet another security guard inside, not as big as Dr Evil on the front desk, but he looked just as scary. "Pass," he asked as he held out his hand to receive it. Danni handed it over and he looked at the pass, then looked at her, the looked at the pass again. He handed it back and asked, "Which floor?"

"Eight, please," replied Danni as she moved inside. She tried to strike up a conversation with him as the doors closed and the lift passed through the various floors. "What's going on? Isn't this a bit over the top?"

"The safety and security of its employees is of the upmost importance to Moskaneft," replied the guard, staring straight ahead and not making eye contact with Danni. She guessed he had been well briefed on the company line.

The lift reached the eighth floor and the doors opened. "Thank you," said Danni. The guard did not reply but just pressed the button to close the doors. The red numbered panel above the lift showed the numbers going down 7, 6, 5… as it made its way back to the ground floor.

There was no-one in yet on her floor, the overhead fluorescent lights clicking into life as she moved down the corridor and the sensors detected her motion. At least she could get some work done whilst it was still quiet, before the hoards entered and the rumour and speculation began. She sat at her desk and switched on her computer. She had to get that report ready for her boss and she only had a few days left before he expected it. God only knew how many boxes of files she still had to log. She would head up to the file room later, but first things, first. *Coffee!*

Danni was fed up of the instant rubbish that they were being forced to drink since the cutbacks and had decided to take in her own jar. There was no way she was going to leave it in here though. Even with her name on it, it would be gone in seconds. She spooned some granules into her mug and poured on the hot water, the rich aroma wafting through the air. *Ah, that smelled much better than that mass catered muck.* She took the mug and her coffee jar back to her desk, hiding the jar in the desk drawer. She searched the BBC News website to find out if anything was being said about David Gordon's death, but it didn't open. She tried again but a message came up: "The site you are trying to access may be restricted, please check with your administrator." She knew the Russians had strict control over what you could access on the web. Facebook, Twitter and Instagram were all access denied, but it looked like they were now on a total lockdown. She tried the news app on her phone but found that the Wi-FI access had been disconnected. Typical of the Russians. They would still be expecting a full day's work from everyone, never mind what was all over the news and going on outside the office.

Danni heard the lift doors open and in walked a couple of the accountants. They came out of the lift in silence, but as soon as the doors closed they started to chinwag, obviously not wanting to speak in front of the security guard for fear it would be reported back. She imagined it was going to be like this all day. She opened her report and started to read through the last few paragraphs, checking her notes to see where she had got to. The lift doors pinged open again, only this time instead of a deathly hush, she heard the dulcet tones of Becky. *Oh great, here we go,* thought Danni.

"Well you're a font of information, aren't you," sniped Becky to the security guard as she exited the lift. There was no reply, unsurprisingly.

Becky spotted the two accountants who had arrived earlier, huddled over a desk in the corner of the office.

"Hey, have you guys heard the news?" she shrieked. "Oh my God, what the fuck is going on there, that is like totally suspicious don't you think? Here one day and found in the woods a few days later. I heard a dog had dug him up. Do you think them upstairs had anything to do with it? It wouldn't surprise me. Who's next for the bullet?"

"You, with any luck," replied Danni.

The two accountants laughed out loud. Becky swung round to see that Danni was standing behind her. She was furious that she was being laughed at. She was normally the one doing the pointing and laughing. How dare she.

"Who the fuck asked you?"

"Well, you did ask."

"Yeah, well, I wasn't speaking to you. Piss off back to *Sleepy Hollow* or wherever it is they usually keep you hidden from view."

Danni laughed; she had finally got one over on Becky. If she wasn't an enemy before, she had definitely made her one now! *Oh well, it was worth it just to see that smirk wiped off her face, even if it had only lasted a few sweet seconds.* She would take her victories where she could.

The office was starting to get busier now and unsurprisingly the only topic of conversation was what had happened to David. Well, that along with the rumours of a cover up following the death on the North Platform. Danni did think it was strange that no formal report had been issued. None of the usual 'lessons learned', no safety bulletins to the other platforms to ensure something similar did not happen again. She would normally have seen the report findings, being part of the ER team, but there had been a deathly silence on the incident since the Russians stepped in. But as they say, there's no smoke without fire and this was only going to add fuel to a fire that was already burning out of control.

Danni didn't want to get involved in the whispering and hearsay, so she headed back up to the file room hoping to get the last few boxes catalogued. She plugged in her earphones and switched to the local radio station on her phone. "And that was Echo Beach by Martha and the Muffins."

Danni laughed to herself. *Well, that song was apt, in more ways than one.* Her job was very boring, and she had been to a resort called Echo Beach in Bali. Mark had whisked her off on a surprise holiday to celebrate their first anniversary. He told her to pack her bikini and plenty of sunscreen but wouldn't tell her where they were going. He had kept it a secret and she had no idea until they got to the airport. It had been so romantic. The beaches, the villa with the balcony overlooking the sea, the seafood cafes up in the hills giving 180-degree views of the stunning sunsets. They had sipped champagne and dined on lobster. Danni had felt like a princess. How could one girl be so lucky? Little did she know what was waiting around the corner.

But all that was in another life. The life before Mark became possessive and then violent. She wondered what she had done to make him behave that way. Was it her or was it him that had changed? She shuddered, a cold shiver down her spine, goose bumps on her arms. Her mother used to say it was someone walking over your grave. She had lots of sayings like that. *Eat up your carrots, they will help you see in the dark. Good things come to those who wait. A little knowledge is a dangerous thing. A good man is hard to find. Well, she had definitely been right on that one!*

And superstitions, she was certainly one for superstitions. Her mother had got them from her mother, handed down from generation to generation. Like saluting a single magpie while saying, 'Hello Mr Magpie, how's your wife and kids?' But it was only bad luck to see one magpie. *One for sorrow, two for joy.* She had shouted at Danni for opening an umbrella inside, and she was not allowed to put new shoes on a table because it would bring bad luck. *A rabbit's foot was supposed to bring good luck, but it certainly wasn't lucky for the rabbit! And what was the story with black cats and them crossing your path? Was that lucky or unlucky?* Danni couldn't remember.

Danni shook herself out of her daydream and got back to work. How long had she been daydreaming? She looked at her watch, it had only been five minutes but had felt much longer. There was only half a dozen more boxes to go through and then she would be finished. Well, finished in here, she still had to finalise the report. She went to the last rack of files. But hold on, there was another box sitting on the floor next to the rack and the lid was not on straight, like it had been opened and shut again in a hurry. Who else had been in here? Danni had had this room to herself since she had started this assignment. No-one had come in while she had been here and given the hours she had been working it was unlikely anyone was still in the office after she left that would have access to the area. Unless it was one of the managers who could get access through the door from the boardroom.

She lifted the lid from the box and peered inside. *Nothing suspicious, just a box of files. But wait a minute, what's this?* A single sheet of paper tucked in between two of the folders.

She pulled it out. It was a hand-written scribble in blue biro. The writing was terrible, all scratchy and at an angle, like it has been written in a hurry. She read it.

"I fear for my life and for the lives of those who work here. The Russians are planning something, and they want me gone. If anything should happen to me, please tell my wife and kids that I love them. DG."

DG? David Gordon. Whoa! What the hell? Had Danni just found his last testament? She read it again, over and over. What was she supposed to do with this?

The access panel to the room beeped into life and she heard the door handle being tried. As she turned to face whoever was coming in, she slipped the piece of paper into her trouser pocket. Her heart was pounding, and she held her breath. There was nowhere to run, she was trapped.

"Holy shit! You nearly gave me heart failure! I didn't know anyone was in here. Good job you're a first aider, I might have needed you to give me mouth to mouth." It was Tony.

"Jesus, Tony. I scared you? You shouldn't creep up on people like that. And what are you doing in here, anyway?"

"I'm looking for some personnel files. Medical records to be exact. Need to find out if Dougie had any medical conditions and what was recorded during his last offshore medical for the incident report."

"Dougie?"

"Yeah, Douglas Henderson."

Danni looked blank.

"You know, the guy who got squished on the North Platform?"

"Oh, right, yeah. I wondered what was happening with that as it's all gone quiet in here. Nobody is saying anything."

"Well I've been summoned by the tyrants for a 'de-brief session', whatever they mean by that. Sounds to me like a 'cover-up' session. There's something decidedly fishy about the whole thing, it just doesn't feel right to me."

Danni could feel the piece of paper in her hand that was stuffed in her pocket. Did she show Tony? Could she trust him? He certainly seemed to be suspicious of the Russians anyway, so maybe he was the right person to tell. She was about to say something when the door from the boardroom opened. She turned quickly, heart leaping into her mouth again.

"I thought I would find you in here, Antony." *Oh no, he was being called by his Sunday name.*

"Did you find the file you were looking for?"

It was Aleksandr, one of the big bosses. He was built like the security guards downstairs: tall, broad, dark hair that was close cropped and a chiselled jaw. Eyes that were so dark they looked black, dead.

"Not yet, Danni here is helping me so should have it in a jiffy."

He looked Danni up and down like she was something he had just scraped off his shoe. Danni felt another chill down her spine. He was creepy, unnerving. She wouldn't want to meet him in a dark alley, although she had a feeling that was probably just the sort of place he would hang out. He looked like an assassin, like he could, and would, kill someone with his bare hands, just for the fun of it.

"We are ready for you now. Do not keep us waiting." He turned and walked back out the door he had come in.

"Well, he's a bundle of joy," said Tony.

"Shh, he might hear you."

"Are you going to help me find this file before he comes back in here and just shoots me? I reckon I've got five minutes tops."

"The personnel files are over in the cabinets right at the back." Danni moved through the file room to a wall full of old-fashioned gunmetal grey filing cabinets. The locks had long since stopped working, hence the reason they were now stored in this room. Tony opened the door marked H–F and flipped through the files till he found one titled 'Henderson, Douglas'. He pulled out the file and pushed the drawer shut with a flick of his hip.

"Tony, there is something I need to speak to you about."

"Well, it's going to have to wait, cause if I don't get in there in the next few seconds, they are likely to rip me a new arsehole, although I get a feeling that is going to happen anyway."

"Sure, later then?"

"I'll come find you if I'm still alive!"

Chapter Ten

Offshore on the North Platform

"I'm worried they are not going to pay out."

"Of course they will, they won't want the bad publicity if they don't. Reputation is everything to them."

"But everything has gone quiet. They're not asking questions like they usually do. They know something. The medic is onshore right now with them for a meeting."

"That's just procedure, he was first on the scene. Tony's all right, he doesn't suspect a thing, or if he does, he hasn't said anything to me. I've spoken to him. We are home and dry. We just need to be patient."

"God, I hope so, I really need that money. Alison is due next month and with another mouth to feed, we are struggling to make ends meet as it is. Are you sure we will get our hands on the cash?"

"Dougie said so, didn't he? He's a man of his word. Jeannie's got our bank details and as soon as she gets that cheque and it clears her bank account we are in the money."

"I feel bad, knowing what we've done. I keep waking up in the night in cold sweats. Alison knows there is something wrong."

"You haven't said anything have you?"

"No, of course I haven't, but she's not stupid, she knows something is up."

"You can't breathe a word of this to anyone. If this gets out… well, I dread to think what the consequences would be. Listen, you heard what Dougie told us, he was going to die anyway. All we've done is help him to help his family, make sure they are provided for. He didn't have long and this way, everyone benefits. Do you want his family suffering any more than they have to?"

"No."

"Just keep your mouth shut and if you have to speak to someone about it then speak to me. No-one else, not even Alison. OK?"

"OK."

"Right, get back to work before any one wonders where you've got to."

Chapter Eleven

Danni slumped down onto the one and only chair in the file room, the weight of what she had just found was heavy on her shoulders. Her legs were no longer able to hold her upright. She pulled the sheet of paper from her pocket and read it again. She had to get out of here, it wasn't safe with the Russians next door in the boardroom; after all it was them that David had feared. She went back to her desk and down the back stairwell, trying to avoid contact with anyone. She slipped the note from her pocket into her handbag, looking sheepishly over her shoulder as she did it to make sure no-one saw. She shut the bag in the desk drawer, locking it and putting the key in her pocket.

"Danni."

She jumped.

"Have you finished upstairs?" asked her boss.

"Almost."

"Then what are you doing down here?"

"Erm, I have a migraine, I need to go home." Danni needed to get out of here and it was the first thing she could think of.

"Well that's not really convenient. There's going to be a minute's silence for David at twelve o'clock and they want everyone in the conference room to mark it."

"I'm sorry, I can't help it. I need to go."

She stood up, took the key from her pocket, opened the desk drawer and grabbed her handbag and snatched her coat from the back of her chair.

"I'll be in early tomorrow," she said as she started walking. "I'll be fine, I just need to lie down in a dark room." *Well that bit was true!*

"Fine! Just make sure that report is finished and on my desk by 5pm tomorrow."

"Right, boss." She waved him off and made for the lifts clutching her bag tightly like her life depended on it.

As she headed for the lift she suddenly panicked. *What if they were still searching bags? Would they be searching them on the way out too?* She couldn't take that chance. She veered left and into the toilets, slamming the toilet cubicle door behind her. She took the note from her bag, folded it in half four times and stuffed it down her bra. She was definitely keeping this secret close to her chest.

She buttoned up her coat and pulled her scarf tight round her neck, making sure her secret was well and truly covered up, camouflaging it as best she could. She pulled open the main door to the toilets and Becky fell into her.

"Fuck's sake, watch what you're doing," sniped Becky.

"Well look where you're going then."

"What's with the coat and bag, where are you off to? Skiving again?"

"If you must know, I have a migraine and I'm going home."

"Just seeing your face gives me a migraine."

"Oh, whatever Becky, I don't have time for any of your shit today."

She barged past her out into the hall and pushed the button for the lift.

"Fuck you," Becky shouted back over her shoulder.

And fuck you too, thought Danni, but she wasn't about to get into a slagging match with Becky. Right now, she had to get out of here, the sooner the better.

The lift doors opened, and she was met by the same security guard who had been there in the morning. She wondered if he had been stuck in there all day. He looked pissed off but probably no more than he had done first thing, so that could have just been his normal expression.

"Ground floor please."

He looked straight through her, the same look she had got from Aleksandr earlier. *Were they all taught that in school when they were younger?*

He pushed the button and the lift doors closed. Danni would have felt self-conscious anyway, being stuck in the lift with a brute like this but knowing what she knew she felt even more so. She stared straight ahead, not wanting to make eye contact.

It seemed like an eternity before the lift doors opened, like she had entered another time zone. She dropped her head and walked out into the main reception area. It was still manned by the security guards and she could see that the reporters and TV cameramen had not relented and held their positions even in the cold and sleet. Anything to get that picture, that story that would hit the headlines tonight.

"Miss, you cannot go out that way. Please come with me."

She felt a hand on her shoulder and she stopped dead in her tracks, her heart jumped into her mouth.

They know!

She held her breath as she turned to face Dr Evil.

"This way." He placed his hand on the small of her back and guided her away from the front door, round the back of the reception desk and down a dark corridor.

This is it, she thought. *They know that I know. I'm a dead man walking.* She half closed her eyes and gritted her teeth, waiting for it to happen. A blow to the head, a knife stab in the back. *Surely not a bullet, unless he had a silencer?* He looked like someone who would know where to get a silencer.

"You can use the emergency exit door. We have cars waiting to take you away."

Of course, they wouldn't do it here. Not with camera crews and reporters waiting outside. How would they dispose of the body? No, better to take her somewhere secluded. Like they had done with David. Oh God, this was it!

Dr Evil pushed the bar down on the emergency exit door and ushered Danni out into the ground floor of the multi-storey car park that was situated behind the office block. Her legs would barely function. He directed her to the line of waiting cars. They were queued up in the car park, away from the prying eyes of the cameras. He opened the rear door of the first car and Danni reluctantly got in.

"Where to, Miss?"

Surely you know where you are taking me? she thought. Or maybe this was just a masquerade to disarm her, put her on the back foot and lull her into a false sense of security so she didn't see it coming.

"Rosemount, please." Although she had her suspicions that was not where she would be going.

The driver pushed the ignition button and the car sped off out of the car park, whizzing past the cameras at speed so they could not get any photographs. It was like a scene from the news on TV when a politician had been found pocketing tax payer's money, or a criminal had just walked free from court and they were desperately trying to keep their faces out of the papers.

The car didn't stop at the traffic lights but shot out into the oncoming traffic and turned right onto Market Street. Horns blaring, arms being waves and obscenities being shouted.

OK, so they were trying to kill her in a car crash and make it look like an accident.

The car sped through the next set of lights, which were thankfully on green, up the hill past the Douglas Hotel towards Union Street.

"Stop here!" Danni shouted.

"But I thought you were going to Rosemount?"

"Change of plans; I need to get out here."

"OK, but I'm going to have to charge you the full fare."

Danni opened her bag, took out her purse and pulled the last ten-pound note from her purse. Not much in exchange for her life.

"Will this cover it?"

She threw the tenner onto the passenger seat as the car pulled up outside the doors to the deserted Aberdeen market.

The car had barely come to a halt when Danni opened the door and jumped out.

"Wait, Miss, your change."

But Danni was not hanging around. She ran up the hill and around the corner, not looking back, across Union Street and into the St Nicholas Shopping Centre where there would be more people to hide amongst. Only then did she dare to look behind her to see if anyone was following her.

She walked into a clothes shop and weaved through the racks of clothes to the back of the store. She picked up a top, but she wasn't interested in it, she was watching to see if anyone was following her.

"Can I help you, Miss?" Danni nearly jumped out of her skin as the sales assistant approached her from the side.

"Are you OK?"

"Sorry, you gave me a scare. I'm just looking, thanks."

"OK, if I can help you with anything just give me a shout."

The sales assistant walked off and Danni looked back towards the main entrance. She hadn't seen anyone follow her in. Her breath started to return to normal and her heart rate was beginning to slow.

She made her way out of the shop and headed back into the shopping centre, into the lunchtime crowd of office workers rushing around to pick up a sandwich or just get out and stretch their legs before returning to their desks for the afternoon shift. It was busier than usual with eager shoppers starting their Christmas shop early, bustling around to the Christmas music that would be piped out on repeat over the next few weeks, making the shop workers want to lose their will to live. The Christmas decorations had started to go up weeks ago and the shop fronts already had their displays of jolly Santas, reindeer and fake snow. There were tinsel garlands and giant baubles hanging from the centre's ceiling. There was no escape, it was everywhere you looked. Christmas was the last thing on Danni's mind at the moment. She had to get out of here, get back to the safety of her flat and then she had a big decision in front of her. What should she do with the letter? Her mum had been right. *A little knowledge is a dangerous thing!*

As she pushed out through the centre's big glass doors she was caught up in a whirlwind of people, banners and placards. There were hundreds of them marching and chanting. The ones at the front had megaphones and were rallying the troops.

"What do we want?"

"An end to poverty!"

"When do we want it?"

"Now!"

Danni wanted to head left towards Rosemount, but she was quickly swallowed up by the crowd and swept along from Schoolhill, up Upper Kirkgate towards Marischal Square. She fought to get free of them, but the crowd were determined. They were on a mission and she was worried she would be trampled. She was claustrophobic and had an overwhelming feeling of being crushed. She started to panic, hyperventilating. She couldn't see where she was going or where to put her feet. The path of least resistance was to let the crowd carry her, go with the flow and try to move her way to the edge, to break free of their clutches.

As the crowd curved right into Marischal Square, Danni could hear the roar getting louder. Flashing blue lights were visible, their reflections bouncing off the glass fronted buildings like strobe lights, making her disorientated. They were being met by Aberdeen's finest, the boys in blue, who had been sent to disperse them. The noise of the crowd was deafening as they made a push towards the waiting police line. Suddenly there was a massive surge of people and Danni lost her footing, tripping and stumbling towards the ground. She grabbed the person next to her trying to stay upright and pulled him down. And still the crowd kept coming. Somehow she stayed upright, but the man she had grabbed was on the floor, rolled up in a foetal position and being trampled by a heard of wild protestors. She could hear his cries but there was nothing she could do. This literally was survival of the fittest. She clambered over placards, bags and bottles, discarded by the angry mob as they rushed forward. People were being sent flying, crashing to the ground while others desperately fought to stay vertical.

Danni was being pushed closer and closer to the front. She could see the police line ahead of her, some of them with their telescopic batons extended, thrashing through the air trying to make contact with as many heads, legs and bodies as possible. Others had canisters of PAVA spray flicked open and poised, ready to send their liquid stream into the faces of their unsuspecting victims, immediately incapacitating them. Several had already been discharged as men and woman alike dropped to their knees, hands flailing at their faces trying to wipe the stinging, burning liquid from their eyes.

From behind the police lines, more police officers started to push through, lifting up the victims of what would later be described as police brutality on the news, and manhandling them into police transit vans waiting behind the scenes. Those in the vans would be transported to Kittybrewster, but their cells were filling quickly so others were being carted directly down to Queen Street the police headquarters, which was just around the corner, their feet barely touching the ground.

Danni fought hard to get back from the front-line, but a further surge of the crowd shoved her forward and she tripped over a body lying on the floor, clutching their head and screaming. She found herself at the feet of two officers who grabbed an arm each, scooping her up and dragging her through the police line. One was taller than the other. She was being lifted higher on one side, making it difficult for her to keep her feet and walk. Danni started to protest but they were not for listening.

"No, please you don't understand, I'm not one of them."

"Shut it," said the taller one. He must have been over six foot and although lanky, had a vice like grip. The other one was much shorter – about five foot eight – and stockier in build. *The little and large of the police force.*

"But I'm telling the truth, I was on my way home when…"

"Yeah, yeah, we've heard it all before. You can tell it to the custody sergeant."

She struggled to break free, but her attempts were futile. They were not letting go.

Danni was dragged, kicking and screaming down the lane towards the ugly towering building of Queen Street Police Station. They manhandled her past the main entrance and round the back to the custody suite. The place was inundated with police and protestors, queuing up to be booked in, some refusing to give their details resulting in having their pockets and bags searched for wallets and purses and any form of identification. The seasoned rioters had left their personal possessions at home, but many were already known to the police. Knives and metal bars were handed to the sergeant who recorded the details and placed the items into evidence bags, their owners, after being frisked, were trailed off into the holding cells.

Danni reached the front of the queue.

"Name."

"Look, I was trying to tell your officers, this is all a mistake. I wasn't part of the demonstration, I got caught up…"

"NAME."

"I shouldn't be here…"

The custody sergeant looked at Danni and sighed. "Look here, Missy, the sooner you co-operate the sooner you will be out of here. NOW, NAME."

"Dannielle Ross."

"Address."

"64 Esslemont Avenue."

"Date of birth."

"14th December 1986."

He looked at the arresting officers. "And what is she being charged with?"

"Breach of the peace."

One of the officers had already taken her handbag from her and he placed it on the counter. "Empty your pockets."

Danni panicked. What if they searched her? *They might find the note.* She stood there, not moving, in shock.

"I won't ask you again, now empty your pockets."

Danni rummaged in her coat pockets and pulled out a crumpled tissue, fifty-three pence in coins and half a packet of polo mints. She placed them in the box that had appeared on the counter.

"And your other pockets."

"There's nothing in them."

"Let me see."

Danni opened her coat and pulled her pockets inside out confirming they were empty. Thank God she had stuffed the note into her bra. *Surely they wouldn't search any further!*

"Remove your watch."

Pushing the catch of watch's bracelet, it popped open and she slid it from her wrist over her hand and laid it in the tray with her other belongings.

"And your belt."

Danni looked down and undid the buckle of her belt, pulling it free from the loops and placing it in the outstretched hands of the sergeant.

"Boots too."

She pulled off her boots and looked down, thankful there were no holes in her socks.

"Take her through to cell number eight."

Danni opened her mouth, ready to protest but given the death stare she was faced with she realised it was useless. She allowed herself to be frog-marched down the white corridor. An officer unlocked a security gate and she was shown to her room for the evening.

"You might as weel git comfy quine. Ye ah'll be here for i'night an yer case ah'll git seen tee in t'morning," said the shorter officer in a broad Aberdonian accent. Danni flinched as the cell door was slammed shut behind her.

She surveyed her residence for the night. Whitewashed walls, a raised concrete platform with a blue vinyl covered mattress and matching blue blanket. A metal sink was attached to the wall and a similar metal toilet only just hidden from view of the cell door behind a low screen wall. She turned as she heard the sliding peephole slam shut. She was all alone. How the hell did she end up here? One minute she was fearing for her life and now she was in police custody! *Could this day get any more ridiculous?*

She collapsed onto the mattress. It was as thin and hard as it looked. She guessed they were not designed for comfort. She raised her right hand to her chest and felt the folded piece of paper still in her bra. At least they hadn't found that, or she would really be in for a grilling tomorrow. She decided to leave it there in fear that someone might look in at the wrong time and find her with it. All she could do now was get her head down and try to sleep the rest of this ludicrous day away.

Chapter Twelve

Danni was running. Running from the monster. The monster who wanted to kill her. She was in the woods. The path was muddy, and she was struggling to keep her feet. It was raining, and she was slipping and sliding as she ran and ran. She could hear his shouts over the rumble of the thunder.

"Where are you, bitch? You can't hide forever. I'll find you!"

Lightning cracked and lit up the sky, casting shadows from the trees. Their branches were grabbing at Danni, trying to stop her as she pushed through the undergrowth. She had to get off the path, had to find somewhere to hide. Her heart was drumming in her ears, her lungs burning. She tripped over a branch and fell down a bank into a ditch. She started crawling on hand and knees as pain shot through her left knee. The sky lit up again, the lightning closer; it was overhead.

There!

A hole in the trunk of a dead sycamore tree, just big enough for Danni to crawl into. She crouched, pulling her legs up tight against her chest, head bowed down against her knees. She tried to control her breathing, but she couldn't slow it down. She had to; he might hear her. She heard the crack of a branch breaking underfoot. He was close, too close. She couldn't run now; he would see her.

"Danni!"

The voice sounded closer.

"Danni!"

The lighting cracked again.

Danni woke suddenly, startled by the loud crack. But it wasn't lightning she had heard, and she wasn't in the woods. Where was she? It was white, bright, the light shining overhead was glaring.

"Danni?"

She rubbed her eyes and sat bolt upright. She turned to face her monster.

"Miss Ross. Are you OK?"

The bolt of the cell door cracked open and a police officer walked in. Danni wrenched herself from one nightmare into another. She took in her surroundings and the memory of yesterday's escapades came flooding back to her.

"You're free to go."

"What?" replied Danni, still not quite in this world.

"We've reviewed the CCTV from the protests yesterday and we are satisfied you were not one of the instigators. You're free to go without charge." It was a different police officer from yesterday.

"You can collect your possessions from the front desk." He motioned towards the door and Danni stood up, pulling her coat tight around her neck. She walked out into the corridor, keen to escape from this hell hole. The sooner she was out of here the better. The officer followed her to the custody desk where her belongings were already sitting on the counter.

"Is this all your possessions?" asked the custody sergeant. It was the same one that had booked her in yesterday. She wondered who he had pissed off to have to pull a double shift.

Danni picked up her bag, pulled the zip open and rummaged inside. Her purse, keys and make-up bag were all in there, along with all the other bits of paper she meant to clear out ages ago. Both phones were there, her own one and her work mobile that was showing several missed calls.

She pulled on her boots, picked up the fifty-three pence, tissue and packet of polos, along with her belt and watch and shoved them all in her bag, not wanting to spend any longer in here than was absolutely necessary.

"Yes, that's everything."

"Sign here." He handed her a pen.

She scrawled her name on the form and made for the exit door. She pushed, but the door didn't open. She tried again but still it wouldn't budge.

"Hang on, Miss, I'll need to buzz you out."

The sergeant pressed a button on the wall behind his desk and the lock of the door clicked. Danni pushed and this time the door opened. She marched out without looking back, hoping she never had to return any time soon.

It was early morning and still dark outside. She rummaged in her bag for her watch and saw that it was 7am. As she fastened it to her wrist her mobile phone started ringing. It was her work mobile. As she went to answer it, she noticed there had been several missed calls.

"Hello?"

"Danni, where are you?" It was Tony.

"I've been worried sick. You said you wanted to speak, and I looked for you after my meeting, but your boss said you had gone home with a migraine. I came past the flat but there was no-one home. I've been trying to reach you all night."

"It's a long story and I don't have time right now. I'll call you in a bit, OK?" She hung up on him. Before she did anything, she needed to get home and take a long, hot shower and wash the smell of stale sweat and desperation from her body. She could smell it in her hair.

Tony called back but she ignored him, hitting the decline button. A few seconds later she received a text. It was Tony. He wasn't going to give up in a hurry.

"Call me back. I need to know your OK :)"

What was with the smiley face?! And it's 'you're', not 'your'. Does no-one understand basic grammar nowadays?

She shoved the phone back in her bag and headed out onto Queen Street. It was bitterly cold and blowing a hooley but at least it wasn't raining. Thankful for small miracles, Danni pulled the collar up on her coat and, with the wind at her back, made her way home.

She headed past the scene of yesterday's demonstration. The council had done their best to clean up but there were still banners and placards lying on the pavement and stuck to the railings outside Marischal College. The statue of Robert the Bruce was waving a placard which read 'People against Poverty' whilst donning a very fetching traffic cone at a jaunty angle. She continued onto Schoolhill and onwards to Rosemount Viaduct. The streets were quiet, not quite rush hour yet. A couple of taxi cabs passed by, but she disregarded them, instead relishing the fresh air after being cooped up all night. At the speed she was walking, it only took her fifteen minutes when it would normally take around twenty. Even walking at speed, the cold was still biting, the glow from the streetlights doing nothing to warm her. She turned into her street, stopped at the front door and reached into her bag, scrambling for her keys. They were in here somewhere. *Why is it when you need them you can't find them?* She dropped her bag onto the doorstep and bent down and searched inside, pulling out her purse and both phones. *Where the hell where those keys?* Using her free hand, she felt along the bottom of the bag. *There*, she grabbed them. As she pulled them out and stood to open the door a hand touched her shoulder.

She screamed and turned, striking out with the hand the keys were in and knocking her assailant to the pavement.

"Bloody hell, Danni!"

Danni was ready to run, but she recognised that voice.

"Tony, where the hell did you come from? You shouldn't sneak up on people like that."

"That's the second time you've almost attacked me. What's up with you?" Tony scrambled back to his feet.

"What the hell are you doing here?"

"You're not answering my calls and when you do, you hang up on me and you haven't replied to my text. I needed to make sure you were OK. You seemed upset yesterday and you haven't been home all night…"

"Have you been watching my flat?"

"I came by a couple of times last night and I spoke to one of your neighbours. They knocked at your flat door and no-one answered. And look at you, you don't look like you've been home."

"That's 'cos I spent the night inside."

"What do you mean… inside?"

"You know, inside. Like banged up. Inside a cell. At Queen Street."

"How on earth did you end up in there?"

Danni looked over her shoulder. "Look, I'm not discussing this out here. You better come upstairs." She slid the key into the lock and turned it, opening the door. She switched on the light switch, but the stairwell remained in darkness. Her bloody landlord still hadn't been round to fix it. Tony pulled his phone from his pocket and shone the torch up the stairs.

"After you."

The stairwell was painted a disgusting orangey-brown colour with dark green linoleum on the stairs themselves. The banisters were painted brown too, with several coats of paint making the struts look thicker than they actually were.

Her flat was on the first floor and as they entered it felt warm compared with the cold of the stairwell outside. Danni hung up her coat, went through to the kitchen and switched the boiler back on. The timer had only just switched it off.

Tony followed her into the kitchen. "Wow! Is your landlord a Dons fan?"

The kitchen units were white, but the walls were painted a bright red over woodchip wallpaper. The floor was a red and white tile effect linoleum, the colours of Aberdeen Football club.

"He's a season ticket holder."

"I thought as much. Now, are you going to tell me what's going on?"

"Before I say anything, I need a shower. I need to wash the smell of Queen Street off me. You can wait in the living room."

She walked into the bathroom, shutting and locking the door behind her. She opened the shower cabinet and turned on the hot water, turning the temperature up to high. She began to undress, removing her boots and socks. She unzipped her trousers and let them fall to the floor, stepping out of them and then kicked them into the wash basket in the corner. She undid the buttons of her blouse, slipped it off, rolled it up and threw it on top of her trousers. She was going to have to wash everything twice to get rid of the stink. She put one hand up her back and undid the clasp of her bra and as she removed it, the note fell to the floor. She picked it up, unfolded it and placed it on the toilet cistern. She looked in the mirror, but it was already steaming up. She wiped it with her hand, looking at the tired features staring back. She had aged overnight. Her reflection became hazy and started to fade as the steam yet again fogged up the mirror. She looked back at the note and shouted through the closed door, "You better get the coffee machine on; I have a feeling we are both going to need something strong when you hear what I have to tell you."

Danni let the scalding hot water hit her skin. It was hotter than she would normally want it, but it was the only way to get rid of the smell of last night. *Scald it off!* Her skin was turning pink with the heat, but she didn't care. She wanted to stand in the shower for hours letting yesterday wash off her, but she knew Tony was waiting impatiently, and she couldn't put it off any longer. *After all, a problem shared is a problem halved.* That was another one of her mother's sayings and she had already decided that Tony was the only one she could share this with. He was the only one who had been worried about her. Plus, he already suspected there was something up with the Russians following the incident on the platform. Maybe he had found out more during his meeting with them yesterday.

Danni grabbed a big, fluffy white towel from the heated towel rail. She dried herself and wrapped it around her, grabbing a second smaller towel to dry her hair. She unlocked the door, picked up the note and dashed through to her bedroom not wanting to let Tony see her in a towel. She pulled on her jogging bottoms and a T-shirt and sweatshirt and tied her hair back in a ponytail. She didn't care what she looked like. After all, they were both going to have more things to worry about when she dropped this bombshell on him.

She left the bedroom and walked into the living room. It was a decent-sized room with alcoves either side of the fireplace which housed a gas effect fire. The shelves of the alcoves were bare except for Danni's collection of CDs, DVDs and one photograph of her with her mother. The photo was one of the personal effects she had managed to flee with, and she hadn't bothered to buy anything else as she wasn't sure how long she would be staying. She needed to be ready to leave again at short notice. The walls, like the kitchen, were also adorned with woodchip wallpaper painted magnolia but with paint test patches along one wall. Her landlord had given her permission to paint the living room, but she was not to touch anything in the shrine-to-the-Dons kitchen. The carpet was beige, and the three-piece suite was actually dark blue in colour but was covered by cream coloured throws to fit in with the rest of the decor. Tony was standing by one of the armchairs looking out the window, a mug of coffee in his hand. A second mug was sitting on the table, the steam rising. *At least he had put it on a coaster.*

Tony turned to face her. "Are you going to tell me what this is all about or do I have to guess?"

"You'd better sit down for this."

"OK…" Tony sat on the armchair and Danni sat on the settee. She picked up the mug of coffee and blew on it before taking a sip.

"What's going on?"

"I don't even know where to start, but here goes." Danni pulled the note from the pocket of her jogging bottoms and handed it to Tony.

"What's this?"

"Just read it."

Tony scanned the note, looked directly at Danni and then back at the note. He read it out loud. "I fear for my life and for the lives of those who work here. The Russians are planning something, and they want me gone. If anything should happen to me, please tell my wife and kids that I love them. DG."

"What the fuck? Is this for real? Where did you find this?"

"In the file room, in one of the last boxes I was cataloguing."

"But who… how… what the fuck?"

"I know, it's a lot to take in. I only found it yesterday, just before you went into your meeting. This is what I wanted to talk to you about."

Tony stood up and walked to the window, still holding the note in his hand.

"We need to show this to the police."

"No way, I'm not going back there."

"Oh yeah, that's right. What were you doing spending the night at Her Majesty's pleasure?"

"You're never going to believe this, but I was arrested for breach of the peace."

"Breach of the peace? You?"

"Yeah, yeah, I know. It's a bit of a long story, but basically after I found the note I had to get out of the office, but the TV crews were still outside, and the security guard took me out the back exit. I was ushered into a car and my mind was going overtime so I thought he knew more than he did and was arranging to have me bumped off. So, I jumped out of the car on Market Street and ran into the shopping centre."

"Wait a minute. You thought you were going to be bumped off?"

"Yeah, well, it's obvious that's what happened to David. Anyway, I was scared I was being followed so I hid in a shop for a while and when I left, the Against Poverty march was on and I got caught up in the crowd. A fight broke out with the police and I got arrested. Only I was released this morning without charge."

"Hang on, I can't get my head round this. You thought you were running for your life and then ended up getting arrested? Surely a police cell was a safe place to spend the night?"

"Not for me, but that's another whole story and I'm not going into that right now."

"You're not on the UK's most wanted list, are you?" laughed Tony. "Did you rob a bank or something? Is your dim and distant past catching up with you?"

"Like I say, that's not for today." *Or any other day*, she thought, and she certainly hoped her past was not catching up with her. She could have done without her brush with the long arm of the law.

Tony stared at her. He was intrigued and wanted to ask more, but it was clear she was not in the mood for discussing her personal life.

"What do we do about this note then? We need to tell someone. It says others could be at risk."

"Let's wait and see if the police find anything in their investigation into David's death. There's no point getting involved if we don't have to."

And Danni wanted to avoid any more contact with the police. She was already worried that by being arrested she had given Mark a lead to follow. Would he be checking the police database? What could he find out? She had changed her name, but did he already know that? Had she covered her tracks well enough?

"OK, agreed. We wait to see what the police come up with, but if their investigation concludes it was suicide then we need to rethink this."

"If we do anything about this then we could be in danger. Who knows? Maybe we are already. What if the Russians find out about this?"

"How could they? David's been gone for a while. He must have hidden the note the day he disappeared. If they had found it, they wouldn't have just left it lying about, would they? Incriminating evidence like that. No, they don't know about this and I'm guessing that you and I are the only ones who do. We need to act normal. Whatever normal is. Go into work like nothing has happened. I've got a mate on the police force, I'll speak to him and get him to give us any updates on David's investigation."

"OK, but keep my name out of it."

"Sure, but what's your problem with the police?"

"Like I said before, I don't want to discuss it!"

"OK, OK, whatever. I'll just say that the jungle drums are beating at work and I'm curious if there is more to David's death than meets the eye."

"Fine. Look, you better head into the office. I'm staying put, I need to get my head around this. I'll phone in sick, tell them I've still got a migraine. Unless you think that will look suspicious?"

"I'm heading back offshore on the late flight today; I was only back because the Russians wanted to talk to me about Dougie's death on the platform. I've still got two weeks of my rota to complete."

"What's the story with that? You said you thought it wasn't an accident."

"Yeah, that is what I think, but that's not what I've told them. As far as they are concerned, it was an accident and they are treating it as one. They are putting it down to not following procedures, that the lifting gear wasn't checked before slinging the container and it was past its certified date and was faulty. There are a lot of nervous people on the platform as they are sure someone will be fired for it. They wanted to talk to me about Dougie's health and if I was aware of any issues, as apparently the post mortem showed he had a brain tumour. There is no record of it in his file – which is what I was checking when I saw you in the file room the other day – and he certainly didn't tell me about it. We are not sure if he even knew about it, but it could have been a factor. It was his name on the lifting plan and he signed off on it as the supervisor, but maybe he hadn't checked properly. We'll have to wait and see what happens. Of course, there are now rumours offshore that he did know, and he topped himself so his wife would get the insurance money, but no-one will ever know for sure."

"Do you think he did?"

"I think it's a definite possibility, but I'm not going to risk chancing his pay-out by saying anything. It's just another secret I will have to keep for now. Like the note."

Danni had more than just two secrets to keep and she wasn't going to be sharing them with anyone any time soon. She had become a master of disguise, hiding in plain sight. Blending into the background and not being noticed. She would just have to keep her wits about her.

"At least with the investigation ongoing into David's death they are going to want to close this out quickly. They have enough on their plates that they are not going to notice whether an admin assistant turns up for work or not."

"OK, so maybe I'm overreacting, but after yesterday's encounter with the police you never know what could happen." And it wasn't just yesterday's encounter she was worried about.

"Let me know if your mate turns up anything on the investigation. When are you back onshore?"

"I'm back in two weeks but I'll be in touch before then."

"Don't email me, we can't put anything in writing that they could see."

"Hey, I'm not that stupid!"

"And don't call me on my work mobile. I'll give you my personal number, just don't give it to anyone else."

"Who am I going to give it to?"

"I don't know, I'm just saying, don't give it out, OK?"

"OK, I'm beginning to think there is more to you than meets the eye, with all this cloak and dagger mystery going on. Who are you hiding from?"

"What?! No-one!" He was getting too close to the truth, she had to get him out before he started asking more questions.

"Here, give me your mobile and I'll put my number in your contacts."

He pulled out his phone and gave it to her. She typed in her number and handed it back.

"DR? Like doctor. Could you get any more cryptic?"

"Like I said, I don't want anyone else getting my number. And now I really am starting to get a migraine, so if you don't mind." She motioned towards the door.

"OK, OK, I can take a hint!"

Tony headed back out into the dark stairwell. Danni waited until she heard him go down the stairs and the bang of the main door shut then closed the flat door and headed back into the bathroom. She was going to have to have another shower. She could still smell the stench of last night's sleepover in the cells. She needed to get some paracetamol too as her temples were starting to throb. Unsurprising, given everything she had going on in her head right now!

Chapter Thirteen

"I don't know anything, honestly. Please, just let me go and I won't say a thing. Please!"

"You know too much, and you need to be... dealt with."

"NO, NO, PLEASE, I beg you. I won't say a thing. PLEASE! You've got the wrong person!"

"Deal with her."

Danni knelt on the floor, looking down the barrel of the gun into the eyes of her killer. She pleaded for her life, but she knew what was coming. There was no remorse in those eyes. *Black. Dead. Lifeless.* He adjusted his aim and squeezed the trigger. *BANG!*

Danni woke with a jolt, her hand instantly reaching for the gun in her bedside drawer. Her heart was racing and nerves on edge.

The radio alarm clock clicked into action. "And that was *Here Comes the Rain Again* by the Eurythmics, fronted by Aberdeen's one and only Annie Lennox, and it's definitely fitting for today given the weather outside. If you haven't looked out yet then I suggest you stick your head back under the duvet, stay in bed and stay tuned to Radio Aberdeen, your home for local news and the sounds of the '80s."

She had been having these vivid dreams for nights now. The stress of carrying these secrets was playing on her mind and emerging as full-blown nightmares. She wondered if Tony was suffering the same fate. Knowing him he was probably sleeping like a baby.

"And speaking of the news, here is Alastair with the latest round-up."

"Thanks Martin. Police Scotland have reported that twenty-two protestors were arrested after yesterday's Against Poverty rally which culminated in brawls with police officers in Marischal Square. Several people were injured including three police officers who required medical treatment at Aberdeen Royal Infirmary. None of the injuries were serious and only two people remain in hospital under observation. Of the twenty-two arrested, ten were later released without charge. The remaining twelve were reported to the Procurator Fiscal and will attend Aberdeen Sherriff Court later today. In sport, Aberdeen look to continue their winning streak against arch-rivals Celtic today…"

Danni hit the snooze button and did as the DJ suggested, sticking her head back under the duvet. *I was one of the ten*, she thought. Aberdeen's finest were non-discriminatory when it came to keeping up their arrest figures. No-one counted how many were wrongly arrested! In today's climate they had been given an edict to arrest first and ask questions later. After all, they had to keep the streets safe for the law-abiding public.

It was Saturday and she didn't have to go into the office, but as she had missed most of the last two days, she thought she had better make an effort. Her boss would go ballistic if she didn't get that report finished. She was supposed to have it on his desk yesterday. She didn't want to give him an excuse to give her her P45, although with everything that had been going on that might be a welcome gift. Well it would be if there were any other jobs out there to be had. After Tony had left yesterday, she had showered and then nipped out to the shops to pick up some groceries. Milk, bread, some soup for lunch and a newspaper. The front story was 'an exclusive' about how oil companies have spent the last year slashing spending and firing workers to protect profits, only to find their hard work blown away as the oil price dipped to a new all-time low. Operational efficiencies have gone some way to helping the situation, but the oil price will continue to drive the share price. 'Further, painful cost reductions will be required if they are to ride out the storm' was the strap line. *Surely they couldn't get rid of any more people? Everyone seemed to be doing the work of two people as it was, but how else were they going to reduce costs?*

She switched off the alarm before it went off again and threw back the covers. *Holy shit, it's Baltic. Cold enough to freeze the balls off a brass monkey.* Another of her mother's sayings. Her feet hit the cold floor and she tip-toed through to the kitchen, not wanting to touch the floor any more than she had to. She switched on the heating. It wasn't set to come on till later as she wouldn't normally be up at this time on a Saturday. There was a film of condensation on the kitchen window. The flat was supposed to be double-glazed but she had her suspicions that the window was long since passed its useful date. She could see her breath in the air. Before leaving the kitchen, she pressed the button to set the coffee machine into action and then jumped into the shower. *Aggghhh!* The water wasn't quite hot yet. She hadn't given it time. Cold needles pierced her skin. It was only seconds before it heated but if felt like forever. At least she had finally got rid of the stink of the cells from her hair. Her clothes had been washed and were hanging up on the clothes horse in the kitchen. She had added an extra dose of detergent to the wash to get rid of the smell and had then worried that she would be mopping up soap suds as they flooded out of the machine. Thankfully it hadn't come to that. She rinsed the shampoo from her hair and dried herself, then dressed in a pair of jeans and a sweater. The office would be dead. She had been in the last few weekends working through the files and hadn't seen a soul, so it didn't matter what she wore as no-one would see her.

She jogged most of the way to work. The rain had faded to a mild drizzle but was still just as drenching. The Christmas lights had been switched on on Union Street, but they did little to lift her spirits. They were the same ones as last year with their twelve days of Christmas theme. And, just like last year, many of the bulbs were out or missing altogether. The six geese were no longer laying and there were only four gold rings. Santa had not paid a visit to Aberdeen Council recently.

When Danni arrived at the office, she noticed that the Russian mafia security had been removed, along with all the reporters and camera crew. They had given up on their exclusive story and had gone off to harass some other poor soul. Tom, the usual weekend security guard was back on duty. Tom was in his mid-sixties, short and dumpy with a healthy head of grey hair, a matching beard and ruddy cheeks. He could have passed for Santa himself and Danni was sure he had attended the odd children's party in his life. He had a similar cheery personality to the big man.

"Morning, Tom."

"Morning, Danni. I didn't expect to see anyone in today. No rest for the wicked, eh?"

"Something like that."

Danni placed her hand on the biometric scanner and waited for the light to turn green. Nothing happened. She tried again, still nothing.

"The system is down at the moment. It's being updated this weekend to remove everyone who has been let go. They didn't expect anyone to come in. Thought they would all be Christmas shopping or heading off to the Dons game."

"Oh, right. I really need to get an urgent report finished. If I don't do it today, then my name will be next to be removed from the system."

"Well, I'm not supposed to let anyone in, but since it's you." He took a swipe card from the reception desk drawer and swiped it through the machine to activate it. He handed it to Danni and motioned towards the door. He pushed a button to open the sliding glass door and Danni walked through.

"It's one of the cleaner's cards, but I know he's heading to the game and he won't be in. They are on a different part of the system, so their cards are still working. I'm afraid the lifts are out of order too so you're going to have to take the stairs, but the swipe card will give you access to all of Moskaneft's floors. If there's any problem, just call down to reception."

"Thanks, Tom, I owe you one."

"No problem, Danni, you have a good day now."

Danni headed for the stairwell. She had just jogged all the way here; the last thing she wanted to do was scale eight flights of stairs, but that's just what she would have to do. She stood at the bottom, hands on her hips, contemplating the challenge ahead and then started the climb. She stopped briefly for a rest at the halfway mark on the fourth floor, caught her breath then pushed on up the stairs.

She made it to the eighth floor and swiped her borrowed pass card on the reader. The door unlocked, and she made her way to the other end of the corridor. First things first, she was desperate for some caffeine! The lights switched on as she made her way along the floor and the motion sensors detected her movement. They would switch off again in five minutes if there was nothing more to detect. She switched on the kettle and went to her desk drawer to get her jar of proper coffee. If she had to be in here, she wasn't going to settle for that weak brown piss they were trying to pass off as coffee.

While she waited for the kettle, she looked out the window into the darkness and caught her reflection staring back at her. Was that really her? She looked like she was carrying the weight of the world on her shoulders. Bags and dark circles under her eyes. The stress was starting to take its toll on her face. The kettle came to the boil and clicked off, the steam fogging up the window and masking her reflection. She poured the hot water into the mug, stirring twice and rinsed the spoon under the tap, replacing it back in the cutlery drawer. As she walked back to her desk, she couldn't help but think about the note she found and what had happened to David. There had been little more on the news other than the desperate appeals for information from Police Scotland. Danni was sure that no-one would come forward. If the Russians had dealt with him, they would have covered their tracks. *What if there was something more in the file room? Something else to link them to his death.* She'd had to get out of there sharpish and she had not been back in there since. Maybe there were more notes, more evidence. She had to look.

Danni headed out into the emergency stairwell where the doors had automatically swung open when the security system had been shut down. She ran up the two flights of stairs to the tenth floor which was in darkness. *No-one was up here, so that's a good start.* She swiped her pass to enter the room, but nothing happened. Damn it, of course it wasn't her pass, Tom had given her one of the cleaner's. They wouldn't have access in here. Danni was about to head back downstairs to get her own pass from her bag when she remembered the system was down. *But wait a minute, if the system was down, maybe, just maybe the door was unlocked...* She tried the handle and, to her surprise, the door opened. *So much for security!* They really didn't expect anyone to be in here today.

She closed the door behind her and switched on the light. Nothing happened. She flicked it again, still nothing. Maybe shutting down the system had fused them. She wouldn't be surprised; they had always been a bit dodgy. Flickering on and off. They hadn't been upgraded to the new motion sensor lighting. That would cost too much money and since hardly anyone came in here, they would just have to do with the old fluorescent tubes. She took her phone out of her pocket and switched on the flashlight app and made her way down through the racks of files. The box where she had found the note was still lying on the floor, the lid balancing against it. It didn't look like anyone had been in here since she last left. Danni rummaged through the files in the box, flicking through the pages then holding each one up and shaking it to see if anything would fall out. *Nada. Not a thing.* She was about to place the last file back in the box when she heard a noise. She ducked behind the shelving rack and switched off the light on her phone. She could hear muffled voices. Russian accents. She snuck over toward the wall that adjoined the boardroom so she could hear better, and slid into a tight space behind a filing cabinet, pressing her ear against the wall.

"The office is clear, there is no-one here. A cleaner was on the eighth floor but he must have left as the lights are out. There is no record of anyone else entering the building."

"Good. We need to discuss our plan for the South Platform. It is bleeding us dry. Moscow is unhappy. They want something done, and soon. What do you suggest?"

"Shut it down. Permanently. I have some friends who can make the arrangements. They know people who will be 'willing' to help if you know what I mean?"

Laughter.

"Ah, yes. Blackmail and intimidation can get you a lot of willing help."

More laughter.

"Make the arrangements and let me know when everything is in place."

"*Da.* Consider it done."

Shut it down permanently? What did they mean? This was definitely not good. She had to get out of there before anyone found her. Why had she come into the office today of all days? She felt like she was a magnet for bad news, like it was attracted to her, seeking her out. First the incident on the platform, then the note and now this. But what was this? What had she overheard? They were going to shut down the platform. Lots of companies were shutting down platforms that weren't making money. There was nothing sinister about that; it was just business. But it was the way they had said it. *Shut it down. Permanently.* And using words like blackmail and intimidation. *Who were they going to blackmail? And for what gain?* She should stick to her gut reaction that this was bad and get the hell out of there.

Danni's instinct now was to run but she forced herself to wait until she heard the Russians leaving the boardroom. She was scared to draw attention to herself, so she kept the light off and made her way out of the file room in the dark, using her hands to feel along the shelves and guide her back to the door. As she scrabbled down the aisle, her foot caught the box that was sitting on the floor, sending her flying on to all fours.

Shit!

"What was that?"

"What?"

"I heard a noise back there."

"Go check it out."

Fuck! Fuck! Fuck! They were going to find her and then she would end up with the same fate as David. Danni slid down the aisle to the back of the room and crouched down behind a file cabinet.

"It must have come from in here."

She heard the door being opened, held her breath and shut her eyes. This was it. She was going to suffer the same fate as David.

"What are you doing here?"

Danni's heart was racing, pounding in her ears.

"Sorry, I didn't realise anyone was up here. Just doing the hourly floor check." It was Tom's voice.

The door shut closed again.

"Have you seen anyone? I thought I heard something."

"No, just you two. I just came through the emergency doors, that's probably what you heard."

"OK. Make sure no-one else enters this building today. The security upgrade is not finished yet."

"No problem, sir, you can count on me."

"Off you go then, finish your patrol."

"Yes, of course, sir."

Danni heard footsteps heading down the corridor. *Phew, that was close.* Thank goodness for Tom and his hourly security checks. He might have just saved her bacon. She waited a few minutes then slid out from behind the file cabinet and back out of the file room, being careful this time to avoid the box on the floor. She put her hand on the door handle and waited, listening. It was quiet. She turned the handle and pulled the door open just a crack. Peering out, there was no sign of anyone, so she slipped out and quietly pulled the door shut behind her. She quickly made her way down the emergency stairwell, taking the steps two at a time all the way down to the bottom. On reaching the ground floor she dashed through to reception which was unmanned. Tom was still doing his rounds. She threw the pass he had given her on the desk and pushed the button that controlled the security lock, running to the door before it had time to relock. She flung the door open and ran out into the street right into the path of an oncoming lorry. The lorry driver tooted his horn and shook his fist at her, shouting some expletives that she couldn't actually hear but she certainly got the gist of. She waved at him and mouthed the word 'sorry'. She didn't want anyone to see her leaving the building, so she intermingled with a crowd of passengers who had just came out of the ferry terminal, pulling their suitcases behind them. She stuck with them until they got to Market Street and then snuck off into the Union Square shopping centre where she could get lost in another crowd. The crowd of Christmas shoppers mixed with football supporters heading to the pub for a swift pint – or ten – before the game started. She could certainly do with a stiff drink right now!

Danni pushed her way through the hordes of people, the Christmas music blaring out around her. Jolly, and not quite so jolly, shoppers bumping into her. Wives on a mission to get the Christmas shopping done with their downtrodden other halves trailing along behind them carrying all the bags, looking longingly at the lucky ones who were heading off to the match. A mob of teenage football fans, all wearing red and white replica Aberdeen football tops and waving matching scarves came running through the centre shouting obscenities, closely followed by four police officers who were missing their hats, scattering shoppers left right and centre. She had to get out of this madness and back to her flat, to some sanity and figure out what to do. Should she tell anyone what she had heard?

Who? Tony? He was offshore, and she wasn't calling him on the platform. Anyone could be listening into the conversation. This was going to have to be her secret for now. *Another secret. How many secrets could one girl keep?*

Chapter Fourteen

Danni kept a low profile over the rest of the weekend, choosing to stay indoors. The TV was full of Christmas films and festive cheer which she really wasn't in the mood for. Instead she chose to watch DVDs she had bought from one of the many charity shops. *Ocean's Eleven*, the 1960s version with the Rat Pack, not the George Clooney and Brad Pitt one. The rest were all '80s films. *Beaches*, with Bette Midler and Barbara Hershey, *The Lost Boys*, *The Breakfast Club*, *The Shining* and *Top Gun*. She ordered takeaway and had it delivered to the flat. Honey chilli chicken with fried noodles on Saturday and lamb rogan josh on Sunday. She would normally avoid fast food, but there wasn't much to eat in the flat. She was in desperate need of a proper food shop, but it had started snowing on Saturday afternoon and it was beginning to lie. She didn't fancy slipping and sliding her way back from the supermarket loaded up with bags full of shopping that might end up all over the pavement. The council had been out gritting the roads, but they hadn't bothered with the pavements. She had looked out the window earlier and watched several pedestrians trying to keep their feet as they walked, or rather slid around the corner onto Esslemont Avenue. One had looked like he was auditioning for *Dancing on Ice*. The movements were not natural, and she was sure he couldn't get his leg in that position again even if he tried. He had only just managed to keep on his feet, turning around to see if anyone had seen him, he hadn't noticed Danni looking down from the warmth and safety of her flat. She had already decided to book a taxi for Monday morning to get to work if it continued to snow.

She would need to get in early and finish that report for her boss or risk incurring his wrath. He had demanded it be on his desk on Friday evening. Her intent had been to finish it on Saturday morning, so it would be there when he came back after the weekend, but she had been disrupted by the small issue of the overheard conversation about the South Platform. Danni had thought about this over and over again during the weekend and had managed to convince herself that it was nothing sinister, just business, and that she was being totally paranoid, what with everything else that was going on at work and in her personal life. *After all, what could they possibly do?*

She booked a taxi for 6am. Her boss didn't usually get in until about 8am so that would give her a couple of hours and there wasn't much left to do. She had been through all the files now and just had to summarise the contents of the last few boxes. Although she certainly wouldn't be including any details on the note from David. She still wasn't sure what to do about that if anything. There had been no more on the news and when unexplained deaths go quiet then the most likely conclusion is usually suicide. She wondered if Tony had gleamed any information from his copper mate. She hadn't heard from him since he went back offshore, and she was going on the premise that no news was good news. Just then her mobile phone started ringing. She didn't recognise the number.

"Hello?"

"Hey, how you doing? I'm freezing my nuts off out here."

It was Tony. *Speak of the devil and he shall appear.*

"Listen, I heard from Scotty, my mate on the force. It sounds like they are treating it as suicide. Prominent oil executive is let go from his position, he cracks up, can't take the shame, walks off into the woods and kills himself. They are still waiting for lab results to come back but it looks like he injected himself, an overdose. They found a needle."

"But we know different."

"Which is why I'm calling. You need to tell the police what you found."

"I'm not telling the police anything! Are you on your mobile or the platform phone?"

"My mobile, why?"

"Just don't want anyone listening in to this."

"You really think they had something to do with his death?"

"What do you think? And after what I heard yesterday, I wouldn't put anything past them."

"What did you hear yesterday?"

Damn it. She was going to keep that to herself. "Erm nothing, look, it doesn't matter. I told you before, I can't go to the police."

"You're gonna have to tell me what your problem is with the police. I'm starting to think all sorts about what you've been up to and you really don't want to know what I've been imagining! My mate, Scotty, he's sound as a pound. He's not on the case but he knows the detective inspector assigned to it. They play football together at Goals."

"How many times do I have to tell you? I'm not getting involved with the police."

"OK, OK, I get it, but we have to let them know somehow. It sounds like the case is going to be closed."

"So, you tell them."

"I'm not pissing off the Russians! Look what happened to David. And I need to keep my job."

"So, it's OK for me to get on the wrong side of them but not you?"

Danni was getting angry now. How dare he put her in that position? "OK, I hear what you're saying, but what if he's not the only one? There's been a lot of people who have been made redundant and no-one has heard from them since they left. That could open up a whole new meaning to getting fired! What if we send them the note anonymously?"

"But our fingerprints will be all over it."

"I'm seriously concerned about what you've been up to in the past if the police have your fingerprints on file!"

"No, stupid, the scanner to get into the building has a record of our prints. They could check the note against those records then they would know it was us that found it."

That wasn't the real reason Danni was concerned. She didn't know for sure, but she wouldn't be surprised if Mark had recorded her fingerprints without her knowledge. It would have been easy for him. He could have taken them off any number of items over the years. A glass, a piece of cutlery. She always wondered where her favourite chef's knife had disappeared to. He had controlled her in so many other ways; it was highly likely. She was relieved they hadn't fingerprinted her when she was arrested. One positive match on the police computer and he could be alerted to her whereabouts. No, she had to protect herself at any cost.

"We could send a copy of the note, that way they have the information just not the original. They'll have to investigate it further, surely?"

"The original would be more convincing, but I guess that could work."

"I'll scan a copy of it on my printer and post it to them tomorrow. What's the detective's name?"

"McWilliam. I don't know his first name, Scotty just calls him Willie. I'm assuming that's cause of his last name, but you never know!"

"Wait a couple of days, then call Scotty to see if there's been any developments. Let me know what he says."

"Will do. So, changing the subject. What's your plan for Christmas? Catching up with family?"

"No, it will be a quiet one this year."

Christmas had been a time that Danni had looked forward to. The magic of Christmas, the excitement and anticipation leading up to the big day. She had revelled in it. But not anymore. Now it just reminded her of the life she had left behind, and of the family she no longer saw or had contact with. She wondered if they lit a candle for her as she had done for them last Christmas morning. It had been on the lead up to Christmas that she had fled. Mark had let his guard down slightly, allowing her out on her own to finish the Christmas shopping and make the arrangements for their perfect Christmas Day, just the two of them, the way he liked it. That had given her space to plan her escape. His division had arranged to go out for drinks when they came off shift that afternoon and she had made plans to go as soon as he left for work. She got up as normal and dressed for work and had breakfast with him. As they went to leave their flat, she made an excuse that she had forgotten her phone and went back to get it. She told him to go without her, she would get the tube into work. He was clearly annoyed but was also distracted with the case he was working on and needed to get to the station early. He told her to text him when she arrived at the office and left. She waited till he drove off and was out of sight, grabbed the small bag she had hidden in the cleaning cupboard and dashed out of the flat. By now she was sure he was tracking her through her phone as he always seemed to know where she had been, often using an excuse that a colleague had seen her. In order to give herself more time, she took the tube to the office as she said she would, sent him a text to say she was there, then left her phone hidden in her desk drawer. Made an excuse she wasn't feeling well and left, never to return. She would be long gone before he realised what had happened.

"Well I'm back onshore on the 23rd and since my wife has now officially kicked me out, I've nothing to get back to. So, I'm thinking, maybe we can be bah-humbugs together?"

Ah, he was married, she had suspected he was.

"Let's wait and see what happens."

"No pressure, like, just thought you might want some company. You shouldn't be alone at this time of year."

Danni wasn't sure if it was her or him he was worried about being alone.

"We don't need to do the whole turkey and all the trimmings thing. Just get a takeaway. Two friends together, looking out for each other. You know that statistically you are at a higher risk of suffering from depression at Christmas than at any other time of the year? Trust me, I'm a medic!"

The way he was going on, she was now convinced it was him he was more worried about.

"OK, OK, stop going on. I'll think about it."

"Great, that's a date then."

"I said I would think about it! And it's most certainly not a date!"

She hung up on him. It sounded like she wouldn't have much choice. He wasn't going to let this one go. *Oh, what the hell, maybe it would be nice to have some company for a change.* Being on her own for so long was beginning to take its toll. She enjoyed her own company most of the time, but he was right, at this time of year no-one wanted to be alone.

Chapter Fifteen

She could hear him, he was getting closer. She pulled her knees to her chest, burying her head into them, making herself as small as possible, trying to control her breath. She was cold and wet and covered in mud from when she had fallen, running from him. The hole in the tree trunk was only just big enough for her to crawl into. The rain was getting heavier, the storm brewing like a witch's cauldron.

"I'll find you, BITCH! And when I do, oh I'm going to enjoy myself. No-one makes a mug of me. You're going to pay for what you've done... LOUISE, I know you can hear me, get out here NOW. Make things easier for yourself, 'cos if you don't and I have to come find you..."

He was getting closer.

"LOUISE!"

The lightning cracked overhead and lit up the darkness. In that brief flash she glimpsed a silhouette of him. What did he have in his hand? *A gun? A hammer?* She couldn't wait around here to find out. If he found her, she would be dead, but not before he had made her suffer. She would have to make a run for it. She had to time it right. After the next flash of lightning, the rumble of thunder would conceal any noise she made. *CRACK…* It was now or never. She pushed forward, clawing her way through the undergrowth, the bushes clawing at her arms, trying to hold her back…

Danni jolted awake, fighting with the sheets she had become ensnared in. The duvet had been kicked to the floor. Lightning lit up the room through the gap in the curtains, followed immediately by a crash of thunder. The storm was directly overhead. She jumped out of bed in the pitch dark and switched on the light. She was gasping for breath and covered in a clammy, cold sweat. This was the second time she had had this same dream. Why was she dreaming about Mark again? Was it because it was the anniversary of her escape? Was it the stress of everything that was going on at work? *Probably a bit of both.*

She looked at the alarm clock. It was 4am. She picked up the duvet that had landed on the threadbare carpet and dumped it back on the bed. There was no point getting back in as she was not going to sleep after that rude awakening. She might as well get ready and head into the office. She booked a taxi for 4:30am through the app on her mobile phone. Thirty minutes would be enough time to get showered and make some coffee.

*

Her mobile bleeped to alert her to a message. Her taxi had arrived outside. She grabbed the travel mug of steaming hot coffee and wrapped up, ready to face the cold. She used her phone to light up the stairwell. Maybe if she didn't pay her rent this month then her landlord would come around looking for it and she could pin him down about fixing the bloody light!

She opened the door and was met with a scene from a winter wonderland. It must have snowed all night as there was several inches of it lying and it was still coming down. Big individual flakes, knitted together to make a cold white blanket, covering everything in sight. It had been bad enough last night when she had nipped out to the post box to post a copy of David's note to the detective in charge of the case. She had been careful not to get her fingerprints on the paper or the envelope by wearing a pair of marigolds. It was probably over the top, but she had to be cautious. She had written on the envelope in large capital letters, trying hard to disguise her handwriting. This could not be linked back to her in any way. The cover letter was brief and was typed, not written.

The taxi had stopped under the orange glow of the street light, its hazard lights blinking on and off in the blizzard. Danni stepped out carefully onto the pavement, her footsteps making imprints in the fresh snow which came up past her ankles. Thankfully she had put on her long boots, otherwise her feet would have been cold and wet already. She picked her way over to the taxi and opened the back door, snow blowing into the car as she got in.

"Jeez, it's wild out there."

"Tell me about it," said the taxi driver.

"The gritters haven't been out yet, I wasn't sure I was going to make it here. I was sliding sideways coming up the hill at Rosemount Place. Good job there is no-one else on the roads 'cos if I'd had to stop, I don't think I would have got going again. Where you off to at this time, airport?"

"No, the office, Salvesen Tower down at the harbour, please."

"Well, at least it's mainly downhill from here, we can probably just slide there," he said jokingly.

He switched off the hazard lights and indicated to pull out. The car slid briefly, then caught traction on the road and moved off. The wipers were struggling to keep up with the amount of snow falling, the driver perched forwards in his seat straining to see the road in front of him. Danni wondered how many people would phone in requesting a snow day today. *Was that still a thing, or had the Russians put the kibosh on that too?*

The streets were quiet, nobody stupid enough to be out and about in this weather yet. The only signs of life were the seagulls and a couple of homeless people who were squatting in shop doorways. Danni hoped they were still alive and hadn't frozen to the spot overnight.

The taxi driver did his best to fight his way through the blizzard and keep the car on the road, making it to the office in one piece.

"Here," said Danni as she paid the driver, "and keep the change," leaving him a tip for his efforts.

"Thanks, Miss, stay safe out there."

"You too."

She got out of the car and traipsed through the snow to the front door. There was no-one at reception. She hoped that they had finished upgrading the system and that she could get in otherwise it was going to be a long wait in the cold. She placed her hand on the biometric scanner and prayed. It turned green and the door slid open. "Thank you," she said to herself as she looked up to the sky. Someone was looking out for her today. She made her way to the lift and up to her desk. She laid the travel mug down, which only had a dribble of coffee remaining after her journey, switched on the computer and sat down. She opened up the report that she had been working on for her boss and pulled out her notebook from the desk drawer to check her notes on the final files.

The report was finished and on her boss's desk before 7am and before anyone else had made it into the office. She hadn't looked up or even stopped for another coffee since she got in but was in desperate need of one now. She took her travel mug through to the coffee area and rinsed it out, before filling it again with another caffeine infusion. She looked out the window and although it was still snowing, it wasn't as heavy as it had been when she got here. Hopefully it would go off soon. She hated snow. Well, that wasn't strictly true. It was nice to look out at if you didn't have to go anywhere. From the lights of the boats tied up in the harbour she could see their decks were being swept clear by their crews, shovelling the snow over the side into the cold, black water below.

It was at this time of year she was glad she had an office job and not an outdoor one. She loathed being cold and wished she had moved somewhere further south instead of to this frozen hell where it never seemed to get above twenty degrees even on what the locals called a glorious summer's day. It was probably about minus twenty out there now with the wind chill factor.

She missed London and her past life. Life before Mark, well, before he became the controlling monster. At least in London it was warmer, and you could get some pretty decent summer days. Sitting outside in one of the many parks: St James's, Hyde Park, Green Park. Catching up with friends, having a picnic or a barbeque. Even at this time of year the weather was better, not so bitterly cold and less snow. And there was much more to do down there. Sure, Aberdeen had the Christmas Village, but it was nothing compared to the Hyde Park Winter Wonderland. Now that was a proper Christmas Village, you could spend a whole day wandering round there taking in the atmosphere. The smells and sounds of Christmas. Mulled wine, spiced cider, hot roasted chestnuts.

Ice-skating, the fun-fair, Santa Land. The twee German-style markets all lit up with their Christmas lights. And the lights on Regent Street and Oxford Street. There was Christmas magic all around London. Aberdeen had probably done its best with the limited funds it had but one street of repetitive German chalets run by Weegies, an ice-rink that you could skate from one end to the other in about three strides, a bar for the adults and a couple of rides to keep the kids happy, didn't measure up to the capital's efforts. It was probably magical if you were under the age of twelve. She was definitely in a bah-humbug humour.

Danni's reminiscing was rudely disrupted by the sound of footsteps and the annoying voices of Becky and her sidekick. Great. If she wasn't feeling depressed before she certainly would be now.

"Oh, it's you."

"Nice to see you too Becky, as always." *Let the repartee commence...*

"You're still here then, I thought they had finally got rid of you when you disappeared last week."

"No, I'm still here, they kept me on specifically just to annoy you."

"Well, you've certainly got that down to a fine tee."

The words 'pot', 'kettle' and 'black' sprung to Danni's mind.

"Well, I'd love to hang around here and make small talk, but—" Danni turned to leave, clutching her mug of coffee.

"Hang on a minute, you're bound to have heard something about what's going on with David. The rumour is that there's more to this than meets the eye. I was just saying that I reckon it wasn't suicide and that the Russians had something to do with it and are trying to cover it up."

If only she knew, thought Danni. "How would I know anything?"

"Well you're always up there with the Russians, you must hear things."

"Yeah, well if I did, do you think I would tell the office gossip?"

"You do know something, don't you? What is it? Did they arrange a hit? They did, didn't they? See, I knew there was more to it."

"I think you're getting a bit carried away there, don't you?"

Only Danni knew she wasn't, and the scary thing was she was closer to the truth than she realised. It was time for Danni to make her escape before she got dragged any further into her conspiracy theories.

"She knows something, I'm sure she does." Danni could hear Becky speaking to her colleague as she headed down the corridor away from them. "She's such a bitch. She enjoys keeping things from me. Like who am I going to tell, I'm no blabbermouth, am I? I can keep a secret."

Yeah, right!

Danni was heading back to her desk just in time to see her boss coming in. He was earlier than usual and looking rather bedraggled, like he hadn't slept all weekend. She was glad she had got in to the office when she did.

"That report better be on my desk, Danni."

Good morning to you too! she thought.

"Yes, it's waiting for you."

"About bloody time, and if I catch you gossiping with the accounts girls again there will be trouble. Do you not have enough work to keep you busy? I can always find someone else if you're not motivated. Don't you realise there are people queuing up for a job like this?"

"I wasn't gossiping, she…" Danni was met by a death stare. There was no point arguing with him when he was in that sort of mood. "No, I mean yes." *What was the question?*

He stopped in his tracks and just glared at her.

"Well… what are you waiting for? Get on with it. And tell Gary to get his butt in here as soon as he comes in. I need to speak to him straight away."

He didn't wait for a response but instead stormed into his office and slammed the door shut so hard that the whole partition wall rattled.

The door opened again briefly.

"And someone get me a damned coffee!"

Slam! The door was almost taken off its hinges that time.

Someone got out of bed on the wrong side, thought Danni. She wasn't sure what had gone down over the weekend, but she did know that Gary's day was about to get a whole lot worse when he arrived. She didn't want to go into that office, but if she didn't fetch him a coffee, he was going to be considerably more grumpy and unbearable than he already was. It was more than her life was worth to ignore his demands.

Becky and her sidekick were still in the break out area and had heard the whole thing.

"Wow, what's got into him? I knew he had a temper but just, wow! Do you think it's got anything to do with what happened to David? He's the legal manager, if anyone knows something then it's got to be him. What do you think?"

"I think I'd better get back to him with his coffee while I still have a job."

Danni grabbed his mug from the cupboard, ladled three spoons of coffee into it and waited for the kettle to boil, praying it would be quick.

Becky, for once in her life, took the hint and headed back to her desk. *Thank God for that,* thought Danni. She didn't want to get back into that conversation again.

The kettle clicked off and Danni delivered the mug to her boss. She knocked on the door and was met with a gruff, "WHAT?"

"Um, your coffee."

"Leave it on my desk and close the door on your way out." He didn't even look up at her.

She did what she was told and got out of there as quickly as possible. The air was frostier in there than it had been outside in the blizzard this morning.

Danni returned to her desk and checked through her emails. She wondered if the postie had been to Queen Street yet. She had posted the copy of the note first class, so it should have got there by now, but then again, the post wasn't always entirely reliable and in this weather, deliveries were liable to be delayed. She questioned whether she had done the right thing in sending it, but it was too late to worry about that now. If the police had just done their job properly in the first place, then she wouldn't have had to get involved. It was too easy for them to write it off as a suicide. She probably would have done the same in their shoes. She could only hope that this would open up the investigation and they could get to the truth, whatever that was.

Surprisingly the rest of the day was relatively uneventful. Gary never made it in to the office, which was probably a lucky break for him. He lived out in the country and had called in to say the snow was blowing and drifting badly. The council had been very helpful in that the snow plough had cleared the main road but had shoved the snow into a three-foot pile blocking the end of his road. There was no way he was going to get to the office in his car even if they cleared the snow drift. *Serves him right for driving a BMW.* His failure to make it in did nothing to appease her boss's mood though. Danni had managed to avoid him, scuttling out of the way whenever she saw his office door open. He had been upstairs all afternoon probably in a *tête-à-tête* with the Russians, but Danni wasn't going up there to find out.

An email flashed into her inbox from the office manager saying that due to the adverse weather if anyone was concerned about their safety in getting home then they could leave the office now so long as it was approved by their manager. Danni's manager wasn't in his office to ask, not that she would have approached him given his foul mood. She was concerned about her safety – not necessarily related to the weather – and she had been in the office since 5am. She wasn't about to look a gift horse in the mouth, so she grabbed her coat and made her escape.

Chapter Sixteen

The snow was relentless all evening, and it was still dinging it down at 11pm when Danni went to bed. She had spent the afternoon tidying and cleaning the flat as she had been lazy all weekend. Washing had been hanging out to dry on the clothes horse in the bedroom for days. The window was gummed up with condensation because of it. She had to switch the heating on for longer than its normal programmed time to try to get everything to dry.

She had set the alarm for the more respectable time of 7am, the radio clicking on just as the news started.

"Police Scotland confirm there has been a significant development into the investigation of the death of prominent oil company executive, David Gordon. Police want to speak to anyone who had been in contact with Mr Gordon in the days prior to the discovery of his body in the woods at Countesswells. Extensive enquiries are ongoing into his last movements and anyone who had seen or spoken to him and may have information are urged to contact Police on 101 or if you wish to remain anonymous contact Crimestoppers on 0800..."

The copy of David's note had obviously reached Queen Street. Had she opened up a can of worms? There was nothing she could do about it now, except hope and pray that there was no way they could trace it back to her.

She couldn't afford to keep taking taxis to the office, so she decided to walk. The snow had stopped falling sometime in the early hours and the temperature had dared to rise above freezing. The thaw was on and the drip, drip, drip from the overflowing gutters would continue all day. Danni wrapped up in her long coat, scarf and gloves, and pulled on an old pair of Dr Martens boots. She stuffed a pair of heels in her bag to change into at the office and grabbed a woollen beanie hat on the way out the door.

She began the long slog into work. The council had finally got around to clearing some of the pavements, but the snow overnight had now melted into a glassy, brownish slush that would make her walk in interesting. But not as interesting as work would be when she did get there.

The police were already in the office and had started to interview the first few arrivals. They had set up camp in the boardroom. As each member of staff arrived, they were greeted by an officer with an official looking clipboard at the front door. Their details were checked, and their names added to his list alongside an allotted time slot which was scheduled in ten-minute intervals. As the stern looking officer checked Danni's pass and returned it back to her; she was advised not to be late for her interview as they had a lot to get through. Her name was written down next to the time of 8:40am. She glanced at her watch; it was 8:05am. She had thirty-five minutes to worry about what she was going to say to them.

As she got out of the lift, she could hear Becky's dulcet tones down the corridor. *Might have known there would be no show without Punch.* She would be loving all the intrigue and speculation and would most likely be instigating most of it.

"I said to Jenny last week, didn't I, Jenny? I said there was more to this than meets the eye. I knew it, I said, didn't I? Someone like that doesn't kill themselves. No, no, no. I reckon they put a hit out on him. You know what those Russians are like. He knew they were up to something and they got rid of him. I bet you that's what happened. Why else would the police be here now?"

Danni slipped past Becky who had her back to her. She was too busy holding court with the rest of the accounts department to notice her. If she wasn't unbearable before, she definitely would be now. She could see the looks on some of her colleague's faces, willing her to disappear or at least just shut the fuck up. But that wouldn't be happening any time soon. Rumour and speculation were something that Becky was incredibly good at and she would be happy to show off her talent for it to anyone who cared to listen – and to those who didn't – for the rest of the day.

Danni retreated to her desk. Her boss's door was open, and the light was on, but he was nowhere to be seen. He had probably been called in early to keep an eye on the interviews in case anyone said anything incriminating. *Great, he was going to be in a good mood.* At least if he was tied up with the police all day, he wouldn't be busting her chops for a change. She almost felt sorry for the police as he would be making their life even more difficult than it already was.

She looked at her watch. 8:15am. She still had twenty-five minutes to go. *Coffee.* That's what she needed to get her through this. Help settle her nerves or add to the adrenaline already building up inside. Either way, she needed caffeine before she met with them. Needed to get her head straight and figure out how to play this. Deny everything, say as little as possible. Get in and get out before they could figure out that she knew more than she was letting on. She took her coffee back to her desk and sat there staring at the blank computer screen. She thought back to her legal training and, although she hadn't focussed on criminal law, she had completed that module. *Just answer the questions as succinctly as possible. Yes or no. Don't embellish on anything. Keep to the point.* That's all she needed to do. *Easy!*

She kept glancing at her watch. The minutes were ticking down. Only five minutes to go. She better head down to the boardroom. She didn't want to piss them off by being late. As she got there the person before her was just leaving. He didn't look too harassed. After all, this was just a formality.

Danni poked her head through the open door.

"Danni Ross?" asked the officer who was sitting in one of the black leather swivel seats at the far side of the boardroom table. His colleague sat next to him was still writing frantically in his black police issue notebook. They had both removed their hats and they were placed on the table either side of them.

She nodded.

"Please take a seat, we will be with you in a moment."

Danni sat down opposite them. This felt more nerve-wracking than the interview she had to get this job and there had been four of them interviewing her then. At least her boss was not in the room. That would have been awkward.

The second officer put down his pen and stuck his thumbs down the arm pits of his stab vest and adjusted it as best he could. He was much younger, looked like he was barely out of school, or old enough to start shaving. He looked more uncomfortable than Danni felt if that was even possible. He had obviously drawn the short straw and had been delegated to take the notes. His older colleague pulling rank knowing full well that the new recruit would also have to type up the reports when they got back to the station.

"First, we just need to take a few personal details. Full name?"

The second officer picked up his pen, turned over a page in his notebook and was poised to start writing again. She wondered if he would have writer's cramp by the end of the day, or maybe his colleague would take pity on him.

"Danielle Ross."

"Date of birth?"

"14th December 1986."

"Address?"

"64 Esslemont Avenue."

Déjà vu, thought Danni. She had been through this before at Queen Street.

"How well did you know David Gordon?"

"Well, I knew him to see him."

"Did you have any cause to enter into conversation with Mr Gordon prior to his leaving the company?"

"No."

"No?"

"No. We weren't exactly on speaking terms. He was the boss. We said 'hi' in the passing and that was about as much conversation as we had." A little voice inside her head reminded her to keep her answers short and to the point.

"But you interacted with him on a daily basis, did you not? You're a..."

He looked down at a sheet of paper with a list of all the employees and their job titles. "admin assistant, so you would have arranged for him to sign documents?"

"Yes, but I just left them with his PA and then picked them up again once he had signed them."

"And his PA is…"

He looked back as the sheet, but before he could find the right name, Danni answered, "Karen Beecham."

"Ah, yes, I see her here." He pointed to a name on the list. "Did Mr Gordon seem distracted to you?"

"Like I said, I didn't really know him."

"What would you say was his state of mind the last time you saw him?"

"I can't remember the last time I actually saw him."

"Were you aware of any issues he had at work or at home?"

"I told you, I've not really had any dealings with him."

The police officers looked at each other, like they knew more than they were letting on. Danni was starting to sweat.

"We have received a copy of a note, anonymously, that seems to be in Mr Gordon's handwriting, suggesting that he had cause to fear for his life. Do you know anything about this? Who it was that he feared? Had you heard him arguing with anyone?"

Danni could feel herself becoming flushed, the red moving up from her neck to her cheeks.

"I don't know anything about that." She tried to maintain eye contact with the officer but failed and looked down at the desk, willing the ground to open up and swallow her. The guilt must be written all over her face. They must know it was her who sent the note or why would they mention it?

"Are you sure? You seem a bit worried, anxious. Is there something you want to tell us? You understand that anything you tell us will be treated in the strictest confidence?"

Yeah, right, like I'm going to tell you anything and implicate myself, thought Danni.

"No, it's just warm in here and you are making me feel nervous, like I've done something wrong."

"Have you done something wrong?"

"No!"

"And you are sure you don't know anything about Mr Gordon's concerns?"

"No."

"You have access to the management suite, don't you?"

"Yes, what's that got to do with anything?"

"Perhaps you found this note and sent it to us?"

"No! I don't know anything about any note."

"You're sure about that?"

"Yes! Why would I lie about that?"

"I don't know, Miss, why don't you tell us? Perhaps you're scared you'll get in trouble with your employers?"

Danni just kept staring at the table.

The police officers looked at each other, the younger one poised ready to write down Danni's response.

"I told you, I don't know anything about it."

"OK. And you're sure you haven't overhead any conversations up there between Mr Gordon and any of the other managers?"

"I just get on with my work. Why are you picking on me?"

"We're not picking on you. We're speaking to everyone in the company. We are just trying to get to the bottom of what happened to Mr Gordon. You do understand the seriousness of this investigation, Miss Ross?"

"Yes, of course. I'm sorry, but I can't help you."

"Can't or won't?"

"What?"

"Can't help us or won't help us? If you heard or saw anything, however insignificant it may seem to you, it could assist us."

"I can't think of anything." Danni was lying through her teeth and she was sure they knew. She just needed to get out of here as soon as possible.

"Are you sure?"

"Yes, I'm sure."

"OK, well if you DO happen to think of anything then please contact us."

He handed her a business card with his number on it.

Danni took the card, pushed the chair back on its wheels and stood up.

"Thank you, Miss Ross, you've been most helpful," he said in a sarcastic tone.

Danni had to stop herself from running out of the room, she couldn't wait to leave. The younger officer was still scribbling in his notebook as the older one leaned over and whispered something to him. They both looked at Danni as she turned to walk out the door, her face getting redder and sweat starting to appear on her brow and upper lip. The younger one was tapping his pen on his notebook like he was contemplating what his colleague had just said. She was sure they didn't believe her, but there was no way she was confessing to sending that note or to knowing anything about it. She wanted – no, needed – to keep herself out of this. She wished she hadn't sent it now, but she had done what she had to do, to get them to investigate it further. It was up to them to do their jobs and find out who killed him, but she didn't want to be involved any further in those investigations. She had co-operated, answered their questions and that should be that. *Shouldn't it?*

Chapter Seventeen

As Danni dashed out of the boardroom she was in her own little bubble, completely oblivious to her surroundings, almost bumping straight into the next victim waiting to be interviewed.

He sidestepped at the last minute, managing to balance his mug of coffee so as not to spill any.

"Hoy, look where you're going!"

"Sorry, I didn't see you."

She looked up. Brilliant, it was her boss.

"I trust you have been helping our boys in blue with their enquiries?"

"What? Oh, um, yes, but I wasn't much help. I don't know anything."

"I see."

He looked Danni up and down, as she tried hard not to look as guilty as she felt.

"I'm just popping in to see how they are getting on, see if there is anything else we can do to assist them."

Checking up on them, and trying to gleam some info, more like, Danni thought. "Right. I'd better get back to work."

She turned and headed off down the corridor before he could respond. She wondered what he knew about David's death. He was thick as thieves with the Russians. Maybe he was in their pockets. Maybe he'd been sent down by them to see if anyone had been finger pointing and speculating yet. He should have waited till they interviewed Becky. They were going to need more than a ten-minute slot with her by the time she got all her conspiracy theories off her ample chest. She wouldn't care that she was jeopardising her job, so long as she was centre of attention for a while.

The phone rang as Danni got back to her desk.

"Hey, what's going on? I hear the police are interviewing everyone." It was Tony calling from offshore. "I take it they got the copy of the note then? And before you ask, I'm alone in the office and I'm calling from my mobile so it's safe to talk."

"Yeah, they were here when I arrived. They are interviewing everyone in the office, asking if we had been speaking to David before his death, if we had any suspicions."

"They've interviewed you already?"

"Yes, I've just been in."

"And what did you tell them?"

"Nothing! I've nothing to tell. I've done my bit, now it's over to them."

"Did they suspect anything?"

"No," Danni lied. She was sure they did, but she wasn't about to get into that over the phone. "It's fine, they still have to interview Becky and she's already been spouting off about her conspiracy theories to anyone who will listen. Maybe they will take her on her word and investigate the Russians, but I wouldn't hold my breath. Whatever happens, I'm sure they will have covered their tracks."

"But at least they are doing something and not just sitting on their backsides, drinking tea and eating doughnuts or butteries or whatever it is they eat. Yeah, hold on, I'm on the phone, I'll be there in a minute…"

"Who's that?"

"I've got to go, someone's just cut off a finger or something?"

"WHAT?"

"I'm joking, but I do need to get back to work. Look, I'm back onshore in a couple of days. Let's catch up when I get back and I'll get hold of my mate, Scotty, and see what the police are saying. OK?"

"OK."

"Are we still on for Christmas Day?"

She had forgotten about their so-called date.

"Let me think about it."

She hung up.

She swivelled round in her seat and looked out the window. The sun had dared to show its face for the first time in days, possibly weeks. It certainly felt like weeks. The sky had also transformed from its stubborn slate grey to a pale blue and the clouds from black to white. The weather was improving, the police were now doing their jobs and investigating David's death and she was going to have company for Christmas. Maybe things were starting to look up.

The police had taken up residence in the office all day. People came and people went. Some were in and out in a couple of minutes and others took longer. The office gossips were doing their best to second guess what had happened to David, with Becky being the main instigator. *Surprise, surprise!*

No-one had seen hide nor hair of the Russians. They were keeping a low profile, hiding out on the tenth floor, in the management suite. Danni had every intention of keeping out of their way with all this going on. She wondered if they were being interviewed too or if it was just the workers that the police were interrogating.

Becky had been beside herself, feeling it was her absolute duty to re-interview everyone as they left the boardroom. She was like a panther, waiting to pounce on poor unsuspecting prey. She wanted to know every detail, verbatim, about what the police had asked and what they had told them. She even had out her own notebook and was scribbling down details and checking them against what others had already said. *Who did she think she was? Nancy Drew?* She was on her own personal mission to get to the bottom of it and solve the murder before the police did. Who needed evidence and motive? All she needed was a few people to concur with her speculations and then her own little fantasy would become gospel. By the end of the day there were two main rumours doing the rounds. The first was that David had committed suicide and had set up the Russians to make it look like he had been murdered to get back at them for firing him. The other was that the Russians had arranged for his demise as he had found out they had been doing something illegal and was going to report them. Either way it was keeping everyone – especially Becky – amused.

The sun had stayed out all day and melted most of the snow. By the time Danni left the office it was dark, and the temperature had dropped significantly, turning the slush into invisible, lethal, ice traps. She almost lost her footing on three occasions just walking up to the traffic lights beside the entrance to Union Square shopping centre. She thought it would be safer to walk up through the centre then cross over Guild Street into St Nicholas Centre, avoiding the icy pavements for as long as possible. At least it would be warmer even though she would have to face the hordes of Christmas shoppers. It was the week before Christmas and the shops were open till at least 8pm every night. The monotonous loop of Christmas songs would soon be over but for now they would continue on repeat: *I Wish It Could Be Christmas Every Day, Last Christmas, Santa Claus is Coming to Town.*

Danni knew that Santa Claus wouldn't be coming to visit her this year. He hadn't been last year either. Not since she had left Mark, and because of him, her family. She would buy herself a small present, wrap it up with a gift tag, the note saying 'Love from Santa xx' and put it beside the fireplace, just so she would have something to open on Christmas Day. She could pretend that someone cared and was thinking of her. She knew her mother would be thinking of her and it made her feel closer to her. She hadn't bought anything yet this year, perhaps she would have a look tonight on the way home. And what about Tony? If he was going to be coming around on Christmas Day, should she buy him something? Would he get something for her? If he did buy her a present and she hadn't got one for him she would feel bad. But what would she get him? She didn't really know him. He had been drinking whisky the night they had gone to the pub. She could get him a bottle of single malt, or was that too much? Aftershave? Socks?

Why were men so difficult to buy for? Mark had been easy. He told her exactly what he wanted and where to get it. She had thought it was great the first few years, took the pressure off finding the perfect gift. That was until the year she had bought the wrong iPhone. She couldn't find the one he wanted. It was limited edition and was out of stock in all the shops and websites she had tried. But the one she got him was very similar. It was even the same colour that he wanted. They had woken on Christmas Day and, like excited schoolkids, had run downstairs in their pyjamas to the tree to see what Santa had brought. They unwrapped the presents from their families and friends first, leaving the presents to each other to last. Mark ripped the paper while Danni (or Louise, as she was then), took the time to pick and pull each piece of Sellotape free before carefully unwrapping. They had even opened a bottle of champagne and were drinking Buck's Fizz to celebrate. The morning had been perfect. Perfect, until Mark opened his gift from Danni. When he realised it was the wrong iPhone and not the exact one he had specified, his mood changed without warning.

"What the fuck is this?"

"I know it's the not the exact one that you wanted, but it's actually the next model up." Danni looked at him hopefully.

"I told you what I wanted. What is wrong with you? You can't even get a simple thing like that right."

"I tried, I really did, but it was out of stock."

Smack.

He slapped her right across the face, knocking her backwards, the glass of Buck's Fizz crashing to the floor, smashing into tiny pieces. Orange liquid spilled into a sticky pool on the hardwood floor.

She was shocked. He had never hit her across the face before, always choosing to hit her in areas that could easily be hidden. She raised a hand to her cheek that was starting to sting, tears beginning to form in her eyes.

"What if I didn't get you what you wanted for Christmas? How would you feel? I work hard to buy you these things and this is how you repay me? Well, that's Christmas ruined."

Danni had dropped to her knees, curling herself into a ball, waiting for the onslaught.

"Get that mess tidied up. My parents will be here for lunch soon, you better not mess that up as well. And stop that insipid snivelling. You're a fucking disgrace. Get upstairs and get cleaned up."

Danni ran upstairs, tears now streaming down her cheeks, making them sting even more than the slap had. She slammed the bathroom door behind her and locked herself in, knowing full well that a little bathroom lock would not stop Mark if he decided to come after her. She looked at herself in the mirror, her cheek already showing the outline of a hand print. If she was going to placate Mark and salvage anything from this Christmas, then she would need to do a really good make-up job so that his parents wouldn't notice. She splashed her face with cold water, wincing as it hit her cheek, and patted herself dry with a towel. The towel felt soft and comforting against her face. For a moment, she just held it there, rubbing her face gently against it, like a small child clutching to its comfort blanket.

She dug out a bottle of foundation from her make-up bag and shook some out onto a blending sponge, her cheek smarting as she began to build up layer upon layer of pale liquid silk. It hid the worst of it, but the red was still showing through. Nothing was going to cover that up completely. She was going to have to come up with a good story.

She changed into the dress that Mark had looked out for her, her pyjamas were damp with the Buck's Fizz that had spilled when she dropped the glass. The dress was not what she would have chosen. Black, three-quarter length with a round high neck and short capped sleeves. Much more demure and conservative than her usual style, but Mark had been very specific about what he wanted her to wear. In fact, he had become quite opinionated about her clothing recently, commenting on everything that she wore unless it was something that he had bought for her. She slipped on the black pumps that Mark liked. He had remarked the night before that heels made her look like a tramp. She fixed her hair, tying it up in a bun and put on the small pearl earrings Mark bought her for her birthday. She barely recognised herself in the mirror, but she knew Mark would approve.

She crept back downstairs, unsure what she was going to be met with. Mark had tidied up the broken glass and was washing out the mop after wiping the floor clean.

"Now that's more like it," he said, admiring her dress as though nothing had happened. He walked up to her while Danni cowered, waiting for the next punch. He took her chin gently in his hand and lifted her face towards him.

"Shame about the slight imperfection, but beggars can't be choosers, can they?" He laughed and let go of her.

"Your cheek has bruised like a delicate peach. You should have been more careful getting out of the taxi last night, especially when you'd had so much to drink. Tripping up the steps in those ridiculously high heels and catching your face on the door handle wasn't the best idea, was it?"

OK, so that was the story they were going with.

"No," she replied. "I'm so clumsy."

"You're my accident-prone little angel, aren't you?" He pulled her towards him and kissed her on the cheek that wasn't bruised. "What am I going to do with you?"

That was the exact moment that Danni realised she had to get out, although it would take almost a year to the day for her plan to come to fruition.

Chapter Eighteen

Offshore on the North Platform

"Have you heard?"

"Heard what?"

"I got a phone call from Dougie's wife yesterday; the company have paid out his death in service money, and she got an extra bonus. Hush money to keep her from making any statements to the press."

"I thought they were questioning it after the post mortem results?"

"They did, but they have no evidence that Dougie knew he had that tumour. And with all the hoo-ha with the heid bummer being found dead in the woods, they don't need any more bad press at the moment."

"So she's got the money?"

"Cheque arrived in the post yesterday with a note expressing their condolences. Bloody cheek, if it wasn't for them cutting all our benefits then Dougie might not have resorted to such drastic action."

"We are in the clear?"

"We are in the clear, and Jeannie's going to transfer our money as soon as the cheque is banked."

"What am I going to tell Alison when she asks where I got the cash?"

"Just tell her the company decided to pay a Christmas bonus this year. It's not that far from the truth. Just don't go over the top spending. I know what you're like when you've got a few bob to spare. We need to keep this low key, so no-one gets suspicious and starts asking questions. OK?"

"OK."

"Don't look so worried. The nightmare is over. Merry Christmas, pal!"

Chapter Nineteen

On the days leading up to Christmas, the office was quiet. The police had been back to take statements from those employees they had not got around to interviewing or who had been out of the office the previous day. There were lots of empty desks with people using up the last of their annual leave, travelling south to spend time with family and friends before the big day. Unfortunately, Danni's boss was not one of them. He was in a foul mood. His wife's family had arrived and were staying for the holidays and he would rather spend time in the office inflicting his Ebenezer, bah-humbug festive cheer on his staff than spend time at home with them. Even Becky had been quieter than normal. Danni had heard through the grapevine that she had had her fingers wrapped by human resources. They had taken her 'detective' notebook from her, and she had been told to keep her opinions about what happened to David to herself, if she wanted to have a job to come back to after the holidays. Becky was also in a foul mood.

The only department who seemed to be full of Christmas cheer was the subsurface department. Their office was covered in decorations. It looked like Santa's grotto. Strings of flashing lights, singing Christmas trees and dancing snowmen. They had even sprayed the windows with fake snow. She had never seen anything like it. Her previous colleagues at the solicitor's office she had worked for in London had embraced Christmas, but not to this degree. The geologists, geophysicists and petroleum engineers were a strange bunch with their own unique brand of humour.

There had been no office Christmas party this year, what with the investigation ongoing. An email had come out from the HR manager stating that it would be disrespectful to the memory of David to be frivolously enjoying themselves whilst David's death was still a matter for the police. More like it was a good excuse to save the company money not having to pay for overpriced dried-up food and copious amounts of alcohol for their so-called valued employees to get drunk on. Everyone had been well-warned not to speak to the press, who were still looking for an exclusive angle on what was happening inside Moskaneft, and they didn't want to add fuel to the fire, so to speak, by paying to lubricate loose lips.

Some departments had organised their own Christmas parties, going out for food and drinks after work, but not Danni's. No, her boss was doing his utmost to portray Scrooge and was making a great job of it. None of her colleagues were going to question his decision and Danni had no desire to spend any more time with them than she had to. Plus, the last time she had gone out for drinks with work she had paid the price with a serious hangover without even enjoying the drinking part.

As she sat staring blankly at her computer screen, her phone rang.

"Hey, what's up? Things quietened down in the office now?" It was Tony.

"Yeah, the police have left. There are still a few people they want to speak to, but they are away on holiday, so they will catch up with them later."

"Are we still on for Christmas Day?" Tony sounded hopeful.

"Yeah, I guess so. It can't hurt to have some company."

"Well, don't sound too enthusiastic about it!"

Danni was trying hard to sound casual but secretly she was quite looking forward to having someone to share the big day with. Even if it was Tony.

"Actually, I have a favour to ask."

"What's that?"

"Well, you know my wife has chucked me out?"

"Yeah." *Oh, oh, what's coming now?* she thought.

"I've been crashing at a mate's place."

"And?"

"And, well I think I've kinda overstayed my welcome. You see, his wife's family are coming for Christmas and they need the room and, well, hotels are expensive at this time of year, even though they say they are struggling, and I wondered if…"

Here we go, she thought.

"Is there any chance I can crash at yours? It would only be for a couple of days over Christmas, just till I sort myself out with a flat. Everywhere is shut now for the holidays and I've not had a chance to do anything as I've been stuck offshore."

Great, she had been put on the spot and she felt sure he had played her. "Tony, look, I said OK for Christmas Day but I'm not sure about…"

"You'd be doing me a massive favour. Pretty please? I'll do all the cooking; you won't have to lift a finger. I'm a dab hand at beans on toast. Only joking! Actually, I'm not bad in the kitchen. I think that's the only reason my wife didn't chuck me out before now!"

"OK, OK, but only until the estate agents open and you can find somewhere else. You can sleep on the sofa."

"Thanks, Danni, you're a good friend. I knew I could count on you."

"OK, stop milking it. But I'm holding you to the offer to do the cooking."

"Absolutely, no problem. I'll even do the food shopping. My chopper gets in this afternoon. So, I'll see you at your flat after work?"

"Doesn't look like I have much choice, do I?"

"Trust me, this Christmas is going to be a good one."

*

When Danni left the office that evening, she switched on her out of office, having dared to ask for Christmas Eve off from her boss. At first, he had not been too enthusiastic about the request. He probably wanted her to suffer as much as he was, but when she offered to be 'on-call' and come in if there was anything urgent, he had relented. She was looking forward to seeing Tony. He was the only real friend she had, and it would be great to have someone to share Christmas with again. She walked home through the shopping centres and immersed herself in the Christmas spirit, humming along to the Christmas songs with a smile on her face. She hadn't had much to smile about recently. She threw some coppers in the collection bucket that was held out by an overly cheery, red-cheeked Santa with a terrible fake beard and the smell of alcohol on his breath. *Someone had been partaking in the Christmas spirit in more ways than one!* Speaking of which, she had better buy a bottle of whisky for Tony to put under the tree. After all, he did say he was going to do the Christmas food shop and the cooking. There was an Oddbins wine merchants on Rosemount Place, just around the corner from the flat and she knew they sold spirits too. She had no idea about whisky, but she was sure they would be able to suggest something suitable. She could maybe even buy a bottle of nice wine or some champagne for Christmas Day.

She was right, they were very helpful in Oddbins. So helpful that she came away with a bottle of malt whisky, two bottles of champagne and three bottles of wine. Well, there was a deal on that if you bought six bottles, the cheapest one was free! They had even thrown in a spice kit to make mulled wine. It had been a while since she had bought any alcohol as she did not enjoy drinking on her own. But now she had an excuse for a few days.

When she arrived at the flat, Tony was already waiting at the door, under the dim orange glow of the street light, with a rucksack and bags of shopping.

"About bloody time, I'm freezing my butt off out here. I thought you would have been home by now."

"Sorry, I had some things to take care of."

"I could hear you clinking all the way down the street!"

"Oh, this." Danni laid down the carrier bag of bottles on the door step. Thankfully they had offered to gift wrap the whisky bottle for her, so Tony wouldn't see what she had bought.

"Are you planning a party?" joked Tony.

"No, they had a deal on and…"

"I'm only joking!" Tony held up his hands in defence. "I was going to buy some wine tomorrow as I didn't have enough hands to carry everything today but looks like you beat me to it."

Danni scrambled to get the flat keys out of her bag and opened the door. She held it open for Tony who was struggling with his rucksack and shopping bags. As the door fell shut behind them, she heard the click of the Yale lock falling into place. The lock might be working but the bloody stair light still wasn't. It was pitch dark, and as their eyes strained to adjust to the darkness Danni reached for her mobile phone to use as a torch.

Something twisted around her leg, tripping her and sending her sprawling onto the stairs, wine bottles clinking in protest.

"FUCK, what the hell was that?"

Meow! It was the neighbour's bloody cat! Danni hated that thing. It was a Siamese with a pointy face and pale blue eyes that looked like the gateway to the soul of the devil. It had hissed and spat at her before.

"Fucking thing, I nearly dropped the wine."

Tony started laughing.

The cat shot off up the stairs.

"It's not bloody funny, fucking thing should be shot for sneaking up on people."

"Well, I think it just lost one of its nine lives," replied Tony.

"I've dropped my fucking phone now."

Tony couldn't keep it in any longer and burst into a fit of the giggles.

"And you can shut up if you still want a bed for the night."

He was trying hard to muffle his laughter as he put down the shopping and got his own phone out of his pocket. He switched on the flashlight and held it under his chin like kids did when they were telling each other spooky stories at Halloween.

"And you can cut that crap out too."

"Sorry, but it was funny."

"Give me that, I need to find my phone."

He turned the phone in her direction giving just enough light to see where her phone had dropped. She picked it up.

"Bloody brilliant, the screen is cracked."

Tony kept his mouth shut. He needed a bed for the night.

Danni stomped off up the stairs with Tony following close behind, trying to balance all the bags and shine the light in the right direction.

They got into the flat without further incident.

Danni switched on the light and stormed into the kitchen, placing the bag of bottles on to the dining table. Tony followed her in.

"At least it's the work phone and not my own."

"Be grateful for small mercies," replied Tony. "What shall I do with this lot?" He held up the shopping bags.

"Stick them on the table for now and I'll sort them out in a minute. First, I need to get out of these work clothes." She wandered through to the bedroom.

"You can open a bottle of wine if you like," she shouted over her shoulder.

"That sounds like a great idea." Tony looked in the bag of bottles. "What's this one?" he said as he pulled out the wrapped-up bottle.

Shit, thought Danni, *he's found his present.* She ran through, grabbing the bottle from him and taking it through to the bedroom.

"It's nothing, it's just a present for a neighbour." *Damn, that was close.* She hid the bottle in the bottom of her wardrobe.

"White or red?"

"Red, and there's a bag of mulled wine spice in there, you could stick it in a pan and warm it up."

"Great, could be doing with a hot drink after freezing my balls off waiting for you."

Tony started opening cupboards looking for a pan.

"They're in the drawer under the hob," shouted Danni.

"Got one."

He found the corkscrew in the cutlery drawer, opened the bottle and poured the contents into the pan. It was an Argentinian Malbec. A bright crimson red whose plum and raspberry aromas mingle elegantly with vanilla notes from the six months aged in French oak barrels. Or so the label said. Was anyone, other than the wine makers and sommeliers, actually able to distinguish these flavours? Tony didn't seem to think so. Wine was wine to him. He tipped in the spices and gave the wine a stir, turning the heat down to a low a simmer. By the time Danni came through he was already pouring out the wine into mugs.

"I didn't want to put it in a glass in case it was too hot."

"This is fine," said Danni, picking up the mug and breathing in the sweet citrus and cinnamon aroma. *Ah, Christmas in a mug.* The smell was good enough to cheer anyone up and Danni could feel her mood start to brighten.

Chapter Twenty

For the first night in as long as she could remember, Danni had slept right through and not woken in a sweat from her terrifying, recurring nightmare. Maybe it was because she felt safe knowing that Tony was asleep next door in the living room, or maybe it was the wine that had knocked her out. Either way she woke feeling content and well-rested.

Tony had made pasta for dinner. The pasta might have been out of a packet, but he had made the creamy mushroom sauce from scratch. He wasn't lying when he said he was a good cook. They had stayed up late, curled up on either end of the sofa with a tartan throw covering their legs. The only light coming from the warm, orange glow of the electric fire and some scented candles placed on the alcove shelves. The smell was not dissimilar to the mulled wine they had been drinking earlier, making the room feel cosy and peaceful. The flicker from the candles were mesmerising as they watched one Christmas film after another. *Elf, The Polar Express, Miracle on 34th Street* and of course Christmas would not be Christmas without *It's a Wonderful Life*. The line 'every time a bell rings an angel gets his wings' always caused Danni to shed a tear.

"That's what I need," said Danni. "A Clarence Odbody."

"What?" asked Tony.

"A guardian angel to look out for me."

"We all need one of them," he replied.

Danni and Tony barely spoke all evening, catching the occasional glance. Smiling and looking away quickly, like lovestruck teenagers, yet feeling strangely at ease with each other. Again, maybe that was down to the wine! They had finished the mulled wine and opened another bottle which in turn led to a third and yet, surprisingly, Danni wasn't feeling the effects. Perhaps she was still drunk!

The smell of frying bacon wafted through from the kitchen, closely followed by the aroma of fresh coffee. Danni's stomach started to growl in anticipation. She threw back the duvet, stepped into her slippers and wrapped a pink fluffy dressing gown around her.

"Morning sleepyhead," said Tony, who was standing over the cooker. "How do you like your eggs?" He was dressed in a pair of jeans, and a checked lumberjack-style shirt.

Wow, she could get used to this. "Fried is fine." A good fried breakfast would fix her right up for the day.

"Coming right up. There's coffee in the pot."

Danni grabbed a couple of mugs out of the cupboard and poured coffee for each of them. She handed one to Tony and sat down at the dining table, one leg tucked under the other, pulling her dressing gown around her, hugging the mug of steaming black java, blowing on it before she took the first sip.

"I hope you don't mind, but I helped myself to a shower. I used one of the towels from the airing cupboard. I would have asked first but you were out for the count and I didn't want to disturb you."

"No, of course, that's fine." Danni raised her hand to her head, pushing back her hair and tucking stray strands behind her ear. She had no idea what she looked like, having not yet looked in a mirror, the draw from the smell of food had been too great.

The table had been set. Plates, forks, knives and glasses. A carton of orange juice, the butter dish and a jar of orange marmalade were also set out. Danni couldn't bring herself to tell Tony that she hated marmalade; she would just avoid it and hope he didn't notice. He certainly had thought of everything when he had been shopping.

The toaster popped, and Tony grabbed the two slices of toast and placed them on a plate on the table.

"Eat up," he said, "the bacon and eggs are just coming."

Danni grabbed a slide of toast, spread a good layer of butter over it, cut it in half and tore off a bite. As she began to chew, Tony walked over with the frying pan and dished up three rashers of bacon and a fried egg. Danni was ravenous and tucked in before Tony could dish up his own.

"Whoa, someone's hungry. I'd better hurry up before you finish and start on mine," he joked.

Danni looked up and smiled, a bright orange streak of egg yolk smeared on her chin.

"You've got something on your face."

Danni wiped her chin.

"The other side," he said as he picked up the tea towel he had been using, leaned over and wiped her face.

They stopped in their tracks for a moment, staring into each other's eyes. Danni looked away, embarrassed, she could feel her cheeks becoming flushed. They continued eating without making eye contact. The only noise was the scraping of cutlery on plates and the satisfied chomping and chewing of bacon. When both of their plates were empty, Danni stood up and carried them over to the sink.

"Leave that, I'll do the washing up," said Tony.

"No, you've done all the cooking."

"Yes, but you're putting me up for the next few days so it's the least I can do. Honestly, you go and get dressed. I thought since you've got the day off, we could have a wander through the town, and I can see this Christmas Village they've been going on about."

Danni laughed.

"I wouldn't get too excited about the village. It's not all it's cracked up to be."

"It can't be that bad surely? Anyway, it's a nice day, the sun is out, and I need to get outside for some exercise. I've been cooped up in the medical office on the platform for the past three weeks and I've got cabin fever."

Some fresh air would be good, thought Danni; she was beginning to feel the after-effects of all that wine after guzzling down her breakfast.

She quickly showered, dried her hair, put on some make-up and got dressed in a pair of jeans, long brown boots and a chunky red cable knit sweater that looked mildly festive. When she walked into the living room, she noticed that Tony had tidied up in there too. He had taken through their dinner plates and wine glasses from the night before and had folded up his pillows and blankets and placed them in a neat pile behind the sofa along with his rucksack. He really was the perfect house guest.

He walked up behind her.

"You ready?" he asked.

"Yes, let's go." Danni was looking forward her day out. It felt good to have someone to spend time with instead of aimlessly wandering around the streets by herself as she had so often done.

They walked out into the crisp air. Danni looked up at the bright blue, cloudless sky and wondered how many kids would be disappointed they weren't going to get a white Christmas this year. As they made their way down Esslemont Avenue she could almost feel warmth from the sun on her back. Tony linked his arm through Danni's, and they strolled through the streets. They made their way down to Union Terrace to the Christmas Village. The sounds of kids laughing and screaming filled the air along with the Christmas tunes: *Here Comes Santa Claus.*

Christmas Eve had always been her favourite day, more so than Christmas Day. The build-up and sense of anticipation was high.

As they walked along the street, they browsed the German market stalls.

"Is it just me or are the stalls all selling the same tat?" asked Tony, who looked completely unimpressed.

"I told you not to get too excited about it, didn't I?"

"Yeah, well, I kind of expected a bit more than this."

The stalls were a repetition of cheap Christmas ornaments that you have could have your name painted on, costume jewellery, scented candles and scarves.

"Well we are in a recession."

"Surely, they can do better than this? Ah, that's more like it." Tony had spotted the beer tent. "Fancy a drink? Hair of the dog? The sun must be over the yardarm somewhere."

The smell of hot cider and mulled wine was wafting out into the street.

"Actually, that's not a bad idea." Danni felt like she wasn't quite on this planet, probably still riding on the alcoholic high of last night. A nice hot beverage would go down a treat.

Tony queued at the bar while Danni found a free table outside in the sun. She cleared the empty plastic glasses from the table and placed them on top of the already overflowing wheelie bin. Seagulls were fighting over cold chips and remains of burgers they had picked from the bins. *Welcome to Aberdeen and its flying rat population.*

She used a napkin to wipe the wooden picnic bench seat and sat down, taking in the scenery. The beer garden overlooked the Union Terrace gardens. In the summer, it would be blooming with roses and a floral crest depicting the city's coat of arms. At this time of year, it was less colourful, but they had set up a magical Christmas Tree maze. Hours of fun for the family. In the sunlight Aberdeen was a different place. The sun's rays reflected from the grey granite buildings, making them look like they were sparkling. In fact, it was so bright she wished she had brought her sunglasses. They were something she hadn't had to worry about for months now. She reached into her handbag hoping to find a pair, but they had long since been removed. She was disappointed as she carried everything else around in her bag.

Tony came back with the drinks. A hot apple cider for her and a large German draft beer in one of those oversized beer mugs for him.

"Cheers," he said as he clunked his glass against hers.

"Slàinte," she replied.

"Well this is nice."

She smiled at him. This was nice. Danni had to pinch herself as this felt almost too good to be true. After everything she had been through with Mark, and the lonely past year, maybe it wasn't just the sun that was shining on her, but maybe fortune was shining down on her too.

They spent a few hours in the beer garden, totally engrossed in each other and oblivious to everyone else around. They ate giant bratwurst sausages and chips covered in cheese for lunch. Tony insisted on taking a selfie of them attempting to eat the sausages. As they drank, they chatted about nothing in particular, but eventually the subject got around to David and what was happening with the investigation. Tony had called his mate in the police, who had told him they were no further forward. They still had a number of people to interview, but so far, nothing of any real help. He did however, let slip that David had died from a drug overdose. They had found a needle beside him and it had been tested. He, or more likely someone else, had injected a lethal dose of morphine. Scotty had said that if they could find whoever had sent them the note that would at least be a lead.

"You didn't say anything, did you?" Danni asked, beginning to panic.

"Of course not," he replied. "If I say anything now, I'll be implicating myself."

"So, what's their next step?"

"Probably nothing till after Christmas and they finish their interviews. He did say that the Russians were their number one suspects but without any more proof they were heading down a dead end. There were no fingerprints on the needle apart from David's, but they probably put the needle in his hand after they injected him to get his prints on it. Make it look like he committed suicide. But if you were going to do that, why would you wander out into the woods to do it?"

They sat in silence for a while, contemplating what would happen now.

As the sun started to dip and the temperature dropped dramatically, they decided to make tracks and head for somewhere indoors. The inner warmth from the alcohol was starting to wear off. They headed down Union Street, which was busy with last-minute shoppers, mainly men, scurrying around trying to find something for the wives. The centres would stay open late trying to flog anything they could to the hopeless husbands.

They headed left onto Belmont Street and found a cosy bar that also served food. The bar was already heaving with festive revellers, but they managed to find a table near the back away from the bar where it was a bit quieter and they could hear themselves think. It was a traditional-style pub with dark wooden panelling and dark green carpets that were threadbare and sticky from years of spilled beer and wine. A very harassed-looking waitress came over with a couple of menus.

"Hi, I'm afraid there will be a bit of a wait for food, we are absolutely swamped tonight."

"No problem," replied Tony. "We're not in any hurry, are we?" He looked across at Danni who shook her head, already studying the menu. Drinking through the day always made her hungry.

The waitress took a notepad and pen from the black apron tied around her waist. "I can take your drinks order now and come back for your food order."

"Lucy! These are for table eight and table ten will be up shortly," a voice shouted from the hatch through to the kitchen.

"Sorry, I need to get these," said the waitress. "You'll probably get your drinks quicker if you order direct at the bar." She walked off before they had a chance to answer.

"What will it be?" asked Tony as he stood up and removed his leather biker's jacket, draping it over the back of his chair.

"Better stick to cider, I think," replied Danni. "Don't want to start mixing my drinks."

The waitress walked past them carrying two plates of fish and chips that smelled divine.

"If the waitress comes back, can you order me that?" asked Tony.

Funny, thought Danni. That was exactly what she fancied on the menu, but the smell as it went past confirmed her choice.

By the time Tony got back with their drinks she had managed to get the waitress's attention and placed their food order.

The noise was getting louder in the bar with more and more people arriving. Town would be a nightmare tonight. The number of bars in Aberdeen had reduced dramatically over the past year with many having to close their doors, unable to make money. Those that had survived would be full of rowdy drunks, forgetting they were celebrating Christmas and starting fights because someone spilled a drink down them or looked at them the wrong way.

They had finished their first drinks and Tony was fighting through the crowds to get back to order another round when their food finally arrived.

"Sorry about the wait," said the waitress who was looking even more harassed. "You're lucky, that's the last two portions of fish too."

She put down their plates. The fish was massive and was hanging off either end of the plate. Danni's first thought was that there was no way she was going to eat all that.

"Thanks, it looks delicious."

"I'll be right back with some sauces and vinegar."

Danni tried to get Tony's attention, but he was busy texting someone on his phone.

She didn't want his food to get cold, so she walked over and tapped him on the shoulder.

He turned around and quickly shut down his phone.

"Food's here."

"OK, thanks." He seemed distracted. "I'll be right there."

"Anything wrong?"

"What?"

Danni pointed at his phone. "Something important?"

"Oh, um, no. Just replying to a mate I haven't seen for a while. You better start eating before it gets cold, I'll be right there."

Danni walked back to the table, concerned that something was wrong. She sensed that Tony seemed different, preoccupied. She wondered who he had been messaging. *Maybe it was his wife.* He had told her that they had separated but maybe that wasn't the whole truth.

By the time he arrived back with their drinks he was back to his normal cheery self.

"This looks good," he said as he put down the drinks, his beer sploshing on to the table. "Oops!"

Danni handed him a napkin to mop up the spillage.

"Thanks," he said, licking the sticky lager from his fingers.

"Is everything OK?" she asked.

"It's only a little spillage, I'll survive," he laughed.

"No, I don't mean with that, I mean about your text message. You seemed… troubled."

"Oh, no, that was nothing… So, have you been a good girl this year for Santa?" he asked, quickly changing the subject.

"I guess I'll just have to wait and see what he brings."

"Yeah, right…" He took a sip of lager.

"You sure you're OK?"

"Yeah, I think the beer is starting to take its toll, but this will help." He smiled and tucked into his fish and chips.

"Pass the tartare sauce, will you?"

Danni handed over the jar and watched as he opened it and spooned a huge dollop of sauce on to the side of his plate.

"Eat up," he said as he picked up a chip, dipped it in the sauce and stuck the whole thing in his mouth in one go.

Danni picked up her fork and knife and cut into the fish, the steam rising from it as the batter split open.

"Careful, its hot," said Tony, fanning his mouth with his hand.

They ate the rest of their food in silence, the noise in the bar getting so loud that they were having to shout to be heard. Danni got stuck about halfway through her massive plate of food, but Tony polished off all of his and what she had left. He signalled to the waitress to get the bill.

"It's too loud in here," he shouted to Danni. "Shall we head back to the flat?"

"Yeah, all this food and drink is making me sleepy."

Tony took the bill to the counter and handed over cash. "Keep the change," he said as the barman took the payment.

He took Danni's hand and pushed through the crowd, keeping her close behind him so she didn't get squashed. As they headed out the door Danni was knocked to the pavement by a group of legless, scantily clad females who could barely walk in their high heels.

"Watch it," one of them shouted. Her skirt was half way up her bum and her chest was hanging out the front. Lipstick was smeared over her face from snogging anyone that had even looked at her sideways. The group click clacked off down the street trying to hold each other up but failing miserably. They looked like two octopuses having sex, arms and legs everywhere.

Tony bent down to help Danni to her feet, lifting her up in one swift move. He was strong for his size.

"You OK?" he asked.

"I am now," she said. "My hero." They looked into each other's eyes, gaze held for a moment before they both laughed. He kept his arm around her as they started to walk back towards the flat. Danni felt safe and protected with him. Something she hadn't felt in a long time.

It was dark and cold but at least it was still dry. The cold air hit Danni and suddenly she felt very drunk. She clung tighter to Tony, finding it more and more difficult to put one foot in front of the other. She had definitely had too much to drink. They staggered back to the flat, waving and yelling 'Merry Christmas' to everyone they passed.

Danni struggled to get the key in the door but got there eventually after the fourth attempt. She brushed along the corridor using the walls to hold herself up and then stumbled up the stairs, falling in a heap on the landing. She got a fit of the giggles and couldn't get up. Tony struggled to lift her. It was like lifting jelly, she kept slipping through his fingers. He finally got her to her feet and threw her over his shoulder in a fireman's lift. He took the key from her, opened the flat door and dropped her down onto her bed, losing his balance and landing on top of her. They lay there for a second, gazing into each other's eyes and then he kissed her. He stopped suddenly and pulled back.

"Sorry, I shouldn't have done that," he said as he pushed himself off her and stood up.

"I've just remembered, we drank all the wine last night, I'm just going to nip round to the shop and get some more for tomorrow."

He headed out the door before she could say anything.

Danni lay there trying to figure out what had just happened. She hadn't been with anyone since Mark, scared to let anyone in, but Tony was different. *Wasn't he?* She managed to get to her feet and swayed over to the bedroom window to shut the curtains. As she looked out the window, she saw Tony heading up the street with his phone to his ear. Who was he calling? Was it her, his wife? She had no right to feel jealous, but she did. She was starting to fall for Tony. He looked up, as though he was aware she was watching him, and she shut the curtains quickly, ashamed that she had been caught spying on him.

She struggled out of her clothes, and into her pyjamas, leaving them where they fell on the floor. She crawled into bed, the sheets feeling cold as she pulled them up around her. A few minutes later she heard the flat door open as Tony returned.

"I got a couple of bottles of that Malbec we had the other night," he shouted.

She was embarrassed about the kiss, so she pretended she was asleep.

"Hey, you OK in there?" He pushed open the bedroom door and saw she was already in bed. He watched her for a few seconds to make sure she was breathing, then pulled the door towards the frame, leaving it slightly ajar so he could listen out for her in the night.

He put the bottles of wine on the dining table and then went through to the living room and made up his bed on the sofa. It was actually quite comfortable even though his feet were hanging off the end. He switched on the TV, turning the volume down low so as not to wake Danni. Suddenly he wasn't tired. He had too many things on his mind, all swarming together, making no sense. What were his feelings towards Danni? He shouldn't have kissed her. He didn't want things to be awkward between them. Hopefully she was too drunk to remember. He lay there thinking about her. The smell of her was still on his shirt and he breathed it in.

Danni opened her eyes. She couldn't get up because then Tony would know she wasn't actually asleep, so she lay there with one eye open and one eye shut trying to stop the room from spinning. *Helicopter head.* That's what her old flatmate from university had called it. Thoughts were jumbled in her mind. She thought about the kiss and closed her eyes, trying to remember the way his body had felt against hers. *Strong and warm and protective.* She wondered what tomorrow would bring. After all, it would be Christmas Day. She closed her eyes and made a wish. If anything was going to happen, then the magic and spirit of Christmas would help make her wish come true. Tomorrow was going to be a day to remember.

Chapter Twenty-One

He had only just rolled into bed and was drifting off. It had been a long and difficult day and all he wanted to do was go to sleep and forget about it when his phone bleeped to alert him to a message.

He opened WhatsApp.

"Is this her?"

He sat up in bed, switched on the bedside lamp and looked at the photo. He rubbed his eyes and studied it hard. There was a resemblance. He clicked on the photo with two fingers and enlarged it, zooming in on just her. The face was familiar, but she looked different if it was her. The hair was brown, not blonde, and it had been cut shorter to shoulder length. Her hair had been half way down her back which had annoyed him as he thought it was untidy. He had made her tie it up in a bun when they went out as it looked more stylish and sophisticated instead of flyaway and carefree. He quite liked the shorter, darker hair.

He stared at the photo a bit longer. Yes, it could be her, but he would have to see her in the flesh to make sure.

He replied to the message. "Think so. The jocks want help from Scot Yard for murder inquiry. B up soon. Keep an eye on her. B in contact."

Chapter Twenty-Two

He was up to his eyeballs in debt and had taken out loans that he was never going to be able to repay. And now things were going from bad to worse. He had gone to a money shark in the city. A so-called friend who was in a similar position had given him his details. He had made the call and the Russian accent on the other end had told him to meet him in a dark and dingy pub off Crown Street.

The Russians were running things now. They had offered to pay off all his debts and give him money to tide him over. He would not have to pay them back a single penny. Instead they would look for him to repay them in some other way. He would be at their beck and call. Some would say he had sold his soul to the devil. And they would be right. Why had he taken money from the Russians? They had supplied him with a pay as you go mobile that was untraceable. He was to carry it with him at all times and they would let him know how and when the debt was to be repaid.

His wife had no idea. She had gone mad this Christmas, buying presents for the kids. The same kids that the Russians had threatened if he did not do exactly what they said. She spent all of the 'bonus' he had received from work. Little did she know that he would be paying for that for the rest of his life.

And he knew the threat was serious too, as the friend who had introduced them was already paying the price for not following orders. His boy had ended up in hospital after a hit-and-run incident outside his school. Thankfully he had made a full recovery – a few broken bones and a concussion – but it could have been so much worse. No-one could say for sure that the Russians were involved but it was unlikely to have been a coincidence.

He had received orders from them before. He was a helicopter pilot and they had required a 'colleague' to be picked up from a remote location and transferred to Aberdeen without trace. He had said it was impossible. He couldn't just take a helicopter out without his bosses asking questions. He was told he would have to make it possible.

He had concocted a story about a warning light that was flashing intermittently and that he needed to take out the chopper for a test flight. There had been so much noise in the press recently about the safety of helicopters for transferring oil workers, that his employers hadn't really questioned his request. After all, safety was paramount, or so they kept preaching.

He thought that was it, that he had fulfilled his part of the bargain, but that was just the start of it. He had been forced to move goods around the platforms without being manifested. He had no idea what was in the bags and boxes he was taking on his flights and to be honest, he really didn't want to know. And he was pretty sure the Russians had been people trafficking, transferring folk between platforms, again with no record of them on the paperwork. He had wondered what he would be asked to do next, but he had not considered the unthinkable.

His phone rang. The one the Russians had supplied. He left the living room where his wife was busy wrapping the parcels from Santa for the kids. They had gone to bed early under the pretence that Santa would not come until they were asleep, and the sooner they were asleep, the sooner he would come.

"Yes," he whispered, fighting back the feeling of dread as to what he was about to be instructed to do. They had told him this day would come but he had not expected it so soon. "But it's Christmas, please just give me one more Christmas with my family," he begged them.

But his words fell on deaf ears. The debt was to be paid off in full early tomorrow morning. He was given his instructions and reminded what would happen to that lovely family of his if he did not comply. The phone went dead.

Chapter Twenty-Three

Christmas Day

Danni lay awake, listening for any movement from next door. She had thought about nothing except the kiss since she woke. She had already decided to pretend to Tony that she didn't remember anything about it. She didn't want things to be awkward between them. Especially not on Christmas Day. Maybe things would happen later but for now she was willing to just let them run their course.

She got out of bed; her head was pounding. Two days of drinking was beginning to take its toll. She needed paracetamol and coffee. She snuck out of the bedroom, treading carefully to avoid the squeaky floorboard, but she didn't need to as she heard the shower running. She looked into the living room to see that Tony had already tidied up his bedding. But what was that on the windowsill? She walked over to take a closer look. It was a small plastic Christmas tree, about a foot tall, with tiny red and gold-coloured baubles and a sparkly gold star on top. As she bent over to look closer, she noticed a small parcel beside it. It was a square box, about two inches by two inches.

It was wrapped in red and white Christmas paper depicting Santa, reindeer and penguins. There was no label on it. She was about to pick it up when she heard the shower switch off. She tip-toed out of the living room into the kitchen not wanting Tony to know that she had seen it.

As Tony came out of the bathroom, Danni was standing in the kitchen switching on the coffee maker.

"Merry Christmas," he said. He was naked except for a towel wrapped around his waist, beads of water glistening on his chest. Danni's cheeks flushed as she realised she was staring at him. She shook her head and blinked her eyes.

"Erm, Merry Christmas," she replied, dropping her gaze to the floor.

He walked over and pecked her on the cheek, before turning and heading into the living room.

"I'll just get some clothes on; I feel a little under-dressed."

Danni continued to blush as she watched him. She noticed a tattoo on the back of his left shoulder, but that wasn't what was fixing her attention. He obviously worked out. That six-pack was impressive.

But that tattoo looked familiar. *Was he ex-army?* Mark had a tattoo that looked similar to Tony's. Mark had been in the army before he had joined the police, long before he had met her. He had never spoken of his time in service, but Danni knew he had been stationed in Iraq. She often wondered if what he had seen there had affected him and that was why he had become so controlling over her. PTSD, that's what they called it nowadays, wasn't it?

But she didn't want to be thinking about Mark, today of all days. She pushed the thought from her mind and headed into the bathroom. As she opened the door, swirls of steam escaped. She quickly shut it behind her, keeping the warmth in the room. The bathroom mirror was fogged up and she wiped it with her hand to see her reflection. God, she looked rough, and she was still wearing the make-up from yesterday. Well, half of it anyway. Her eyes were smudged and puffy and her lips stained pink from the remainder of the lipstick. *Oh my God!* She had just let Tony see her looking like that. *What an embarrassment.* Yet, he hadn't said anything. Didn't seem to notice at all. Or maybe he was just too polite to mention how rough she looked.

She pulled a face wipe from the packet and removed what was left of the mascara, eye shadow and lipstick. She squeezed toothpaste out onto the toothbrush and cleaned her teeth and cringed as she realised that when Tony had bent over to kiss her, he might have smelled her morning breath. She was going to have to do better than that if she wanted to impress him! She jumped in the shower and turned the temperature up. She would steam herself clean.

She left the bathroom and dashed through to the bedroom so that Tony wouldn't see her. He looked round as he heard the bathroom shut.

"I hope you like scrambled eggs?" he shouted through.

"Yeah, thanks," she replied.

"Not sure if your head's anything like mine, but I couldn't face a fry up."

"Me neither, eggs and toast will be great."

She got dressed, blasted her hair with the dryer and made herself look more presentable.

As she walked back into the kitchen Tony was already dishing up the eggs. Slices of toast were stacked between the salt and pepper shakers.

The smell of eggs started to turn her stomach and she could feel the bile rising. *Oh God, please don't let me be sick in front of him*, she thought. She swallowed as she tried to control the feeling. Pouring a small glass of orange juice and taking a sip, hoping the sugar fix would help. She picked up the fork and poked at the eggs but didn't feel ready to attempt to eat any.

"Something wrong?" asked Tony as he sat down opposite and guzzled down forkfuls of pale-yellow egg.

"I think I just lost my appetite," replied Danni as she made a dash for the bathroom.

A few minutes later she sheepishly emerged, looking decidedly green around the gills.

"Someone can't take her alcohol," laughed Tony.

"Oh, don't!" She couldn't bring herself to look at him, too embarrassed to make eye contact.

She shuffled back through to the kitchen, sat down at the table and pushed the plate of eggs away from her like it was poison.

"Well if you don't want them, I'm not letting them go to waste," said Tony as he took the plate and began shovelling down the eggs before they got cold.

Danni picked up the mug of coffee and took a sip. The orange juice hadn't helped but maybe the caffeine would. *Or maybe that was wishful thinking.*

"I was going to suggest some Buck's Fizz to kick the day off, but perhaps not?" joked Tony.

Danni remembered the last Christmas she had drunk Buck's Fizz in the morning and felt even more sick, her stomach turned, and she had to make another dash to the bathroom.

Surprisingly, by the time she re-emerged, she was starting to feel better. Her empty stomach rumbled, and she felt like she could possibly eat something and keep it down. She sat back at the table and smiled embarrassingly at Tony.

"Better now?" he asked, smiling back.

"I certainly hope so," she replied.

She attempted to eat a piece of dry toast. She waited a minute and when it didn't reappear, she took another bite.

"I know what we need," said Tony as he pushed back his seat and carried the empty plates over to the sink. "Some Christmas cheer, and I don't mean the alcoholic kind."

He put down the plates and turned on the radio catching the end of *I Wish It Could Be Christmas Everyday* which was swiftly followed by The Pogues and Kirsty MacColl with *Fairytale of New York*.

Halfway through, the song stopped and an announcer came on.

"We interrupt this recorded programme to bring you breaking news. A helicopter has crashed into an offshore platform in the northern North Sea."

Tony and Danni both stared at each other.

"According to eye witnesses from a nearby support vessel the crash happened at approximately 8:05am this morning when they were alerted by the sound of the aircraft. No flights were scheduled to the platform, today being Christmas Day. Contact with the platform has not been established and there are reports of several explosions and flames reaching over 100 feet in the air. It is thought that a crew of approximately forty-six people are onboard Moskaneft's South Platform, which is currently shut-in awaiting decommissioning."

"WHAT THE FUCK?" shouted Tony.

"Moskaneft's platform?" questioned Danni. "Did I hear that right?"

Tony looked at his watch. It was 9:30am. The crash had happened over an hour ago, while they had still been sleeping off the aftereffects of the previous day and night.

Danni suddenly felt very sober.

"Why haven't they called me?" she questioned. "I'm on the emergency response team." She ran through to the bedroom, searching for her bag that was lying on the floor beside her bed where she had dropped it last night. She grabbed her phone and through the broken screen she could make out she had five missed calls. The phone had been switched to silent.

"Shit! They've been trying to get hold of me," she shouted through to Tony.

"I'll call a taxi. I'm coming to the office with you," he replied.

She tried to call the office, but her phone wasn't working properly after the bloody cat had made her drop it. She found her own mobile and dialled the office. It was engaged. She hung up and tried again. Still engaged. They had probably taken the phone off the hook.

She tried a third time. A recorded message answered.

"You have reached the offices of Moskaneft. We are presently dealing with an incident and our emergency response team have been mobilised. We wish to assure you that the safety and wellbeing of our employees is our number one priority. If you are calling about a relative, please contact the relative support team on 0800 111 2233. If you are a member of the press, please contact the media support team on 0800 111…" Danni hung up.

"Shit! They've called out the relative support team," she shouted through to Tony.

"They can't get a taxi to us for another thirty minutes."

"Let's go, maybe we can flag one on the way."

They both grabbed their coats and ran out of the flat. As they reached the street they started jogging.

"I can't believe this has happened," said Danni. "And on Christmas Day. What the hell was a chopper doing out in the field today? They don't normally fly today, do they?"

"No," said Tony. "The only flights today would be emergency flights for medivacs."

"I know it's not your platform, but I'm really glad you are onshore right now."

"Me too," replied Tony as he reached out and took her hand.

"Taxi!"

"What?"

"Look, there's a taxi coming."

He released her hand and ran out into the street to flag down the taxi.

"Come on!" he shouted as the taxi stopped.

Danni ran across the street and jumped into the back on the driver's side as Tony slid in the passenger side.

"Merry Christmas!" said the taxi driver. "Where you off to in such a hurry, you haven't burned the turkey already, have you?" he laughed.

"We need to get to the harbour as quick as possible," said Tony. "Salvesen Tower."

"Here, isn't that where Moskaneft have their offices?" questioned the driver. "Have you heard the news, it's all they are speaking about. The wife called me, and I've been watching it on the Sky News app between pick-ups. Terrible tragedy. They're saying it's a terrorist attack."

"We need to get there as quickly as possible, can you put your foot down?" asked Danni.

"Sure, you guys work for them then?"

"Yes, look, just drive, will you?"

As the driver pulled out and swung the car around, Tony opened the Sky News app on his phone. The picture that greeted him was one he would rather not have seen. It reminded him of the scenes of Piper Alpha from thirty years ago. He had only been a kid when it happened, but he would never forget the pictures on the news. It was one of those tragedies that you remembered where you were when it happened. Like when Princess Diana died, or when the twin towers fell on 9/11.

"Look," he passed his phone to Danni.

"Oh my God! It's a ball of flames," exclaimed Danni. "Do you think anyone survived?"

"I really hope so, but it doesn't look good, does it?"

"You guys know anyone on the platform?" asked the driver.

"I'm not sure," replied Tony. "Possibly."

"We just need to get to the office, so we can do whatever we can to help," replied Danni.

"Yeah, sure. Sorry." The driver focussed on the road ahead.

It didn't take long to get to the office; the roads were empty, everyone safe at home opening their Christmas presents and starting to cook their turkeys.

A media frenzy was already in progress. It was just like when David's death had been broadcast, only worse. The press would be having a field day. *First the managing director is found dead, a worker is killed on one of their platforms and now this. Was Moskaneft cursed?* Danni was beginning to think so.

As they got out of the taxi, cameras were trained on them. Camera flashes were going off left, right and centre and microphones were shoved in their faces.

"Do you have any information on the incident?"

"Sources are saying there are no survivors, would you care to comment?"

"We are hearing this is a terrorist attack, can you confirm?"

They were bombarded by questions, none of which they knew the answers to.

Tony used his coat to try to shield Danni's face from the cameras as they pushed through the crowd, but it was too late, they were already live on the news. Their faces would be repeated every ten minutes as the news unfolded and they showed the same footage over and over again.

When they got inside, they were greeted by Dr Evil. He was obviously at the beck and call of the Russians to head up their security. He recognised Danni from before and motioned for her to scan into the building.

He raised his hand out towards Tony in a stop motion.

"And who are you?"

"I work here!" replied Tony, clearly irritated. "Who are you?"

"Only emergency response team members are allowed in the building," he replied.

"It's OK, he's with me. He's an offshore medic, he's here to help," replied Danni.

"Sorry, I have strict instructions as to who can enter."

"Look, I have my pass here, somewhere..." Tony rummaged in his jacket pockets. "Shit, I've left it at the flat. But here, I have my driving licence, you can check me against the system. I'm the medic from the North Platform."

"I don't care if you're Dr Doolittle, you are not coming in."

"Wait there," shouted Danni. "I'll go up and tell them you're here. Get them to give you access."

"Take a seat Mr..."

"Mr Black to you," said Tony who was getting more impatient by the second. "And I'm fine standing."

Danni dashed over to the lifts, pushing the button repeatedly like it was going to make the lift come faster.

As the doors opened, she called back over her shoulder, "Don't worry, I'll see you upstairs."

Danni exited the lift on the seventh floor where the conference room would have been transformed into an incident room by now. It was chaos. People were busy on phones and writing up information on the dry wipe boards.

"Thank God you made it!" It was Mike, the same controller who had been on duty during the incident on the North Platform.

"We are struggling to get hold of people. Everyone's away with it being the holidays. Can you help Kathy over there on the information log? She'll show you what to do."

"Yeah, sure. What the fuck has happened?"

"We don't have all the details yet and we have had no contact with the platform. If you've seen the news, then you probably know as much as we do." He pointed to a TV in the corner of the room that was switched to mute on the Sky News channel. The same footage of the platform in flames that they had seen on their way to the office was being shown.

"Listen, Tony Black, the medic from the North Platform is downstairs. I, um, bumped into him at the front door," she lied. "He wants to help."

"Well, what's he doing downstairs? Get him up here, we need all the help we can get."

"Security won't let him up."

"For fuck's sake, do they think I've got nothing better to do than vet who is coming into the office? That's their bloody job." He reached for a phone. "I'll call them now."

Danni took off her coat and headed over to help Kathy who was frantically collating bits of paper and trying to update the computer screens around the room with different information. How many vessels were in the area, who had been called out, police and coastguard contact details. There was so much to keep track of and not enough hands to do it.

"Actually, Danni?" Mike shouted over.

"Yes?"

"You have access to the personnel files, don't you?"

"Yeah, the files are with the legal documents upstairs."

"Can you get up there and find the phone numbers for everyone on this list? Call them and try to get as many people in here as possible."

He handed her a list of about thirty names. She scanned down it. Most of them were managers.

"We haven't been able to get hold of anyone in personnel and we can't get into their system online to get the info. Technology is great if you can work the damn thing! Oh, and leave the file room door open, I'll send someone else up to help you when I have a spare body."

He turned and went back to berating Dr Evil for being a jobsworth. That's not exactly how Danni would have handled it. He was particularly scary looking, and she wouldn't be surprised if he was waiting for Mike down a dark alley anytime soon. She dumped her coat and bag on the nearest chair, took her pass out of her bag and headed up to the tenth floor.

Chapter Twenty-Four

anni was ensconced in the personnel files trying to get to grips with their filing system, or lack of one. What should have been an alphabetical system was turning out to be rather complicated. It seemed that whoever had sorted the files had perhaps been dyslexic, with files in the wrong folders and in the wrong sections. It was going to take her ages to track down the ones she needed. She wanted to get back downstairs to find out what was going on. She could be more help down there.

"I've been sent up here to help. I told them I would be better off downstairs, you know among the thick of it, where the action is. After all, I am giving up my Christmas Day. But no, no, I end up stuck up here with you."

Danni didn't even have to look up, she knew that grating voice anywhere. It was Becky. *Whose bright idea was it to put the two of them together?*

Danni ripped the list in half and held out the bottom half towards Becky.

"Here, start looking for their files and write down all their listed phone numbers."

"And now I have to take orders from you… Merry Christmas indeed. You know that I haven't even had time to open my presents yet?"

"People are dead, and you are worried about your presents! How shallow can you get!"

"I'm only saying. Like, why do they have to blow stuff up on Christmas Day, have they no respect for the sanctity of Christmas? Like I know they don't really celebrate it or anything, but why wouldn't you? Don't they want turkey and presents and stuff?"

Danni just shook her head and kept looking through the files. It was clear that Becky had no idea about the significance of Christmas to the terrorists, and she was pretty sure she had no idea what the true sanctity of Christmas was either, but by some twisted turn of fate they had been thrown together. The quicker they got all the details they needed, the quicker she could be rid of her.

"If you just shut up for two minutes and get on with this, then we don't have to spend any more time together than is absolutely necessary," said Danni as she shoved Becky's half of the list into her hand.

"Whoa! Well, Santa obviously missed someone out last night. Can't say I'm surprised though, who would want to visit your ugly face?"

"For fuck's sake, Becky! Can you just think about someone other than yourself for once? People's lives are actually on the line here."

Becky made a face and grabbed the list from Danni. "Who died and made you God?" sneered Becky.

"Really? You think that's appropriate, considering what's happening offshore right now?"

"Sorry, I didn't mean it like that," Becky apologised.

Danni glowered at Becky who finally took the hint and shut up.

They worked through their respective lists in silence. Once they got to grips with the filing system, they found the files and the numbers that they needed. They were almost done when they heard voices from the room next door.

"Hey, listen. Do you hear that?" said Becky. "Is that the Russians?"

"Yes, it's the boardroom through there."

"Wow, no wonder you spend so much time up here. I bet you hear all sorts, I need to get myself a pass for in here. You must know heaps of things that they've discussed."

"It's none of my business..."

"Shh, I'm trying to listen." Becky moved over and put her ear up against the wall. "You can hear better if you do this."

"I don't think you want to do that," replied Danni, remembering what she heard the time she had listened in to the Russians' conversation.

The voices were getting louder.

"I told you I would take care of it."

"And a fine job you have done."

"We no longer have to worry about the cost of decommissioning that platform!"

Sounds of laughter.

"How did you convince him to do it? No, on second thoughts, the less I know the better."

"Let's just say there are ways and means of getting people to do whatever you want."

"They are already reporting this as the work of terrorists, so we can help them with that."

"Do not worry. There is no link back to us. This time the terrorists are good for something. Their weapon of choice has been cars and lorries, so why not a helicopter? They used planes for 9/11."

More laughter.

"Moscow will be happy when they realise how much money you have saved them."

"And we won't get the blame for any of this as how can we control terrorists?"

"Here's to ISIS and its war against the free world. Good timing to do this on Christmas Day. Very symbolic. There was always going to be casualties, but we kept the number to a minimum. After all, how would the terrorists know which platform was best to target?"

Further laughter.

"I need to get downstairs, make a statement to the press. Condemn this terrorist attack. This attack on our beliefs and our industry. Send our heartfelt condolences to the families, etcetera, etcetera. We shall meet later to raise a glass to our comrades."

Danni and Becky stared at each other.

"Did you hear that?" asked Becky. "They crashed a helicopter into the platform!"

"Keep your voice down," whispered Danni.

"But didn't you hear what they just said?"

"Shut the fuck up, they'll hear us. Come on, we need to get out of here."

"But we need to tell someone."

"Move! We can't let them know we were in here."

Danni grabbed Becky's arm and dragged her out of the room into the corridor.

"Good morning, ladies, can we be of assistance?"

They stopped dead, frozen in their tracks, and turned to come face to face with two of the Russians. She had seen the taller one before, he had spent time in the office. He had short blond hair, shaved close to the bone in a military-style cut and piercing blue eyes. She did not recognise the smaller one who sported a matching haircut. He had a tattoo on the right side of his neck, like a spider's web. They were dressed in almost identical dark blue suits with white shirts and red ties. It hadn't escaped Danni that they were wearing company colours, like a uniform.

"Erm, we are just going back down to the control room to help," said Danni.

"I see," replied the taller of the two.

"And I suppose you want us to believe that you didn't hear our conversation."

"What? I don't know what you are talking about! We were just in there getting some phone numbers from the personnel files and now we are going back downstairs to help in the incident room," replied Danni, trying to keep her voice from wavering.

"We're going to call the police and tell them exactly what you've done!" shouted Becky. "You won't get away with this, you know!"

Becky turned to run towards the emergency exit door but before she could get her hand on the handle she slumped to the floor.

Danni dropped to the floor beside her. She turned to face the Russians to see the smaller of the two had a gun in his hand with a silencer attached. *The cowards had shot her in the back!*

Danni rolled her over and felt for a pulse, but there was nothing there. She was gone. She had wished Becky dead before, but she hadn't actually meant it. She pushed back strands of hair from her face and looked into her cold, dead eyes. "You silly girl, you never could keep your big mouth shut, could you?" she whispered to her. She cradled her body for a few seconds, but the Russians motioned for her to get on her feet.

"Leave her. Get up. You will do as we say unless you want to end up like her."

Danni had a feeling she was going to end up like Becky whatever she did. It was only a matter of when and where.

"On your feet." The smaller Russian motioned with his gun for her to get up. She did as she was told. Her best chance of getting out of this was to do exactly what they said and bide her time. Hopefully she would stay alive long enough to plan an escape.

"In there." He pointed to the file room.

Was this where she was going to meet her maker? The room that had become a sanctuary for her over the past few months was now going to be her mausoleum.

"Get rid of the body while I deal with her," said the taller of the two.

Danni's last glimpse of Becky was of her body slumped over the shoulder of the smaller Russian in a fireman's lift, her golden yellow hair hanging down his back. Becky would have been annoyed that her flowing locks were no longer flawless, but dishevelled, tangled and stained with crimson red blood.

As Becky's body disappeared out the emergency exit door, they entered the file room and the door was closed behind them. Danni stood there, facing the remaining Russian. Her breath was shallow, and she struggled to swallow. Was this it? Had she escaped from one persecutor only to end up in the hands of another? *Out of the frying pan into the fire.* She heard the voice of her mother and her endless sayings enter her head.

"Sit down," demanded the Russian, pointing at the only chair in the room. The one with no arms and a rip in the material. She did as she was told.

A few seconds later the door to the room opened and Tony was shoved inside, falling to his knees. Dr Evil, the security guard from the front desk, was stood behind him with a gun pointing at his head.

"Ah, Mr Black, so good of you to join us. Your timing is impeccable. You are just in time to do the honours."

"Tony, what's going on?" Danni asked, confusion in her voice.

"Silence!"

"Roll up your sleeve," demanded the taller Russian.

Danni looked at him questioningly, wondering what was about to happen.

"This will not hurt. When you wake up you won't remember any of this. And if you do, then I trust you are clever enough to keep your mouth shut, unlike your unfortunate friend."

Dr Evil removed a small, black leather case from his inside suit pocket, unzipped it and removed a syringe and a vial of liquid. He passed both to Tony.

"I assume you know what to do with these?" the first Russian stated.

Tony took both items from Dr Evil and hung his head. Tony looked up at Danni and whispered, "I'm sorry."

"No, not you!"

"I said silence!"

Danni looked away from Tony. Had this all been a ruse to get close to her? Keep tabs on her after she found David's letter? She had thought they were falling for each other, but maybe that's what he wanted her to think. If that was the case, she had certainly had the wool pulled over her eyes. Her feelings had been genuine. She thought she would never trust anyone again, not let anyone else in after what happened with Mark. But she had, and this is what she got for her troubles, for trusting again.

"Get on with it. We haven't got all day."

He inserted the needle into the top of the bottle and drew up the liquid into the syringe. He flicked it a couple of times to remove the air bubbles. He leaned forward and whispered in her ear, "Trust me," then expertly slid the needle into her vein above her wrist in one fluent movement. Danni thought he had done this before. Had he been the one that had injected David? As she watched the clear-coloured fluid leave the syringe and enter her bloodstream, she thought of what had happened between them. The room started to spin. She remembered their kiss last night, remembered the feeling of his body against hers. Her heart started racing.

Thoughts swirled around her head.

Tony.

Her mother.

Her friends from London. She loved London. Why had she moved from there?

Mark.

Mark was the reason.

What if this was down to Mark? Did he know where she was? Had he found her?

A low buzzing noise entered her head, then everything went black.

Chapter Twenty-Five

Tony watched as Danni slumped in the chair, unconscious. He had quickly calculated how much morphine to give her. He had to give her enough to knock her out, so the Russians would not suspect, but not enough to kill her. He hoped he had guessed her weight correctly. He knew what was likely to happen now and he would have to be clever if he was to get them both out of here alive.

"Very professionally done, Mr Black," said the first Russian. "Now I trust you can self-medicate?" He motioned to the syringe.

Tony looked around, there wasn't much to work with, he would have to be quick. Only one of them had a gun that he could see. He reinserted the needle into the vial of morphine and drew back the syringe. A larger dose would be needed this time and he would just have to hope it took effect instantly.

He placed the syringe on the floor and began to roll up his shirt sleeve, going through the motions for the benefit of the

Russians. He bent over with his back to them to pick up the syringe and in one swift move he turned, plunging the needle into the thigh of Dr Evil and knocked him to the floor. As he swung round, he snatched the lamp from the table, smashing the bulb and sticking it into the neck of the first Russian. As he grabbed at his neck in shock, Tony punched him in the face and then kicked him in the balls. He let out a gasp of breath and fell to the floor, clutching his crotch and his face at the same time.

Tony never thought he would ever kick another man in the balls, knowing how much pain that would inflict, but hey, needs must!

He lifted Danni from the chair and over his shoulder, much the same as the time he had carried her up the landing when they had come home drunk from the pub. He had to get her out of here without bumping into any more of the Russians.

He pushed through the doors into the emergency stairwell but as he took his first couple of steps, he could hear footsteps below. He couldn't risk it, so he quickly about turned and headed down the corridor to the main stairs. The lift was not an option as he didn't have his pass and it was locked down because of the ongoing incident. He had been on his way to find Danni when he had passed the boardroom and overhead the same conversation as she and Becky had heard. He was surprised they hadn't killed him there and then, but he had been useful to them, for a short time anyway. He was thankful he had been the one to inject Danni, as God knows how much morphine they would have given her. At least she had a chance if he could just get her out of here and up to the hospital.

He headed down the stairs, almost dropping Danni and having to stop several times to adjust her over his shoulder. As he got towards the bottom, he heard voices and ducked out of the stairwell onto the third floor. They would have to hide until the coast was clear. The floor was deserted, the previous tenant having vacated the premises a few months back as they were no longer able to afford the rent. There were wires hanging from the cable trays in the suspended ceiling and plastic sheeting had been used to separate areas of the floor where partition walls had once been. As he carried Danni through the floor looking for somewhere to hide, he noticed that the windows at the back of the building looked out over the carpark. Maybe he could get them out through a window. He carefully lowered Danni down onto the floor, instinctively placing her in the recovery position. He tried the window, but it didn't open. It was shut fast. *Bloody health and safety!* All the windows had been sealed shut to stop anyone falling or jumping out the window. *Bang goes that idea!*

He pushed through the plastic sheeting into a corridor and to his surprise found an emergency exit door that led directly out on to the top floor of the carpark. He ran back to Danni, who was still unconscious, and lifted her back over his shoulder. As he pushed the fire door open, an alarm sounded. *Oh, great!* He had just alerted the Russians to where they were! He dashed out the door, ran out into the carpark and down the first ramp. *Where to now?* He headed down the next ramp just as someone was walking away from their car. He recognised her, she worked in the office. *What was her name? Sheena? Sheila? Something like that.*

"Hey, I need help here! Danni has collapsed, I need to get her to hospital. I need your car."

The woman stepped back away from them, wary of what she was seeing. She reached for her phone from her bag. "I'll call an ambulance," she replied.

"There's no time, we need to go now. She's unconscious. Please, Sheila, I need your keys."

"How do you know my name?"

He had guessed correctly; he was normally good with names.

"It's me, Tony. I'm one of the offshore medics. I've seen you in the office."

Sheila approached them slowly, but Tony could see a look of recognition on her face. "Oh yes, sorry, I didn't realise it was you."

"Please, I need to borrow your car."

"Yes, yes, of course," she said as she rummaged for the keys in her oversized handbag.

"Hurry, she's unconscious, we don't have long," Tony said anxiously, looking over his shoulder in case the Russians were already on their tail.

Sheila found her keys and handed them to Tony.

"Thanks," he replied, as he beeped open the lock and placed Danni on the backseat of the red Volkswagen Golf.

He jumped into the driver's seat and, without stopping to fasten his seatbelt, started the engine and sped off. The wheels screeched as he raced down the final ramp, out of the carpark and into the street.

Sheila stood there watching, wondering if she would ever see her car again. Some Christmas this was turning out to be!

The media circus was still camped outside the office door. They all turned when they heard the sound of tyres screeching and saw the Golf leaving the carpark and speeding off down the street.

"Who was that?" asked one of the news reporters to his cameraman.

"I don't know, but I got it recorded."

Tony floored the car through the traffic lights onto Market Street. Thankfully, being Christmas Day, there was no-one else on the roads. As he sped onto Union Street the incessant *ting, ting, ting* of the seatbelt warning alarm was beginning to get on his nerves. He reached over with his left arm, flailing at the seatbelt and pulled it across his body. It kept jamming as he was pulling it too forcefully. "AGGGHHHH, fucking thing!" he screamed as he made one last attempt and got enough slack to fasten it. The Christmas lights overhead blinked on and off, mocking him. This was not the sort of day he had planned.

As he headed up Union Street, he suddenly remembered that Union Terrace was blocked off because of the Christmas Village. He hit the accelerator and sped up, ignoring all the traffic lights and turned sharp right into Golden Square. There was a delivery lorry blocking his path so instead he drove around the circular car park the wrong way, exiting onto Crimon Place then down onto Skene Street. He twisted and turned right and left and eventually made his way out onto Westburn Road where he could see the lights of Aberdeen Royal Infirmary looming in the distance. He didn't wait for the traffic lights to turn green but slid round the junction and into the accident and emergency carpark. He abandoned the car in the ambulance bay, knowing full well the dangers of doing that – after all he was a medic – but right now the only thing he was worried about was Danni. He left the keys in the ignition; they could move it themselves!

He lifted Danni out of the backseat and ran through the sliding doors into the reception area.

The receptionist, who was wearing reindeer antlers and a jolly Christmas jumper, leaped from her seat behind the reception desk as Tony practically slid to a halt in front of her.

"Quick, she's unconscious!" he screamed at her.

"What's her name?" asked the receptionist.

"Just get a fucking doctor, will you!" shouted Tony.

With that a nurse came through the door from the treatment area. She was also dressed festively with tinsel in her hair.

"What's going on?" she asked, clearly irritated by the disruption.

"She's unconscious, she's taken morphine."

"And where did she get the morphine?"

"Never mind that, she needs naloxone, now!"

"This way, she needs to go to resus," said the nurse and motioned through the swing doors whilst grabbing a trolley, which Tony carefully placed Danni onto.

They hurried down the corridor, where the strong smell of disinfectant hit Tony and was beginning to make him nauseous, the brightness of the artificial lights causing his eyes to strain.

"In here." The nurse motioned as she pushed open the door to the resus area. There were two other patients already in there, hooked up to monitors with nurses and doctors attending to them.

Tony helped wheel the trolley into the room where the nurse began checking her vitals and hooked her up to a monitor.

"You said she had taken morphine? How much has she taken?"

"I don't know," said Tony. He knew exactly how much she had taken but he wasn't getting into that conversation.

"How did she get hold of it?"

"I don't know, I found her unconscious with the bottle and got her in here as quickly as I could." Tony was going to have to think quickly as to what he could say to the nurse, as he couldn't exactly tell her he had been forced to inject her at gun point. Or could he? If he did, then he would spend the next few hours being interviewed by the police and right now he just had to make sure Danni was OK. He had to tell someone about what had just happened but not like this. He would call his mate Scotty; he would know what to do.

A doctor appeared through the door, wearing green scrubs, with a stethoscope around his neck.

"OK, and what do we have here?" he asked as he adjusted his glasses on his nose, looking from Danni, to Tony and finally to the nurse.

"Suspected overdose. This gentleman found her and brought her in. Her temperature is slightly high, her breathing shallow and she's unresponsive."

The doctor took a pen torch out of his pocket and shone it in Danni's eyes.

"Pupils are pinpoint. Let's give her 400 micrograms of naloxone to start with."

Tony knew Danni was in safe hands now. He had told them all he could but now he had to get out of here before they started asking more questions. She should be safe here, but would he? The Russians were bound to be looking for them. It was better if he left, less likely for them to be found if they separated. He was sure the nurse was suspicious of him and was probably away to call the police. He had to get out of here. As he made his way out of the treatment area and back through to reception, he stopped in his tracks, as he was faced with the images of what was left of the South Platform on the TV in the waiting area. The sound was turned down, but the drama of what was unfolding was unmistakeable. If anyone had survived, then it was only by the grace of God. The footage showed plumes of smoke rising from what was left of the burning platform. The picture then changed to outside Moskaneft's office, with the media circus and— *Wait a minute*, thought Tony. He stopped dead. They were showing footage of himself and Danni arriving at the office. Their faces were all over the news. He had to get out of here fast, before anyone recognised him. Questions would definitely be asked, and he didn't know how to answer them. He couldn't quite comprehend what had just happened in the past hour or so. He had to get his head straight, figure out what to do. Get hold of Scotty, he would have the answers.

He pulled his phone out of his pocket as he dashed through reception.

"Excuse me, I need some details from you," said the receptionist.

He kept walking, dialling Scotty at the same time.

"Sir, you need to fill in this form."

He turned and glared at the receptionist.

"Hey, aren't you the guy that was just on the telly?"

Shit, he'd already been recognised. *Time to get out of here.* He ran out of the door into the carpark just in time to see the Golf they had arrived in being winched onto the back of a tow vehicle.

"Hoy, mate, this anything to do with you?" asked the driver. "You know you can't just leave it here? They need access for the ambulances for people who are actually sick."

Tony pulled his hoodie up over his head and made off in the opposite direction. He would look like any other loser who had just come out of hospital.

"Some people are so inconsiderate. And on Christmas Day, too. You realise I'm missing my kids opening their parcels because of you…" The tow truck driver was shouting after Tony, but he wasn't listening. His head was filled with other thoughts. Thoughts of how Danni had looked at him with disgust as he had been forced to inject her. The loathing in her eyes. But he didn't have any option. If he hadn't done it, then they would both be dead by now, of that he was sure.

Chapter Twenty-Six

The sun was out, but the wind was bitter and cut through him as Tony headed out of the hospital grounds. He had tried Scotty several times, but his phone just kept going to voicemail. On the fourth attempt, he left a message. "Scotty, it's Tony. Give me a call as soon as you get this. Some weird shit is going down and I don't know what to do. I need your help." That should get his attention. He was probably still sleeping off a hangover from Christmas Eve.

Tony wasn't sure where to go now. Back to Danni's flat? Or would the Russians be looking for them there? They would have been able to track down Danni's address from her file. He headed back in the direction of the flat, keeping an eye out for anyone suspicious, although they irony was that he was the suspicious looking one. He crossed the road and wound through the streets, left and right, always checking if anyone was following. He stopped in a shop doorway and waited for the man walking behind him to pass.

"Merry Christmas!" said the man, who was laden down with bags of presents. He wasn't one of them.

"Merry Christmas!" replied Tony, making sure to avoid eye contact.

He let the man get around the corner and out of sight before he started walking again. He passed house upon house, lit up with Christmas lights and saw the excitement on faces of children as they opened the presents that Santa had left for them.

Suddenly a door burst open beside him. Tony flinched, but when he turned, he saw a small boy of about six years old, pushing a blue bike out the door in his pyjamas and slippers.

"You can't go out dressed like that," shouted a man's voice from inside the house. An arm reached out and grabbed the little boy, pulling him back inside. The man smiled and waved at Tony, but he just lowered his head and kept walking.

"Merry Christmas to you too, pal," muttered the man.

Tony made his way onto Whitehall Place and stopped at the corner leading onto Esslemont Avenue. He waited for a few minutes, crouching down beside the large metal refuse bins, watching the flat to see if there was any activity. After ten minutes there was no sign of any one and he was really starting to feel the cold. The tips of his fingers were numb despite having shoved his hands as far as he could into his pockets. He jogged over to the front door of the building and found it was off the latch. Had they not pulled the door properly shut behind them when they had dashed out this morning? Or had someone been looking for them already?

That question was quickly answered when he pushed through the door and crept up the stairwell to find the flat door had been forced open. They hadn't wasted any time. He slid up against the wall and waited, listening. There was no sound coming from inside the flat, so he pushed the door open with his foot. Still no noise, so he entered the flat. They had definitely been here. The place had been ransacked. The settee cushions were on the floor and the contents of his rucksack had been tipped out and gone through. In the kitchen the cupboard doors and drawers were left open and in the bedroom the mattress had been tipped over against the wall and clothes had been pulled from the wardrobe and lay strewn all over the floor. The drawers from the bedside cabinet had been thrown onto the bed. Tony wasn't sure what they had been searching for, if anything in particular, but they had certainly been thorough.

He walked back into the living room, grabbed his clothes from the floor and stuffed them back in his rucksack. As he swung it over his shoulder his eye caught a glimpse of the little Christmas tree decoration he had put up the night before. It was lying on the floor next to one of the seat cushions. He bent down and picked it up and placed it carefully back on the table. Some of the tiny baubles were missing and the star on top was squashed and sitting at a jaunty angle. The tree looked like how he felt. Battered and misshapen and unsure of its purpose in life. This was certainly a Christmas he wouldn't forget in a hurry! As he was about to stand up, he noticed the present he had left out for Danni sticking out below the corner of the settee. At least they had had the decency not to open it. More likely it had been knocked to the floor and kicked under the settee before they had seen it. He picked it up and put it in his inside coat pocket, wondering if he would ever see Danni again to give it to her.

He pulled his hoodie back over his head as he left the flat, looking both ways before heading out into the street. About the only thing going for him at the moment was the fact that the weather for once was co-operating. It wasn't raining, and the sun was out. It was actually turning out to be quite a nice day, ironically!

He headed west, out of the city. Managing to pick up 4G signal, he checked the bus timetable online. The number 19 would take him out to Peterculter where Scotty lived. First Bus were running a reduced service, but there were buses every hour or so. He had been out to his flat once before and was hoping he could remember where it was. Hopefully he would be there and not sleeping it off on a mate's couch somewhere.

He headed along Great Western Road, past the large Victorian granite buildings, most of which were now bed and breakfasts; the rest had been converted into flats. This had been a more affluent area of Aberdeen, but the number of 'for sale' signs and 'vacancy' signs on the B&Bs painted a different picture. Several of the larger B&Bs were boarded up, their owners suffering from the downturn in the oil industry, unable to keep up the payments on their hefty mortgages. In the past they would have had regular clients who rented rooms by the week or for months at a time. Now they were competing with the hotels who had dropped their prices so much that they couldn't afford to compete. Many of the previously distinguished-looking buildings were now showing signs of neglect. Grass growing out of the guttering. Broken window panes. Doors in need of a good coat of paint. He could have laid low in one of the abandoned buildings, but his instinct told him to get out of town.

He kept walking into Mannofield without seeing another living soul. He heard a vehicle in the distance and turned to see the No. 19 double decker bus travelling towards him. He jogged to the next bus stop which was about 100 yards away. He rummaged in his jeans pockets and found some change. Hopefully the buses still took cash, as everything seemed to be paid for electronically nowadays. He didn't want to use his bank card. He wasn't sure how the Russians would get access to it, but he wasn't going to take any chances.

The bus pulled up and the door opened. The bus driver looked about as happy to be driving as Tony was to be on the run.

"Merry Christmas!" he grunted. "Where to?"

He was wearing a badge that showed his name was Norman and that he was 'happy to help'. Tony thought he looked like he was anything but that.

"Culter please, beside the shops." He thought he would get his bearings from there and hopefully find Scotty's flat.

"That will be £5."

"£5, are you having a laugh?"

"Sorry mate, flat rate for Christmas Day, you're lucky there are any buses running at all. I voted against running a service today and look where I am now."

So that was why he looked so 'happy to help', thought Tony. He dropped five £1 coins into the money collector and took his ticket from the machine. The only other person on the bus was an elderly woman who was wrapped up in a bright red woollen coat and a red headscarf. With the grey hair poking out and the glasses perched on the end of her nose she could have been mistaken for Mrs Claus. She had two brightly decorated Christmas bags on her knee. One blue and one pink. Tony assumed she was going to visit her grandchildren.

He made his way up the steps onto the top deck which was empty and sat right at the back so that he could see anyone else getting on. That way he would have time to force open the emergency exit window right behind him should it prove necessary, although he felt he had exited through enough emergency exits today.

The rest of the journey out to Culter was uneventful. The bus only stopped twice. Once for the old lady downstairs to get off in Cults, wrestling with her bags of presents, and once more in Milltimber for two teenage boys to get on. They came upstairs, joking loudly about what they had been up to last night and trying to trip each other up. They stopped for a second to stare at Tony, and then bundled into two seats nearer the front and continued their conversation. They looked quite alike, and Tony thought they must be brothers. The older of the two playfully slapping his younger brother around the head.

"Hoy," said the younger one, "stop that or I'll tell Dad what you were up to last night!"

"You say anything about that, and your life is over. I still have that photo of you from the party, do you want me to make it viral?"

"You bastard, you said you had deleted it."

"Maybe I have, maybe I haven't, but do you want to find out?"

"OK, OK, your secret's safe, just don't show anyone that picture or Dad will find out."

Tony looked back out the window as the road passed over the new Aberdeen Western Peripheral Route. The AWPR had finally been completed a year behind schedule and probably ten years too late if you listened to local businesses. Work started on the road two years late after initially being given the go-ahead by ministers, but there had been numerous petitions and several court cases around the route and those petitioning against it had managed to delay the project significantly but not stopped it in its tracks. Eventually a petition was raised against the protestors, stating that they were threatening the economy.

Today the road was quiet. There were a few cars on it. *Probably families travelling to visit relatives*, thought Tony. He saw the sign for Peterculter just before the BP petrol station. It was closed off with traffic cones, shut for Christmas Day. The two boys got up and pushed the button to alert the bus driver to stop at the next bus stop, leaving Tony as the only remaining passenger. The bus continued through the village and when he saw the Co-op shop, he knew he was close to Scotty's flat. He pushed the button and made his way downstairs. The driver pulled up at the stop outside The Richmond Arms which was better known to the locals as Black's. Tony stepped off the bus and the door shut swiftly behind him. The bus pulled away, indicating right up Malcolm Road where it would then turn up into Johnston Gardens to the terminus, turn around and start its route back into Aberdeen.

Tony recognised the pub. Scotty had taken him here the last time he was out. It was Scotty's local, so his flat couldn't be far from here. He looked both ways, trying to get his bearings. He remembered it was downhill to the flat, so he started walking down the street and ended up on Millside Street. Yes, this looked familiar. He continued down the road but was then faced with a large housing complex. Blocks of flats to the left and town houses to the right. It was definitely a flat he was looking for as it was on the top floor but there were so many flats; which one was it? He checked the names on the intercom of the first block of flats he came to, but there was no Scott listed. He kept walking to the next block but again, no luck. He tried calling Scotty on the phone again. It rang several times but went to voicemail. How the hell was he going to find him in this rabbit warren?

He was just about to put his phone back in his pocket when it rang.

"Tony, mate, what's up? I've missed several calls from you, you OK?" said a half-asleep Scotty.

"Did you not get my message?"

"No mate, I'm just up, was working the late shift last night then went back to Willie's for a few beers. No idea what time I got home, or how I got home, come to think of it," he laughed.

"You in your flat right now?"

"Yeah."

"What number is it?"

"Eh, what you on about?"

"What number is your flat? I'm on…" he looked around for a street name, "Millside Terrace. Is that close to you?"

"Yeah, I'm just down the back of there. What you doing out here? It's Christmas Day. I thought you'd be at home with Kirsty."

"Long story mate. I'll tell you all in a minute but right now just tell me how to find your flat."

Scotty gave directions to Tony and a few minutes later he was ringing the intercom button.

"You found it then," joked Scotty.

"Just buzz me up, will you?"

"OK, OK, keep your hair on"

The front door clicked, and Tony pushed the door open. He took the stairs two at a time to the third floor where he found Scotty's flat door off the latch.

As he walked in, he was immediately met by the stale smell of beer and leftover kebabs. The place stank. He walked into the kitchen where Scotty was stood in his boxer shorts and socks leaning on the worktop waiting for the kettle to boil. There were empty pizza boxes and foil containers with the remains of some congealed orange coloured mixture which had probably once been curry. Empty beer bottles and cans were lined up on the windowsill and some had spilled onto the floor.

"Man, what a mess. You sure the party wasn't back here last night?" asked Tony.

Scotty looked up bleary-eyed and rubbed his chin where the stubble was coming through.

"Batchelor-hood clearly suits you."

"What are you doing out my neck of the woods on Christmas Day?" retorted Scotty. He looked up as the kettle clicked off. "Coffee?"

"Yeah, I'll need one of those, and so will you when you hear what I have to tell you. In fact, we will both probably need something stronger before I'm finished."

Chapter Twenty-Seven

Tony talked Scotty through what had unfolded in the past few hours. They had moved into the living room, which was just as much of a mess. The kitchen wasn't the only room to be littered with empty takeaway containers. Tony moved a pile of clothes from the only other chair in the room onto the floor so that he could sit down. He wasn't sure if the clothes were ready to be put away or ready for the wash. Scotty lived like a pig.

"Let me get this straight," said Scotty, "you think your employer has killed your boss, blown up a platform and overdosed your girlfriend with morphine?" He shook his head in disbelief. "Is this some kind of sick joke? Because it ain't funny, mate."

"It's no joke, and she's not my girlfriend," replied Tony. "Look, if you don't believe me, maybe this will help." He picked up the remote control for the TV, switched it on and tuned in to Sky News. The pictures of the wreckage of the platform were still on continuous loop.

"Holy shit!" exclaimed Scotty. "When did this happen?"

"This morning, I just told you."

"I'm sorry, I can't take this all in. And you're saying that Moskaneft is behind all of this?"

"YES! That's exactly what I'm saying. Come on, we have to get back to the hospital and make sure Danni is OK."

"Danni, the girl you injected with morphine, but she's not your girlfriend."

"Yes! Have you not been listening to what I've been saying?"

"I'm listening mate, but I'm just not believing what I'm hearing."

Tony was getting increasingly agitated and frustrated. How could he convince Scotty to take him seriously?

"The note!"

"What note?"

"The police received a copy of a note written by David Gordon claiming that he was in danger."

"How do you know about that? We haven't released that information to the press."

"How do you think I know about it?"

"You found it?"

"Not me. It was Danni that found it, but I've seen it. She sent a copy to the police and she still has the original. Unless the Russians found it when they did over her flat."

"You have evidence you've been keeping from the police?"

"I just said, it wasn't me that found it. It was Danni. And for some reason that she won't tell me about, she's scared of going to the police."

"We need to speak to Danni."

"That's what I've been trying to tell you! She could be in danger. We need to get to her."

"I need to call this in."

"No, you can't do that. Not yet. Not till we figure out what to do. You call this in now and I'm sitting in a police interview room and meanwhile Danni is still out there in danger."

"OK, we'll keep it between us for now, but if things kick off, I'm calling it in."

Scotty disappeared through to the bedroom and came back dressed in jeans, a black turtleneck jumper and trainers.

"Right, let's get to the hospital then," he said as he picked up his car keys from the hall table and grabbed a black puffa jacket from the hook beside the door. He checked the pocket for his warrant card. "We might be needing this," he said as he transferred it to his jeans pocket.

They got into his Vauxhall Corsa, which had seen better days and which was also in dire need of a clean out. The footwell was filled with empty Coke cans, crisp packets and sandwich wrappers.

"You're disgusting, no wonder you can't find a girlfriend," said Tony as he wiped what looked like a mixture of crisp and biscuit crumbs from the passenger seat before getting in.

"Yeah, yeah, whatever," replied Scotty, who was oblivious to the mess.

He turned the key in the ignition, but the car didn't start. He turned it again, nothing. Third time lucky and the engine fired into action.

"She likes to keep me guessing," joked Scotty.

He shifted the gears into reverse and sped backwards, spinning the car round and into first gear while Tony was still reaching for his seatbelt.

"You might as well forget that," said Scotty. "The belt doesn't fasten. Been meaning to get it fixed but just haven't got around to it."

"You do know it's illegal, don't you? You know, you being a copper and all that?"

"It's all right, as long as I don't get stopped. And even if I did, this usually does the trick." He patted his pocket where he had put his warrant card.

The car spluttered up the hill and then burst into life as they turned onto North Deeside Road and headed east into Aberdeen. They took the same route that Tony had taken on the bus and turned left onto Anderson Drive. The drive was quiet with only a few cars out and about. Scotty overtook them at speed as Tony kept clutching at the seat belt.

"It's OK, I've had training to drive like this you know," joked Scotty.

That was a small comfort to Tony.

They passed Rubislaw Den and onwards up by the fire station. At the next traffic lights, they turned right onto Westburn Road, down the hill and into the main entrance to ARI. They screeched into the A&E carpark and abandoned the car across two spaces. The car Tony had used to get to the hospital was long gone. He felt a tiny tinge of guilt for poor Sheila who probably wouldn't get her car back now till after the holidays and would be waiting for its return to the office, oblivious that it had been towed.

As they entered the reception area, the same receptionist that had been there earlier was still behind the desk. Scotty flashed his warrant card at her and asked for the whereabouts of Danni.

"You were in here earlier," she said, looking at Tony. "You're the guy that was on the telly."

"What's she on about?" asked Scotty.

"Long story, I'll tell you later," replied Tony.

Scotty turned back to the receptionist.

"Danni Ross? Where is she?"

"Has this got something to do with the Moskaneft

platform blowing up?" asked the receptionist, hoping for a bit of juicy gossip to tell her colleagues during their break.

"Miss, if you could just tell us where to find Danni please. This is urgent police business." Scotty tapped his finger on the desk to emphasise the importance.

"Yes, sorry, of course." She looked disappointed that the gossip wasn't forthcoming. That was OK, she could make something up to tell her friends.

"She was transferred up to the High Dependency Unit."

"Where is that?" asked Tony, looking around for any signs to direct him.

"Along the corridor, turn left, take the lift to the sixth floor."

Tony was already on the move before Scotty had a chance to thank the receptionist for her help. He ran after Tony, who was already through the first set of swing doors and running down the corridor.

Tony pushed the button for the lift, then continued to push it several more times like that was going to get the lift there any quicker.

"Hey, steady on mate," said Scotty.

The lift doors slid open and they got in, Tony pushing the button for the sixth floor as impatiently as he had pushed the lift button. The doors seemed to take an eternity to close.

"Come on, come on!" shouted Tony, with his finger on the button.

Finally, they were on the move. Tony was pacing round the lift like a caged tiger.

"You need to calm down man," said Scotty. "She must really mean something to you, I've never seen you like this."

"You don't understand. I was the one that injected her. If something has happened to her, then it's my fault. I need to know she is OK."

"I get it, I really do, but you need to calm down, take a

breath." Scotty put his arm on Tony's shoulder in a gesture of reassurance.

They looked at each other, then they both turned to face the lift doors, willing them to open.

Chapter Twenty-Eight

"Miss Ross, good to see you awake. How are you feeling? Do you know where you are?"

Danni opened her eyes and struggled to take in her surroundings. There were tubes coming out of her arms and she seemed to be in a cubicle with curtains separating her from the rest of the room.

"Hospital? What happened? I can't be here, it's not safe, I have to leave." Danni started pulling at the tubes in her arm and the sensors attached to her body. As they fell to the floor, an eerie flatline monotone resounded from the display monitor.

"Wait, you're in no fit state to be getting out of bed," said the nurse. "Danni, please, you need to calm down, you need to rest. You were found unconscious, you've been drugged. Morphine was found in your blood. We need to get the doctor to check you over."

"Morphine? Drugged?"

Danni tried to remember what had happened, but her head felt fuzzy, like she was suffering from the hangover from hell. She closed her eyes and rubbed them, trying hard to remember. Where had she been? What had happened? Something important, she knew it was important. Something bad had happened.

Work.

She had been at work.

There had been an explosion on the platform.

No, not an explosion. A helicopter. That's it, a helicopter had crashed into the platform. She and Tony had gone to the office.

It was the Russians. The Russians had caused the helicopter to crash.

Becky! Oh my God, they shot Becky!

Tony. He was there.

Had he done something to her? Was he working for the Russians?

Trust me.

Was that what he had said?

Trust me.

But he had done this. He had injected her. He had put her in hospital. How could she trust him?

Danni had to get out of here. She threw back the bedcovers.

"Danni, please, get back in bed."

"No, no you don't understand, they will find me here, I need to leave now!"

Danni leaped from the bed and ran out of the ward and down the corridor, the hospital gown barely covering her modesty. As the nurse called for security, Danni made her way to the emergency staircase and headed downwards to the ground floor. She knew where the accident and emergency department was, as she he had to chaperone a couple of colleagues there in the past in her role as a first aider. People were coming and going from there all the time. It was full of druggies and drunks and Aberdeen's down and outs. No-one would take any notice of her, she would blend in, just another patient. She should be able to find some clothes and get out of there.

She waited in the stairwell for two nurses to walk past, they were chatting about the Christmas Eve party last night.

Christmas Eve, thought Danni. *That means today is Christmas Day.* Danni's memory was sketchy, but she remembered being at the flat with Tony. They were having breakfast. She had been sick. *Oh no, the embarrassment!*

Tony had put on the radio and they had heard about the platform. That's why they had gone to the office.

The nurses continued chatting.

"Did you see the state of Matt from radiology?" said the blond nurse.

"I know, he was bladdered. What was in those cocktails they were dishing out?" said the brunette.

"I don't know, and I don't think I want to. I think a few people will be needing sick bowls today, and I don't just mean the patients!" They laughed as they walked past the stairwell, neither of them aware of Danni hiding behind the door. They had just come out of the changing room. If she was quick enough, she would get to the door before it closed.

Yes, she made it.

Danni tried all the locker doors until she found one that opened. *Bingo!* A set of scrubs. She removed the gown and quickly changed into the scrubs along with a pair of trainers that were lying under the bench. She looked in the mirror that was fixed to the inside of the locker door. Her face was pale, with large brown circles under her eyes. She looked like she hadn't slept in weeks but felt like she hadn't been awake for days. She tore off the hospital wristband and made her way back out into the corridor.

"Danni? Is that you?"

Danni turned in shock, the last thing she needed was to be recognised. It was Stuart, a guy she had known briefly a while ago. He had gone out with her friend Mel, but the relationship had ended acrimoniously after only a few months when he had been seen out in town with several younger girls, on several different occasions. Stuart had been what many people would call 'Aberdeen Oil Trash'. When times had been virtuous, he had been among the good and great of Aberdeen. Living it up on champagne and caviar and buying drinks for everyone in the bar, just to show off how much money he had. Now, of course, times had changed, those days were long gone and so were the bars he had frequented. When Danni had known Stuart, he had rugged good looks, a chiselled chin and a boyish charm, but now he looked dishevelled and withdrawn. His once-prominent six pack was gone and replaced by skin and bone; a man half his size now stood before Danni.

"Stuart. Hi. Good to see you." It wasn't, but right now Danni just had to find a way to get out of here as quickly as possible and without drawing any further attention to herself or being seen by anyone else.

"I didn't know you worked here? I thought you worked at Moskaneft. Did you get made redundant too?"

"Long story. I had to go for an X-ray, and they managed to lose my clothes, so they gave me these scrubs." Danni had to think quick despite her head still being foggy.

"That's shocking, I hope you're getting some compensation from them? Do you still keep in touch with Mel? I really messed up there."

"Actually, sorry Stuart, I don't mean to be rude but now is not really a good time and I just want to get home, do you mind if we catch up some other time?"

"Sure, no worries, I totally understand. Who wants to be in here on Christmas Day? Not exactly what I had planned, although to be honest I didn't really have anything planned. Microwave meal for one in front of the telly is not exactly how I'd pictured spending Christmas, but instead I ended up having to take my neighbour in to A&E 'cos he fell down the stairs drunk and knocked himself out. Good job I was at home and heard him or he could still be lying there now. He's not getting home tonight so I'll come back tomorrow. Do you still live in Rosemount? I can give you a lift."

Stuart's appearance may have changed, but his chat had not. He still spoke constantly, not letting anyone getting a word in edgeways. *Why say ten words when 100 would do? AGGHHH.*

He was probably the last person she wanted a lift from but with no phone and no money, how else was she going to get home? She could have walked; it wasn't that far, down Westburn Road, cut through Victoria Park, onto Belvidere Street, down Rosemount Place and on to Esslemont Avenue. It would probably only take fifteen to twenty minutes, but she was already beginning to feel weak and dizzy and she knew she had to get out of there before people started looking for her. Plus, she could see out the door that it was beginning to snow and she had no coat.

As Stuart paused to take a breath, she replied, "Thanks, a lift would be great. Is your car out the front?" She bowed her head and grabbed onto Stuart's arm as she steered him out into the waiting area and through the automatic doors. She needed to steady herself, but she was also aware of the security cameras. If they were looking for her then they would be looking for a single female, not one leaving at the end of a busy shift, arm in arm with her boyfriend.

She practically manhandled him out the door.

"Where are you parked?"

"Over the back, there." He pointed to the rear of the carpark.

Danni was looking for his Range Rover, but she didn't see it. The only car parked there was an old Fiesta with a missing front bumper and the passenger side wing mirror was none existent.

"Bit of a come down from the Rangie, I'll admit, but since the company shut its doors this is all I can afford, and I'm even struggling to afford this."

He retrieved the car keys from his jeans pocket and unlocked the doors. Danni jumped in the passenger side and sat there shivering.

"You look frozen," said Stuart.

"Yeah, can you put the heater on?"

"I could but it doesn't actually work, and neither does the radio. It's a bit of a bucket of shit really, but it goes, and it gets me from A to B. There's a jacket on the back seat, put that on. It's not that clean but it will be warm."

It was a fluorescent yellow work jacket, like the kind you see council workers wearing. Danni remembered the joke, *How many council workers does it take to dig a hole? Ten. One to operate the digger and nine more to stand around and watch.*

"Are you working for the council now?"

"Harbour Board," said Stuart. Right enough, the jacket did have a faint whiff of diesel and fish about it. Still it was better than nothing.

Stuart started the car and they pulled out of the carpark just as the security officer came out the front door of A&E. Danni dropped her head and looked away from him. He stood there looking out into the carpark, annoyed that yet another patient had escaped. He was going to get it from his boss. This wasn't the first patient to disappear on his watch.

They made their way towards Danni's flat. Stuart continued with the mind-numbing chatter as he always had, but Danni wasn't listening. She was trying to straighten things out in her head. What had actually happened? What was real and what had she dreamed? She had pins and needles in her arms and her vision was slightly blurry. Her mouth was dry, and she had trouble swallowing. Her heart was racing, and she had pounding in her ears. At least that was drowning out Stuart's continual muttering.

She had to get home, get some clothes. *Then what?* She had no idea what to do, where to go. Was she still in danger? Would the Russians come after her? Had they really shot Becky, or had she imagined that? She didn't know what was real. She couldn't trust her memory. Who could she trust? *Tony?*

"It's this one, isn't it?"

"What?" She looked up to find that Stuart had pulled up outside her flat.

"Yes, thanks," she said as she struggled to undo the seatbelt.

"Here, let me help."

Stuart's hand brushed against hers and she flinched at his touch.

"Sorry. The seatbelt jams, there's a knack to it."

Danni let him undo the seatbelt and stumbled out of the car.

"You sure you're going to be OK?" asked Stuart. "I can come up with you if you'd like?"

"No, I'm fine," replied Danni. "I just need to go and lie down. Honestly, I'm OK." She just wanted rid of him.

"If you're sure?"

She went to take off the jacket, but Stuart shook his head. "Keep it."

Like she needed a fluorescent jacket. She needed to hide, not bring attention to herself.

She turned towards the main door and suddenly panicked as she didn't have a key to get in. Hopefully some of her neighbours would be home and she could buzz them to let her in. But as she got closer to the door, she realised it was off the latch. She pushed the door open and turned to see Stuart leaving. He had waited to make sure she was inside. He tooted the horn and waved as he pulled out. She didn't wave back.

Why was the door off the latch?

There had been complaints before that residents had not been closing the door properly behind them and there was a laminated sign on the back of the door stating, 'SHUT THE DOOR BEHIND YOU'. Since the guy in the upstairs flat had moved out there hadn't been a problem, but now it was sitting off the latch.

She tip-toed down the hall, listening for any noise or movement. She could hear the TV from Mrs Beattie's ground floor flat. She was pretty sure it was her cat she had tripped over a few nights before. As she started up the stairs, the first step creaked and she stopped. Listening again, but still all she could hear was the TV.

She crept up the stairs, keeping her back against the wall while looking up into the stairwell. She turned the corner and noticed that her flat door was ajar. Who had been here? Were they still here? Were they waiting for her? She had nowhere else to go, though. She looked around, but there was nothing she could use to defend herself.

She crept back down and tried the cupboard under the stairs. It was locked, but the door was not that secure. She pushed hard against it. *Nothing.* She tried again, and the door popped open. It was dark in there, but she spotted a tool box on the floor. Opening it, she pulled out a hammer. That would have to do.

Danni made her way back upstairs, avoiding the creaky first step. She stopped outside her flat door and waited, listening for any sign of life in there. By now her heart was racing and the blood was pumping in her ears. She was struggling to hear anything. She tried to slow her breath but to no avail. She slowly pushed the door open with her foot and raised the hammer in her right hand. The lights were off, but her eyes were adjusting to the glimmer of daylight coming through the kitchen window. She tried the kitchen first. The breakfast dishes were still sitting on the table. Cold, congealed scrambled eggs. Danni retched at the sight of them.

Someone had been here. Cupboard drawers were open. Cutlery and cooking utensils had spilled out onto the floor.

She moved into the living room. Settee cushions were scattered over the floor. Tony's stuff was gone. His rucksack and his clothes were nowhere to be found. Had he been back here? Had he ransacked the place? What was he looking for?

She kept the hammer in her hand as she tried the bedroom. She heard a noise. There was someone in there. She lifted the hammer over her head and kicked the door open, ready to take out whoever was in there.

A yellow streak flashed past Danni's legs, out the door and down the stairs.

"Fucking cat," screamed Danni.

She dropped the hammer to the floor as her heart jumped into her mouth. She had always hated that fucking cat and now she hated it even more. It was dead next time she got her hands on it.

She leaned against the wall trying to get her breath back to a normal rhythm, or at least just slow it down a fraction. She was feeling faint. She stumbled into the bedroom but couldn't lie down on the bed as the mattress was off the bed, up against the wall. Clothes were strewn over the floor, the wardrobe practically emptied. Whoever had been here had been thorough in their search.

Her gun!

She looked to the bedside cabinet but knew as soon as she saw the drawer was lying on the bed that the gun would be gone. What had they been looking for?

The note?

Did they know that she knew about the note?

She pulled the remaining clothes out of the wardrobe. On the floor were shoe boxes. Some still contained shoes and others had been opened and tossed to the side. But where was the one she wanted? *Had they taken it?* She pushed more boxes out of the way.

Here! It was still here!

She opened the box and flung the pair of shoes out. She removed the tissue paper that had been used to wrap them and underneath, there it was. The note was still here. They hadn't found it. She still had the proof that something sinister had happened to her boss. She dropped to her knees on the floor, clutching the note. It was the only thing she had that could prove the Russians were up to something. Who would believe her when she told them what had happened to her this morning? The Russians could talk their way out of anything, but not this. This was evidence.

Bang.

That was the main door closing.

Someone was coming. Were they coming for her?

She heard a noise on the stairs. A loud thump and then laughter. Who was that?

She picked up the hammer and hid behind the bedroom door, ready to defend herself.

Chapter Twenty-Nine

The lift stopped at the sixth floor and Tony wrestled his way out before the doors had fully opened. He looked left and right but had no idea which way to go.

A nurse walked out of one of the rooms and Tony ran up to her.

"Danni Ross, where is she?"

The nurse took a step back from him.

"And you are?"

"I need to know where Danni is, is she OK?"

"Are you a relative?"

"Perhaps this will help?" said Scotty who had caught up with them, showing the nurse his warrant card.

The nurse looked at it and nodded her approval that she thought it was legitimate. "She's not one of my patients. If you come with me, I'll find out where she is."

They followed her down the corridor to the nurse's station.

"Which room is Danni... sorry," she looked towards Tony, "what did you say her last name was?"

"Ross, Danni Ross."

The nurse behind the desk looked up the computer and pointed to the right. "She was in Room 5," Tony started heading the way the nurse pointed, "but she left a few minutes ago."

Tony stopped in his tracks and turned back to face her.

"What do you mean she left? She was unconscious when I brought her in, how can she have been discharged?"

"She wasn't discharged. She removed her IV drips and took off. I tried to stop her, but she was having none of it. She headed down the stairs a few minutes ago."

"So, she is OK?"

"She seemed scared. She was ranting, said it wasn't safe, she had to get out of here. I called security, but I haven't heard back from them. I can only assume she has left the building."

Tony and Scotty looked at each other. "What now?"

"Back to her flat."

"Would she go there?"

"I don't know, but I don't know where else she would go so it's a good place to start."

They ran down the same stairs that the nurse had indicated Danni had left by, taking two at a time. Down to the ground floor and back out into the A&E department. They ran out of the building, almost knocking a hospital porter to the ground.

"Hoy, watch where you're going," he shouted, but they were long gone.

It had started to snow. Soft white flakes falling silently from the sky. It was going to be a white Christmas after all.

They jumped into Scotty's car. He put the keys in the ignition and turned them. Nothing. Tried again. Still nothing.

Scotty tried one more time and like before, still nothing. Not even a whimper.

"That's never happened before," said Scotty. "She always starts third time lucky."

He tried a fourth time, but the engine was dead.

"What now?!" shouted Tony, who was looking increasingly agitated.

"I don't know. I know she's not a thing of beauty, but she's never let me down like this before."

Tony flung open the passenger door and got out. He looked around. There was someone coming out of the A&E department heading towards their car. Tony ran up to them.

"Police business, we need your car."

The man jumped back from him.

"I don't think so, mate. Where's your warrant card?"

"Scotty, quick, get over here. Show him your warrant card."

"So, you're not police?"

"He's not, but I am," said Scotty, who had sprinted over before he had to break up a fight. He took his warrant card out of his jeans pocket and showed it to the guy. He looked at it suspiciously.

"I don't know," he said. "I heard on the news that there are a lot of fakes going around. How do I know this is for real?"

"You'll just have to trust us," said Tony as he grabbed the keys out of the guy's hand and threw them towards Scotty.

Scotty caught the keys and took his warrant card back from the guy.

"Contact Queen Street Police Station to arrange to get your car back," shouted Scotty over his shoulder as he pointed the keys at the line of cars sitting in the car park. The hazard lights of a black Astra flashed and the doors unlocked.

They both ran over to the car. As Tony opened the passenger door, he thought that he was beginning to make a habit of stealing people's cars today.

They sped off, leaving tyre marks in the carpark. The man took out his mobile phone and called 999 to report that his car had just been stolen.

Tony barked directions at Scotty as they headed towards Danni's flat. If she wasn't there, then he had no idea where to look for her. She could be anywhere. He had no idea if she had any friends that she would go to. She never spoke of anyone and nobody had called her while he had been with her. She had shut down when he mentioned family, so he presumed she had no contact with them, although he didn't even know if her parents were still alive. She had briefly mentioned that she had moved up here from London but again had shut down when he questioned her about her past. If she ran off back to London, then he would never find her. If she wasn't at the flat, he could get Scotty to start a police search for her. Check the bus and train stations. He doubted she would go to the airport. There would be limited transportation with today being Christmas Day, so she should be easy to spot.

"Turn left, then first right and her flat is on the left," directed Tony as they got close.

"Stop!" he shouted and was already opening the door before Scotty had brought the car to a halt.

He abandoned it on double yellow lines. The traffic wardens wouldn't be working today, and it wasn't his car, anyway, so what did he care if it got a parking ticket?

The main door was still slightly ajar like he had found it previously. He pushed it open and was about to run inside when Scotty grabbed him.

"Hold on, mate."

"But we need to get to her."

"Look, we don't even know she's in there and with what you've told me about these Russians they are not worried about who they get rid of, so let's just slow down and work out what we're going to do."

"I know what I'm doing," said Tony as he pushed Scotty to the side and darted inside.

He heard a noise and before he knew what happened, the same cat that had tripped up Danni a few nights ago did the same to him. It flew down the stairs, scampering between Tony's legs and causing him to lose balance. He flung out his right arm, grabbing for the railing but his fingertips scraped the banister and he fell onto the stairs, kicking the cat in the process.

Scotty couldn't help himself. He burst out laughing. "I told you to wait, but you wouldn't listen."

"I thought you were worried about the Russians, not a bloody cat," huffed Tony.

Scotty helped him to his feet and they made their way up the stairs. The flat door was wide open. Tony was sure he hadn't left it like that, so someone else had been there. Or was still in there.

Scotty held his index finger up to his mouth, indicating to Tony to be quiet. He unzipped his bomber jacket and removed a retractable baton from the inside pocket. Tony looked at him, astounded that he had been concealing that in his jacket. Scotty flipped the baton forward and it extended. He got to the door and entered the flat.

"Police!" shouted Scotty as he moved inside, the baton raised over his right shoulder, ready to take it down on the head of anyone that came at him. He looked to the left into the kitchen. No-one was there.

He pushed open the next door. No-one in the bathroom.

The next door entered into the living room. Again, no-one.

As he pushed the bedroom door open a hammer came thudding down on his arm, knocking the baton from his hand to the floor.

"AGGGHHHH!" he screamed, falling to the floor and clutching his arm in agony.

Tony came running in behind him.

"Scotty, what happened?" He saw him in a ball on the floor, still screaming.

Suddenly the bedroom door flew open and someone lunged at him with the hammer. Tony ducked to the right at the last minute and felt a rush of air pass his left ear as the hammer came down, barely missing him. He grabbed the arm brandishing the hammer and pushed it backwards, hard.

He heard a scream. It sounded female. He jumped over Scotty, who was still writhing about on the floor, and came face to face with Danni.

She lunged at him, pushing him backwards over Scotty. Now they were both lying in a heap. She tried to jump over them, but there wasn't enough room. Tony, having landed heavy on his arse, sat up and grabbed her arm as she tried to get past.

"Danni, wait!"

She clawed at his face, scratching his cheek and drawing blood. She had to escape.

"AGGHHH!" screamed Tony as he grabbed as his cheek with the free hand. He wasn't letting go of Danni, he had to make her understand what had happened. Why he had done what he had. He had injected her to save her, not to kill her!

He wrestled her to the floor, pinning her down so that she couldn't scratch him again.

"Danni, stop struggling. It's me, Tony. I need to explain."

Danni fought back, but he was too strong. She couldn't break free of his grip. His body was heavy on top of her. She felt weak and struggling was futile. Finally, she gave in and lay still.

"You're hurting my wrists," she shouted at Tony.

"Sorry. I'll let go if you promise you will stop struggling and hear me out."

Danni didn't have much choice in the matter; the aftereffects of the morphine were taking their toll. She had no fight left in her.

She nodded. He released her wrists and shifted off her, both now sitting on the floor of the hall, staring at each other and wondering what their next move should be. Before either could speak, Scotty appeared on his feet, still clutching his arm.

"I think it's broken," he whined. A bruise was already starting to appear on his forearm. It was swollen, and he was straining to move his fingers.

"Stop being such a drama queen and put the kettle on," said Tony. "We've got a lot of explaining to do."

As Scotty went into the kitchen, Tony pulled Danni to her feet and helped her through to the living room. He grabbed the settee cushions from the floor and returned them to their rightful place. Lowering Danni down onto one end, he sat at the other. They just sat there, staring at each other. Not sure what to say, or where to begin.

"Are you OK, Danni? You don't look too good?" She was pale and sweat was beading on her upper lip.

Danni lunged forward and threw up on the carpet.

"Whoa! Let's get you cleaned up," he said as he helped her sit back up. "That will be the aftereffects of the morphine."

"The morphine YOU injected me with," replied Danni, giving Tony an evil stare.

"I had to do it. I had no choice. If I hadn't, then they would have, and we would both be dead by now. I did it to save you, not to harm you."

Tony went through to the bathroom and came back with a cold, wet cloth. He went to wipe Danni's face, but she grabbed the cloth from him, determined to do it herself. She was still in the scrubs she had stolen from the hospital. She looked down to see they were covered in puke.

"I need to change," she said.

She tried to stand but was unsteady on her feet, so Tony helped her up and walked her through to the bedroom. They stood there, looking at all the clothes strewn around the floor. Tony bent down and started picking them up, throwing them onto the bed.

As Danni raked through the clothes, trying to find something to wear, Tony noticed a sheet of paper on the floor. He picked it up and looked at it. It was the original note with David's signature on it. The Russians hadn't found it. He folded it up and put it in his pocket before Danni could see. He would need to give this to Scotty for evidence, despite Danni's previous pleas not to involve the police.

"I'll give you some space," he said as he walked out and shut the bedroom door behind him. He also shut the front door, which was still lying open. The lock was broken – they would need to get that fixed – but at least it shut, and the chain would hold it closed.

He walked through to the kitchen to check on Scotty, who was wrestling with the kettle. He was holding his right arm up against his chest whilst trying to operate the tap and get the kettle in place with the left. It was not that easy.

"Here, let me," he said as he took the kettle from Scotty.

"You're going to have to get that X-rayed. Let me have a look," he said as he motioned towards Scotty's increasingly swollen arm.

Scotty kept his arm against his chest and moved away from Tony. He was in a lot of pain and he didn't want anyone touching it.

"Hey man, trust me, I'm a medic," said Tony as he walked towards him.

He took Scotty's arm in his hands and rolled up his sleeve to get a better look.

"HOLY FUCK! That hurts!" shouted Scotty and pulled away from him again.

"You big pussy," laughed Tony. "Here, I'll make you a sling." He took the tea towel that was hanging over the oven door handle and fashioned a sling, wrapping Scotty's arm up and tying a knot behind his neck.

"That will keep it immobile till we can get you to the hospital."

He went through to the bathroom and rummaged in the cabinet, coming back with a packet of paracetamol.

"Take a couple of these. You're going to need something stronger, but that's all we have for now. Shame I didn't still have some of that morphine," he joked.

"That's not even funny," replied Scotty, but he took the paracetamol, pressed two of them out of the packet onto the counter and put them in his mouth. He stuck his head under the still running tap and gulped down some water to swallow them.

"Here, you'll be needing this," said Tony, as he pulled the piece of paper from his pocket and handed it to Scotty.

Scotty took it with his good hand. "What is this?" he asked.

"It's the note. The original. You know, the one that David Gordon wrote before his demise."

Scotty opened it up and read it. He had seen the copy that had been posted to the police and this certainly looked like the original. He searched in one of the kitchen drawers and pulled out a roll of freezer bags. As he struggled to rip one free from the roll, Tony walked over to help.

"What are you doing?"

"Well, it's not exactly an evidence bag, but this will have to do for now."

Tony held the bag open as Scotty placed the note inside. As he went to place it in his jacket pocket, Danni walked into the kitchen dressed in a pair of grey jogging bottoms and a red sweater.

"What have you got there?"

"I found the note on the bedroom floor and I've given it to Scotty as evidence."

"NO, you can't take that!" she screamed and lunged at Scotty, trying to grab the bag from him.

Scotty held firm with his good hand and turned away from Danni, moving out of her reach but banging his bad arm on the counter at the same time.

"AGGHHH, you fucking bastard!" he shouted, clutching his arm in the sling.

"OK, I know you are struggling to trust me right now, but Scotty is with the police and he knows what's been going on and he's going to help us. Right, Scotty?"

Scotty was bent over in pain, but as he managed to straighten up, he looked towards Danni.

"He's right," he replied. "Look, I'm still trying to get my head round this, so I can appreciate you are finding this difficult too, but trust me, we are going to keep you safe and get to the bottom of this."

"Police! I told you no police!" screamed Danni. "You don't understand, he will find me, he'll track me down. He'll kill me!"

"Who will kill you? The Russians? The police are going to know what they've been up to. Scotty will keep you safe. He'll make sure they are taken into custody and they won't be able to get to you."

"Tony's right," said Scotty. "We need to get you both down to the station and get statements from you. Then we can pick them up and get them charged with murder and attempted murder, and I don't even know where to start with the charges with what they did to the platform. Whatever happens, they are going away for a long time and they won't be getting out on bail with those charges."

Danni had to get out of here. She turned towards the door, but as she tried to walk her legs buckled and she crumpled to the floor.

"Where are you going? You're not fit to go anywhere. We'll arrange for a car to come and collect you."

"NO! I can't go to the police station. He will find me!"

"Danni, you are not making any sense. Who will find you? I just told you, the Russians will be picked up."

"It's not the Russians I'm worried about. It's Mark."

"Mark?" Tony and Scotty said in unison. They looked at each other and shrugged.

"Who is Mark?" asked Scotty. "Does he work at Moskaneft? Did he have something to do with the helicopter crashing into the platform?"

Danni hung her head in her hands and shook her head. She was exasperated. Tears were starting to flow. How could she explain to them what had happened with Mark? She had evaded him all this time and now she had survived all this, only for him to find her. She had kept herself off the radar, but how could she hide if she ended up at the police station? By going to the one place that most people would think of as being a safe haven, she would effectively be signing her own death warrant.

What could she do? She had no other option now. She was at the end of her tether. If she went on the run, the Russians would track her down. If she went to the police, then Mark might find her. *Stuck between the devil and the deep blue sea.* Another of her mother's sayings. She pictured the last time she had seen her when she and her husband had visited her in London. She began to cry. Right now, all she wanted was to be with her mother, to feel her warm arms around her, hear her soothing voice say that everything would be OK. Would she ever see her again?

Tears were now streaming down her face and she sobbed uncontrollably. Tony and Scotty looked at each other, not sure what was wrong or what to do to make it better.

Tony put his arm around her and she initially pulled away from him. He tried again pulling her towards him. She had no strength left and she fell into his arms, feeling the warmth of his chest against her face.

"Shh," he whispered as he stroked her hair. "Everything will be OK." He looked over to Scotty, who had managed to fish his mobile phone out of his pocket and was already making a call for a patrol car to come and collect them.

Chapter Thirty

Tony looked out the window of the flat, down into the street below, and watched the patrol car pull up. Two officers stepped out of the car and placed their caps on their heads. The snow was still falling, and it was beginning to lie. *What a Christmas this had turned out to be.* Instead of enjoying his turkey and Christmas pudding, having a few drinks and falling asleep in front of some Christmas special on the TV, he was going to be spending the afternoon down the cop shop. It was one he wasn't going to forget in a hurry.

Scotty had gone down to meet his colleagues at the front door and brief them as to what was going on. Danni was lying on the settee, wrapped in a blanket. The TV had been switched on and the sound muted. The ticker tape on the news channel reported that currently there were no known survivors from the platform. Vessels were still searching the area in the hope of finding someone alive, but so far only a few bodies had been recovered. No-one would have been anticipating a helicopter flight that day, so the crash had come completely out of the blue. It was Christmas morning and most employees would have been given the opportunity of having a lie in with only a skeleton crew on shift. When the helicopter crashed, most of them would still have been asleep and whilst it was little consolation, at least they would have been oblivious to what happened. There was still no news on why a helicopter was in the area, but Tony knew that the Russians had more than a little something to do with it. Had they blackmailed someone into crashing the chopper into the platform? He certainly wouldn't put it past them. They were very persuasive when they wanted to be. Threats and violence seemed to be engrained in their culture, well, certainly in the ones he had met in Aberdeen. But maybe he was being unfair, after all he didn't really know any Russians. He was just going by the stereotype of the way they were portrayed in films.

Tony and Danni made their way downstairs to the police car. They could feel they were being watched by the occupants of nearby flats. Looking down on them, disapproving. They had been alerted by the flashing blue lights to something going on in the street. The resident curtain-twitchers were all there, scared they missed out. Danni still had the blanket around her, and Tony pulled it up around her to hide her face from the prying eyes. Their faces had already been plastered over the TV from when they had arrived at Moskaneft's offices this morning. *Was it really only this morning this had all kicked off?* Tony thought to himself. It felt like a lifetime ago.

They both slid into the back of the police car, feeling like a couple of criminals. Tony had wanted Danni to go to the hospital and get checked over, but she was adamant that she wasn't going back there. At least he had enough medical knowledge to keep an eye on her for now. She was suffering some aftereffects from the morphine, but nothing too serious.

She should make a full recovery, although she would probably feel like she had the worst hangover of her life for a few days yet. He wasn't sure she was up for questioning by the police either, but he had managed to wrangle it with Scotty that he could be present in the interview room with her, purely to monitor her on a medical basis.

They were driven down to Queen Street where he would be interviewed first, whilst Danni was being checked over by the duty doctor. He had already given a description of the Russians who had been at the office to Scotty, and he had sent a couple of cars down to the office to start the search. They would be long gone by now, of that he was sure, but you have to start somewhere. Maybe someone in the office had seen something. Tony had also asked if they could let Sheila know what had happened to her car as he was feeling particularly guilty about that. He didn't feel quite so guilty about the one they had taken from the hospital. After all, he hadn't been driving it.

They arrived at Queen Street and entered through the main reception. This was not the way that Danni had entered it last time she had the misfortune of being in the building. She still had grave reservations about being here, but she didn't really have much choice in the matter. They were escorted through the building by Scotty, who had come with them in the police car. The officer who had been in the passenger seat of the police car drove back the car they had commandeered at the hospital. The corridors of the station had been whitewashed some time ago and were in serious need of a facelift. The paint was grubby, tinged yellow in places and there were black scuff marks. Several noticeboards were on the walls with posters pinned up of the latest police initiatives. *Have you been a victim of physical abuse in the home? Keep your home safe this Christmas. What to do in the event of a terror attack.*

They don't have one about what to do in the event your employer tries to kill you, thought Tony. *Maybe that isn't such a regular occurrence!*

As they walked the well-worn carpet through to the interview rooms, Danni hoped that Mark had no way of finding out where she was. She had told Tony and Scotty about Mark while they had waited for the police to arrive. Not the full story, but enough details so that he understood why she was so scared of going to the police. Scotty had assured her that everything would be fine. Not all police were like that and that they would keep her safe. After all, she was one of their star witnesses and they had to protect her from the Russians, so they were not about to let any Tom, Dick or Harry (or Mark) know where she was. Scotty told Tony that it was likely he and Danni would be taken into police protection after giving their statements. Well, it wasn't like they could go back to work after what they had witnessed and experienced. If they were going to take down the Russians, then they would be needed to go to court and testify against them. That was provided they were able to track them down to bring them to justice.

As they got to the end of the corridor, they were met by a female police officer, who accompanied Danni through to the medical room to be examined. Danni didn't want to leave Tony and held onto him, but Tony assured her he would see her soon. He kissed her on the forehead and watched her be led off by the female PC. She looked so small and vulnerable. He just wanted to hold her in his arms and tell her everything would be all right.

Tony was shown through to an interview room. Scotty arranged for some coffee to be brought through before he began to give his statement. Tony took a sip of the lukewarm, pale brown liquid and almost spat it back out in the plastic cup.

"Sorry about that," said Scotty. "I guess we've got used to it by now. I'll go and see if I can track down some proper coffee for you." He headed off to the canteen.

The interview room was small, dingy and unbearably hot. There was no thermostat on the radiator to control it. It looked like it had been broken off. The heat and the unmistakable smell of stale sweat made the room feel even more uncomfortable than it looked. *Maybe this was a negotiation technique they used on suspects to get them to confess quicker.* Tony was left in the room with a male PC who stood with his back against the wall next to the door. He looked really happy to be on duty over Christmas. Tony attempted to make conversation with him while they waited for Scotty to return but all he got for his efforts were a couple of grunts. Tony bowed his head down onto the table. Suddenly he was very tired. A lot had happened in the past twenty-four hours. Since that kiss on Christmas Eve. *Had that really just been last night?* And now their entire lives had been thrown into turmoil and would never be the same again.

The door opened behind him. He looked up to see Scotty with the same female PC that had been with Danni earlier. She was carrying two mugs of steaming hot coffee and placed them down on the table. Like her colleague who was stood against the wall, she also looked really happy to be there.

"Don't worry, I got you the good stuff this time. You have no idea what I had to do to get hold of this," Scotty joked. "Even managed to wangle a couple of chocolate biscuits." He had carried them in his sling, which had been replaced with a proper sling from the station's first aid kit instead of the tea towel Tony had improvised with. Tony picked up one and unwrapped it. He took one bite, then devoured the rest in one mouthful. He didn't realise how hungry he was. When was the last time he had eaten? *Scrambled eggs at breakfast?* That was all he had eaten today. No wonder he was ravenous.

"Steady on there," said Scotty. "I'll see if we can get you something from the canteen after this, but that will have to tide you over for now." He pushed the second biscuit towards him. Tony was grateful for the sweet, chocolatey biscuit but it had awoken a monster that was starting to growl in his belly.

The door opened again, and they were joined by a colleague of Scotty's who introduced himself as Detective Inspector Warren, or Bunny to his friends. Tony chuckled to himself at the nickname. He was tall with brown hair that was slightly balding and had dark brown eyes. He was clean shaven and wore a perfectly pressed dark blue suit and white shirt with the top button open, no tie. A thick gold chain was visible around his neck and he wore a large gold watch on his left wrist. It looked like a Rolex, but Tony had an inkling it was a fake. After all, who could afford a Rolex nowadays? He was pretty sure a detective inspector's salary was not much better than his own. Unless he had bought it from one of the many pawn shops on Union Street, having been pawned by some poor soul who was desperately trying to put food on the table. Food. Tony's belly started to rumble again.

"Sorry about that," he said, holding an arm over his protesting stomach.

"The sooner we get this over with, the sooner you can get out of here," said Bunny. He took out his notebook and pulled a silver pen from his suit pocket and prepared to start taking notes.

Tony described the events of that morning as best he could. Bunny rarely interrupted, only doing so to clarify details. They wanted this interview to be in Tony's own words with no prompting from them.

"And that's when Scotty, sorry, Detective Scott, called you guys and how I ended up here," finished Tony. Bunny looked at his Rolex. "Interview terminated at 2:24pm."

2:24pm, thought Tony. There was no danger of him getting his turkey dinner now by the time they interviewed Danni and got out of here. But where would they go when they got out of here? They couldn't go back to the flat. It wasn't safe. Not with the Russians still at large. They would cross that bridge when they came to it. Right now, all he wanted to do was see Danni and make sure she was OK. Oh, and get something to eat to quieten the monster in his belly.

Chapter Thirty-One

They found Danni in the canteen with the same woman PC who had met her earlier and brought the coffees through to the interview room. She was dressed in her standard issue Police Scotland uniform, her blonde hair tied back in a neat bun. The canteen was closed but they had found some tins of soup in the cupboard and had heated one up, which Danni was now trying to force down. She knew she should eat something, but the smell of the soup was making her feel queasy. As Tony sat down next to her, she pushed the bowl of soup away from her, unable to force down any more.

"If, you're not going to eat that, can I have it?" asked Tony, who was already pulling the bowl towards him.

"Be my guest," replied Danni.

"Is there any more going?" asked Scotty to the female PC.

She pushed her chair back, stood up and headed off into the kitchen, muttering something about male chauvinist pigs and that her job was out on the beat not in the bloody kitchen.

"Someone's full of the joys of Christmas," joked Scotty, nodding towards the PC.

"How are you, Danni? I hear the doctor has given you a clean bill of health."

Danni nodded. She didn't feel particularly healthy right now.

"You up for giving us your interview?" asked Scotty.

She looked at Tony, who nodded his agreement.

"Don't worry, I'll be with you the whole time," said Tony. "You just need to tell them all you know and then we can get out of here."

"And go where?" asked Danni.

Good point, thought Tony. Where were they going to go? It was Christmas Day. Everywhere would be shut.

"We've got you a room in a nearby hotel for the night and you'll have a police guard on your door, so you don't have to worry. We are reviewing where the best place is to move you to after that."

Danni didn't look especially comforted by that, but she was looking forward to getting some sleep and shutting out this day from her mind, if that was possible.

The female PC came back with two bowls of soup and threw them down on the table, hot red liquid spilling onto the white formica.

"Hey, watch it," said Scotty.

"You're lucky I didn't pour it in your lap," she sneered and walked off in a huff. She was sick of babysitting the overdosed girl and being treated like a skivvy. This wasn't what she had signed up for. If she had to work on Christmas Day, then at least she could have been out on the reccy for the Russians instead of being stuck in HQ.

"Don't suppose there is any bread to go with this?" shouted Scotty after the PC.

She turned around and gave him the finger.

"I guess that's a no, then?"

They watched her leave the canteen. Scotty shrugged his shoulders and pulled one of the bowls of soup towards him, gulping down the first spoonful and burning his tongue for his efforts. The guys finished their soup in silence while Danni watched. Despite not eating much that day, she wasn't at all hungry. All she wanted to do was have a bath or shower and go to sleep in a nice, soft, warm bed. But first she had to endure her interview.

The scraping of spoons in the bowls signalled they had finished their soup. Scotty pushed his chair back and stood up. "Shall we?" he asked as he motioned towards the door of the canteen.

Danni was still a little shaky on her feet and Tony helped her up. They walked through to a different room from where Tony had been earlier. It was nicely decorated with soft seats. Everything was in pale, pastel colours. There was a plant on a small table and a box of toys in the corner of the room. Scotty advised that this was a room they normally used for interviewing children. They thought Danni would feel more comfortable in here than the standard rooms.

"Thanks for offering me the special treatment!" joked Tony.

"Hey, you got a cup of proper coffee and two chocolate biscuits, what more do you want?" laughed Scotty.

But now it was time to get serious again. Detective Inspector Warren, Bunny, appeared with a different female PC. This one smiled and looked happier to be there than the other one. She was there to try to put Danni at ease and to make her feel safer, so she wasn't surrounded purely by men. Bunny introduced himself to Danni and sat down opposite her. There was no table between them to make it feel less formal and try to make her feel more relaxed.

After about half an hour, they had finished. Danni struggled with some details, the aftereffects of the morphine messing with her memory. She remembered breakfast – well, the attempt to eat breakfast – and then hearing the news on the radio. She remembered getting to the office and going up to the file room. She remembered Becky being there and being as annoying as she usually was. *Or usually had been.* She tried to recall exactly what she had heard the Russians say about what happened to the platform, but it was sketchy at best. Then she broke down in tears as she closed her eyes and visualised what had happened to Becky. She physically recoiled at the memory of the gun going off.

"What happened to Becky? Is she dead?" she asked, wiping tears from her cheeks.

"My officers are out searching for her and the Russians as we speak. We'll let you know more when we find them."

Tony knew that Becky was dead but didn't want to be the one to break that to Danni right now, so he kept his mouth shut. The female PC put an arm around Danni to comfort her and handed her a tissue from the box that was sat on the table next to the plant. She continued sobbing for a few minutes.

"Then, the rest is a blur, and I woke up in hospital," she said finally. "Can we go now? I really don't feel very well."

"Of course," replied Bunny. "You've been more than helpful and have corroborated a few things that Tony has already told us. Perhaps your memory will be better in a day or two, so we will need to speak to you again."

Danni nodded slowly, not looking up or making eye contact with anyone.

"PC Thomson, will you make arrangements to transfer these two to their hotel for the night?"

"Yes, sir," she replied and headed out of the room. Tony moved over to sit beside Danni and take over from the PC, placing his arm around her.

"Thank you for your assistance," said Bunny, and stood up just as there was a knock on the door.

He opened it and stepped outside to speak to one of his colleagues. When he re-entered, he had a serious look on his face.

"My officers have searched Moskaneft's offices. They found the Russian that you stabbed with the needle Tony. He was unconscious but is alive and he has been taken to hospital under police guard. That's one that will not be getting away with this." He then turned to look towards Danni, about to deliver the news she didn't want to hear.

"Unfortunately, they also found a female body behind the bins in the alley outside the office. Formal identification has yet to be made, but we believe, from the description you gave us – and personal items found on her – that it is Becky."

Danni hung her head and continued crying. Tony pulled her tighter towards him and she didn't fight it. She let him pull her close. She didn't feel especially fortunate at the moment, but she was in a much better place than Becky.

The female PC returned, sticking her head around the door to confirm that transport had been arranged. Scotty said he would go with them to get them settled, and then he was heading up to the hospital to speak to the Russian, if he was awake, and to finally get his arm looked at and X-rayed.

By the time they left the station it was already dark. A white blanket of snow carpeted the ground. Danni started to shiver as they walked out into the cold towards the waiting patrol car. Tony was carrying the blanket that she had been wrapped in since the flat and placed it around her shoulders to warm her and shelter her from the snow.

Chapter Thirty-Two

I t was a short ride from the station to the hotel they were going to stay in. It was one of the large granite buildings on Queen's Road, which would have been a family home in bygone days but had been converted into a hotel by adjoining neighbouring buildings. By the time they got there, there was already a police presence. They had checked the hotel and had set up seats outside the room that they had been allocated. Normally it would be difficult to get a room in Aberdeen on Christmas Day, but for the past few years there had been more and more available as struggling families decided to spend the day at home instead of splashing out on some fancy meal in some fancy hotel that they couldn't actually afford. As it was, the hotel was only half-booked, so there were plenty of rooms to choose from. Their room was the end of a corridor on the third floor and the rooms next door and across the corridor from them were vacant.

Scotty nodded to the two officers who were waiting outside the room. Both stood to attention as they appeared out of the lift, one dropping their newspaper to the floor and the other returning his phone to his pocket.

The younger officer unlocked the door with the key card and held the door open for them to enter. Danni noticed that both of them were armed. She wasn't sure if that made her feel more or less secure.

"You are not to leave your posts for any reason," stated Scotty to the two officers. "Two armed guards are to be stationed here at all times, are we clear?"

"Yes, sir," replied the officers in unison.

As Scotty entered the room, he let out a whistle. "Wow! Nice room! You guys are lucky, Police Scotland are obviously feeling the Christmas spirit." Danni didn't feel lucky. The room was spacious for a city hotel room and had two double beds. The decor was tasteful in cream and chocolate colours. There was a night stand between the two beds with a decorative glass lamp and a dressing table near the window. A full-length mirror was on the wall and Danni caught a glimpse of herself in it as she walked past. She stopped dead, staring at the stranger looking back. She barely recognised herself. She was very pale, with large dark circles under her eyes and her cheeks were stained with tears. Her hair looked like it hadn't been washed or seen a brush for days. She looked away, not wanting to acknowledge that was actually her.

She sat on the end of the bed nearest the window. Scotty was looking out the window which faced out to the back of the hotel, not that he could see anything in the dark, but he checked anyway and then pulled the brown velvet curtains shut.

"Stay away from the windows, keep the curtains shut and don't leave the room," he said. "If you need anything, then knock on the door and one of the officers will answer. They can organise any food or drink that you need from room service."

Tony nodded his understanding. Danni just sat there staring at the floor.

"Will you be OK?"

"Sure, mate. Look, thanks for everything, we really appreciate it. Not sure we would have got through this without you," said Tony.

He walked up to Scotty to give him a man hug, but Scotty pulled away. "Hey, watch the arm!"

"Sorry, mate! I forgot. You better go and get that seen to."

Scotty held out his good arm to shake hands with Tony instead. "I'll say goodnight then," said Scotty as he made for the door. "I'll be round to check on you both in the morning. Try to get some sleep."

Danni looked up and tried to force a smile, but she was too tired to manage.

When Scotty had left the room, Tony turned to Danni and asked, "How about a nice hot bubble bath?"

He walked into the bathroom, turned on the taps of the bath and picked up the small bottles of toiletries until he found the bath foam. He emptied the entire bottle under the running water and the bubbles started to froth up. When he entered the bedroom, Danni was still sitting on the end of the bed with the blanket wrapped around her.

"Here, let me help you," he said, removing the blanket and hooking an arm under Danni's, pulling her to her feet. Danni didn't object, she didn't have the strength to. And a nice warm bath sounded like just what she needed to wash this day away. The water was about three quarters of the way up the bath with the top quarter full of soapy white bubbles. The mirror had steamed up and she could see the steam rising from the tub. She felt so cold she couldn't wait to get in the water and warm through.

"Do you need a hand to undress?" asked Tony.

"I think I'll manage," replied Danni.

"Only if you are sure?"

"I'm fine, honestly."

"OK, I'll be right outside, so if you need anything just shout. I'm going to check the room service menu and order some food, I'm starving! Any requests?"

Danni shook her head. She still wasn't hungry.

"You need to eat something, keep your strength up. I'll order for you, shall I?"

Danni couldn't be bothered arguing so she just nodded and shut the bathroom door behind him. She looked at the lock and thought about sliding it over but decided against it just in case she needed him in a hurry. She was feeling very weak and was worried she might pass out. She didn't want to have survived all this just to drown in the bathtub!

She slipped out of her clothes, using the sink to steady herself and then stepped into the bath. The water was too hot, and she had to run the cold tap for a while to cool it down to a manageable temperature. When she climbed in and slid under the soft bubbles, she felt safe for the first time in ages. She let the warmth of the water wash over her and heat her skin, finally starting to thaw her out. She closed her eyes and slid underneath the water, enjoying the feeling of being able to shut out the entire mad world that she had become caught up in. She lay there for what seemed like a lifetime. It was an enchanting feeling and she felt like she could stay there forever and never have another worry or care in the world.

Suddenly, there was a knock on the door.

"You OK in there? You're awfully quiet."

She pulled herself back up, her head lifting above the water. How long had she been in there? She had absolutely no concept of time today.

"I'm fine," she replied, "just enjoying the peace and quiet."

"OK, if you're sure. The food should be here soon."

Tony was always thinking of his stomach, she thought to herself.

She lay there a few minutes more, trying to comprehend what today had brought, then decided it was too much to grasp. The warm water was making her feel even more tired. She just needed to sleep; she could worry about it all in the morning.

She got out of the bath and dried herself with one of the giant, white fluffy towels that was hanging on the chrome towel rail. The rail was heated, and the towel felt warm and comforting around her. She slipped into one of the white dressing gowns that were hung up behind the door. It was huge on her and went nearly to the floor. She pulled the belt tight around her and tied it in a knot. She dried her hair with the same towel and wiped the steam from the mirror to see what she looked like. The reflection looking back still did not look like her, but at least she had a bit more colour in her cheeks. In fact, her cheeks were glowing pink. There was no brush or comb in the room, so she pulled her fingers through her hair. She tentatively opened the bathroom door and walked back out into the bedroom. Tony was lying on the other bed and the TV was on in the background. He had opened the mini bar and had helped himself to a miniature bottle of whisky.

"Fancy a drink?" he asked, holding up his glass and jiggling it towards her.

"No thanks," she replied, screwing up her nose at the thought of alcohol.

"I ordered coffee with the food, it should be..." There was a knock on the door.

"Good timing! That will be it now," he laughed.

He went to the door and opened it. Outside was one of the officers with a trolley of food and a pot of coffee.

Tony pulled the trolley inside. "I didn't know what you would like, so I just ordered a mixture. I'll eat whatever you don't want!"

Danni looked at the trolley and shook her head. *How many people had he ordered for?*

Tony could read her expression. "Hey, we're not paying for it, and I haven't had my Christmas dinner. After the day we've had, I think this is the least that Police Scotland can fork out for."

There was prawn cocktail, melon balls, paté and oatcakes, two plates of turkey with all the trimmings, including pigs in blankets and all the veg you could possibly think of. And to finish, there were two portions of Christmas pudding with jugs of custard on the side.

"Well, it would just have gone to waste!" laughed Tony as he grabbed the prawn cocktail and started tucking in.

"Sorry, did you want this?" he asked as he looked up and saw Danni frowning at him.

"No thanks," she said, feeling disgusted at the way he was devouring the prawns.

She looked at the trolley, picked up a piece of melon and nibbled on it. She sat on the edge of the bed, tucking her leg underneath her. She chewed and swallowed and waited a minute. It didn't feel like it was going to come back up, so she braved another bite. Suddenly, she was famished. The effects of the morphine must have started to wear off. She picked up an oatcake and spread a generous amount of paté on it, taking a large mouthful.

"Easy, tiger!" joked Tony. "Careful, small bites to start with till we see how your body is going to react."

Danni smiled, crumbs of oatcake popping out the side of her mouth and slipping out onto her dressing gown. She brushed them off onto the carpet. Leaning over to the trolley, she picked up the plate and fork and ate some of the salad that was on the side: cherry tomatoes, lettuce and shredded peppers, carrots, and cucumber. She picked out the cucumber, having never been a fan of it she wasn't about to start eating it now.

Tony had already polished off the prawn cocktail, scraping the last of the pink sauce out of the bottom of the glass with the tiny spoon.

They both looked at the plates of turkey and then looked at each other. Tony picked up a plate and handed it to Danni along with a fork and knife and then picked up his open plate.

"Budge up," he said as he joined her on the same bed. They sat up against the pillows, plates in their laps. Tony tucked in with gusto, finally enjoying his Christmas dinner while Danni picked at hers with her fork.

"Cheers," said Tony as he raised his glass of whisky, emptying it in one gulp.

"Are you sure you don't want a drink?" he asked Danni.

She shook her head.

"Coffee?"

"I could maybe manage a coffee," she replied.

He poured some from the silver coffee pot into a cup and brought it over to her, placing it on the bedside table. Returning to the mini bar, he removed another bottle of whisky and poured it into his empty glass.

"Pity they don't have a large bottle, I could do with a few more of these."

"Merry Christmas," he said, raising the glass yet again.

Danni raised her coffee cup. "Merry Christmas," she replied.

As Tony sat back down on the bed, he felt something in his pocket. He pulled it out, forgetting that he had picked up Danni's Christmas present from the floor in the flat earlier. "I forgot, what with platforms blowing up, having a gun held to my head, and ending up at the police station and everything else that has happened today. This is for you."

He handed over the small parcel to Danni. She placed her plate of food on the bedside table and took it from him. As she held it in her hands, she recognised it as being the one that she had seen under the tree in the morning.

"Thank you," she whispered.

"Well don't just sit there," he said. "Open it."

Danni looked at him and then looked at the parcel. She picked at the sticky tape holding it shut with her fingernail.

"Just rip it," said Tony. He seemed more excited than Danni about the parcel.

She pulled a hole in the paper and began to tear it open. Inside was a small box, the sort that jewellery often comes in.

She looked at Tony again.

"Come on, open it, I want to see your reaction."

She opened the small box and inside was a silver chain with a pendant in the shape of an angel, its wings spread open, its hands in prayer.

"It's beautiful," said Danni, as she looked from the angel to Tony and back to the angel.

"Your own guardian angel to look out for you," replied Tony. "Although I think you could have been doing with her earlier today."

Tony took the box from Danni and removed the pendant and motioned for Danni to turn around so he could fasten it around her neck. Danni turned her back to Tony and lifted her hair out of the way. As she looked down, the angel sat just above her chest. She closed her right hand around it, holding it tight.

"Thank you," she whispered, not wanting to let it go.

"I thought of you as soon as I saw it."

"You shouldn't have," she said as a tear formed in the corner of her eye.

Tony turned her head towards him, wiped the tear from her eye with his thumb, then leaned forward and kissed her on the forehead.

"Now, now, don't cry," he said. "It was supposed to make you happy, not sad."

"I am happy," she said, "Happier than I've been in a long time."

"Well if a day like today is what makes you happy, then I guess I'm going to struggle for an encore," joked Tony.

"I don't mean what happened today," retorted Danni. "I don't ever want to go through anything like that again. I just mean being here with you, you know…" She tailed off, too embarrassed to say how she really felt about him.

"I know," he replied, sensing her awkwardness.

He kissed her on the forehead again and hugged her close. She lay her head against his chest but did not let go of the angel. She felt warm and safe as she closed her eyes, falling asleep almost instantly. The day had really taken it out of her.

Chapter Thirty-Three

"Have you heard what happened today?"

"Some of it, but I'm sure you will fill me in on the details."

"Well, she ended up in hospital and we could have got you to her there, but she escaped. She's been at Queen Street most of the afternoon and they've got her in one of the hotels overnight. They will be moving her to a 'safe place' tomorrow, probably, but don't worry, because now we have a way of keeping track of her. Are you going to be coming up to Aberdeen soon?"

"I don't know, was supposed to be heading up as part of the murder enquiry but now with the Russian connections, they are calling in the big guns, so I'm not sure if I'm going to be assigned to the case. I've told them I'm available, but it's not down to me."

"Don't worry, we've got eyes on her at all times now and she has no idea. We'll need to bide our time, though, as she will be under police protection until the trial, but they'll be pushing for an early date on that, so it won't be too long to wait."

"I've waited all this time, a few more weeks or months are not going to make any difference now. Just knowing that it won't be long till we are 're-acquainted' will make the wait even sweeter."

"And she hasn't got a clue?"

"Not a scoobie."

"Good, make sure you keep it that way."

Chapter Thirty-Four

When Danni eventually woke, it was 11am. She had not slept so deeply in a long time. She hadn't even dreamed, well, not that she could remember anyway. As she pushed the duvet down, she realised she was not in her own bed, not in her own flat. A sudden panic washed over her. Where was she? What had happened?

"Hey, sleepyhead."

A familiar voice. She turned to see Tony sitting on the bed next to hers. She rubbed her eyes and sat up, taking in the room. The hotel room they had ended up in last night. She lifted her hand towards her neck and felt the angel hanging there. Her guardian angel. Now it was starting to come back to her.

"You went out like a light last night," said Tony, "and you looked so peaceful, I didn't want to wake you."

She could see that he had slept in the other bed, as the covers were all dishevelled.

"Scotty called and was going to drop by, but we thought it better to let you sleep after all you've been through. I told him I'd call him once you were awake. Do you want something to eat?"

Danni looked around the room and saw that the food and plates from last night had been removed and replaced with a new trolley with empty breakfast plates. Tony had eaten already.

"There's still some coffee in the pot if you want some, I think it will still be OK," said Tony as he got up and walked over to the trolley. He poured a cup of coffee, but he could see there was no steam rising from it and the cup didn't feel warm in his hands. He took a mouthful and immediately spat it back out into the cup.

"Sorry, it's cold. I'll order you some fresh, what do you want with it?"

"Just some toast."

"Is that all? You'll need more than that to get your strength up. How about some scrambled eggs?"

She screwed her face up and shook her head, remembering what happened the last time she had eaten scrambled eggs.

"Bacon roll?"

Again, she shook her head.

"You need to eat something else, what about some fruit?"

"I think I can manage some fruit," she replied.

Tony went to the door to speak to the officers who were standing guard outside. The original officers had been replaced in the early hours and he had met their new guards when he had ordered his own breakfast earlier.

Danni threw back the duvet and saw she was still wearing the robe that she had dressed in after her bath last night. She got out of the bed and picked up her clothes that had been neatly folded into a pile on one of the seats. She took them through to the bathroom to get changed. As she closed the door behind her, she heard Tony speaking to the guard.

"And chuck in a couple of bacon rolls, cause if she doesn't eat them, then I will."

She looked at herself in the mirror. She looked vaguely better than she had last night. The dark circles under her eyes were not quite so dark and she didn't look as pale. She felt rested after that sleep although she had no idea how long she had actually been asleep for. Yesterday was a blur. What time had they arrived at the hotel? She had no idea. Thankfully there was one of those small disposable toothbrushes in the bathroom and she squeezed toothpaste onto it and cleaned her teeth, spitting out the excess paste into the sink. She took a glass from the shelf and filled it with water to rinse out her mouth. It was amazing how just brushing your teeth could make you feel so much better. It was like when you went on a long-haul flight and felt rubbish but being able to clean your teeth in the airport toilets made you feel slightly more human again. She had always carried a travel toothbrush with her when she flew. But the last time she had flown had been with Mark. Why did that have to enter her head now? She had enough to deal with without thinking about him. She shut him out of her head and finished dressing.

When she walked back into the bedroom, Tony was sitting in the chair where her clothes had been. He had opened the curtains a tiny bit, so she could see that the sun was out and the sky was bright blue. The snow was still lying and it was going to be a crisp, frosty day. *Perfect weather for Boxing Day.* In previous years in London, Boxing Day would have been spent having a long lie-in, followed by a hearty brunch, then a walk along the river to meet friends at one of the bars where they would top up on the Christmas cheer from the day before. She had no idea what this Boxing Day would bring, but surely it would be more sedate than Christmas Day had been. *Nothing could be as bad as that!*

Her hand instinctively reached up to her angel as she walked past Tony and sat down on the edge of the bed opposite him.

"Thank you for this," she said. "I have no idea if I thanked you last night; it's all a bit of a blur."

"No problem," he replied. "I'm glad you like it."

"I did actually get you a Christmas gift," she said, "but it's back at the flat so I don't know if you will get it any time soon."

"Don't worry about it. But since I'm not going to see it for a while, can I ask what it is?"

She picked up one of the empty miniature whisky bottles and waggled it at him.

"Not only a bigger version of this," she replied, "but also a better version."

"Well, now I can't wait to get my present," he laughed. "I could have done with it last night. I drank the only two they had in the mini bar and I didn't fancy moving on to gin or vodka. I started on the brandy but it's not the same. I needed something to help me sleep, which obviously wasn't a problem for you."

"Sorry about that."

"I'm only joking with you, you needed to rest. I was struggling to get my brain to switch off."

"Did all that really happen yesterday?" asked Danni. "I was hoping some of it was just a bad dream."

"Unfortunately, I don't think it was," he replied. "And it's going to take some time to come to terms with it all, but I guess time is something we will have plenty of, as I doubt we will be going back to work any time soon."

"Is there any word on what happened to the people on the platform? Any survivors?"

"When I checked the news this morning, two have been plucked from the water and taken to the ARI, but I don't know their condition. Other than that, nothing I'm afraid. I can only hope they were still asleep and didn't know what happened."

Danni hung her head and shook it, a shiver raced down her spine at the thought of what had happened yesterday. *How could anyone have planned something like this? All just to save themselves money.* The oil industry had always been a cut-throat business – as she had found out – but what price do you put on a life? Obviously, the Russians didn't place value on anyone else's lives except their own. Everyone was expendable in their mission to make as much money as possible from oil, the black blood that flowed below the surface.

Danni wasn't too disappointed at the thought of not having to go back to Moskaneft. In fact, it was the last place she wanted to go back to. If she never saw the office again, it would be too soon. How could this have happened at her work? It was like something out of a movie, not what you expect from everyday life. And whilst her life was far from straightforward, she could be doing with taking things much easier for a while.

There was a knock at the door and one of the officers wheeled in the food trolley.

"I see your friend is awake now," he said, nodding towards Danni. "Shall I call Detective Scott?"

"Give her a minute to have some breakfast, but yeah, you can let Scotty know we are ready for him."

He closed the door behind him, removing the empty food trolley that Tony had demolished earlier.

"First, you need to eat," he said to Danni as he handed her a plate of toast. There were butter portions and individual jars of jam on a separate plate. She picked up the first one, it was marmalade. She made a face and put it back on the plate. The next one was raspberry, her favourite. She tried to open it, but the lid was stuck, and she had to enlist the help of Tony to get it open. He opened it first time, making her feel even more feeble than she already did.

"I must have slackened it for you," she said.

She spread some jam on her toast and poured a cup of steaming hot black coffee. She felt the coffee warm her from the inside out and took a bite of toast, licking jam from her fingers. It tasted good and her stomach was ready for more. She devoured the toast in a couple more bites and moved onto the second slice.

"You going to eat that bacon roll?" asked Tony, picking it up and taking a bite before Danni had a chance to answer.

"I guess not," she said. She pointed at his face. "You've got something on your chin."

Tony wiped his face with the back of his hand.

"No, the other side," laughed Danni.

Tony tried to lick it clean, but he missed.

"Here," she said, as she picked up a napkin and wiped his face. Tony looked at her and they gazed into each other's eyes. They stayed there for a few seconds, breathing each other in. Tony leaned forward about to kiss her when there was a knock at the door and the officer from earlier walked in.

"Oh, erm, excuse me," he said, slightly embarrassed.

They moved away from each other, the moment gone.

"What is it?" asked Tony.

"Detective Scott will be here in a few minutes, he wanted to let you know."

"Thanks," said Tony. "For nothing," he muttered under his breath.

Danni had already walked over to the trolley and picked up another piece of toast.

"Better eat up before he gets here," she said, pointing at the remains of the bacon roll that was still in his hand.

"I'm suddenly not hungry," he replied, placing it on the plate. He walked over to the bed and sat down. Danni continued picking at the toast, scraping the remains of the jam onto another slice.

"What do you think will happen to us now?" she asked.

"I have no idea," he replied. "Funnily enough, I've never been taken into police protection before. I'm sure Scotty will have things in hand though."

Just with that there was another knock at the door and Scotty walked in.

"That was quick," said Tony.

"I was up at the hospital having a check-up when PC Harris called, so I came straight here."

His arm was now in a cast, supported by a sling.

"It's broken," he said, raising his arm and then wishing he hadn't moved it as he winced in pain. "I spent the rest of last night at A&E getting X-rayed and getting this stupid cast on."

"I'm so sorry," replied Danni. "I thought you were one of the Russians. I was scared for my life."

"Hey, it's OK. You weren't to know."

"Yeah, and after everything you've been through, who could blame you for defending yourself? Right?" said Tony, trying to make her feel better.

"Right," replied Scotty.

"So, what happens now?" asked Tony.

"Well, so far we've only got the one Russian in custody and although we have men on the ground searching for the others, whilst they are at large we need to keep you safe. You'll be moved to a safehouse, out in the countryside, with police protection for a few days and we will assess things again then."

"Do you think you will find the others?"

"I'd like to say yes, but I'm pretty sure they will be long gone by now. With their connections they may even be out of the country and if that's the case, then we have no chance. That's why we need to keep you safe until we know where they are."

"Where in the countryside are we going?" asked Danni.

"We have access to a small cottage on the outskirts of Fyvie," he replied. "It's owned by a family member of one of my colleagues. They are away for Christmas and New Year, so we can get the use of it. It's in the middle of nowhere, up a farm track with only one way in so we can keep an eye on anyone coming or going. We'll stock up with food before you get out there and there is a log fire, so you will be nice and warm."

"Sounds great," said Danni. "Can't wait to get out of Aberdeen and away from Moskaneft."

"What about clothes?" said Tony as he pulled his shirt towards him and sniffed it. "I could be doing with a change of clothes."

"Hopefully what they have in the wardrobes will fit you for now."

"Can't we go back to the flat and get our own clothes?" asked Danni.

"Sorry, but your flat is being treated as a crime scene for now and until forensics have finished with it, we can't let you in. We could get uniform to pack up some stuff for you and ship it out to the cottage in a day or two."

"I guess that will have to do," said Tony.

Scotty took his mobile phone out of his pocket and dropped it on the floor. As he bent down to pick it up, he knocked his broken arm against the corner of the bed.

"Agghhh, fuck!" he shouted. "It's unbelievable how many things I've managed to bash into already," he said, clutching at his right arm.

Tony picked up the phone from the floor and handed it to him.

"Thanks," Scotty said as he attempted to scroll through his address book, looking for the right number. He found it and pressed the call button.

"They are ready to move, so send over the car. Unmarked, of course, we don't want to draw any attention to them." He hung up and wrestled his phone back in his pocket. "I didn't realise how difficult it would be to do everything with your left hand," he said as he saw them watching him struggle.

"The car will be here shortly. The officers will take you to the cottage and they will stay with you until the surveillance team arrives. Don't worry, we will have someone watching the place twenty-four seven. The Russians won't get anywhere near you."

"How can we be worried when we have Aberdeen's finest on the case?" joked Tony. "It's not like the Russians have anything to lose. We've already seen what they are capable of."

Danni looked nervous.

"They have no idea where you are going and, so far, our enquiries have turned up no known sightings of them. They have gone to ground and will be in hiding or might even be out of the country by now. There is no need to be alarmed. Honestly, trust me!" said Scotty.

Trust me! Danni had heard those words before and look what happened then. She clutched her guardian angel and sat down on the end of the bed.

Chapter Thirty-Five

There was a knock on the door and an officer walked in. "We're ready for them now," he said and retreated out of the room.

Scotty walked with Danni and Tony down the corridor and into the lift. The lift doors opened at the ground floor and they were met by a plain clothes officer.

"The car is parked at the side exit," said the officer. He was dressed in jeans and a dark bomber-style jacket. A dark grey beanie hat covered his head whilst a ginger beard covered his face.

He led the way to an emergency exit door at the side of the hotel. The black Ford Escort had its motor running with the second officer sat in the driver seat, his hands held up against the blowers, trying to warm them. He was similarly dressed in a black jacket. He too had ginger hair and a beard. They could have been mistaken for brothers, if not twins.

"This is where I'll say goodbye," said Scotty. "My colleagues will take care of you but if there is anything you need then just call. I'll let you know if there are any developments, but I would expect you to be out at the cottage for a few days anyway."

"Thanks for everything, mate," said Tony, slapping Scotty on the back and being careful not to knock into his broken arm this time.

"Take care, Danni," Scotty said as she headed down the steps and into the back seat of the Escort, the door being held open by the first officer.

"Thank you," she said as she managed a smile towards Scotty.

Tony slid in the back beside her and the officer shut the door. He climbed in the passenger seat and introduced himself as Bob. The driver's name was Adam. With introductions out of the way, the car sped off out the side alley and onto Queen's Road. They turned right onto Anderson Drive and followed the road all the way to Bucksburn, before heading into Dyce and then out into the countryside. Danni had never been out this way before. She pressed her head against the window and watched as the towns of Newmachar and Oldmeldrum sped past. She saw children wrapped up in snow suits being pulled along on sledges by their parents, outside enjoying the sun on a cold but dry winter day. As they moved further out into the countryside, the view turned to that of endless fields blanketed in white, deserted, having been harvested some months back. The trees and hedges were naked, having lost their leaves, the only green coming from the fir trees on the side of the hills. As they passed a farm by the roadside, she noticed cattle in the steading, chewing on silage, the frost hanging onto their breath in the air.

They didn't speak the whole way out but had glanced at each other several times and smiled. Bob turned on the radio to break the silence. George Michael's *Faith* blared out. Danni and Tony looked at each other and laughed. "Faith! Well that's something we will be needing," joked Tony.

"And now with the time at twelve noon, here is the local news."

"Thanks, Martin. It has been reported that only two survivors have been found following the explosion on Moskaneft's South Platform yesterday. They have been taken to Aberdeen Royal Infirmary, but their condition is unknown. It has been confirmed from eyewitness reports that a helicopter crashed into the platform. The explosion had originally been linked to terrorists, but there have been developments in the case to suggest that this was not an act of terrorism. Police Scotland will be holding a press conference later today..."

Bob quickly tuned the radio to a different station. "Sorry about that," he said.

Tony reached over and took hold of Danni's hand. She looked at him, swallowing hard to choke back the tears that were forming. *Those poor people, they had no idea what they had got caught up in, when turning up for work had become a matter of life or death. All of them, pawns, but in a game of Russian roulette, rather than chess, with the Russians only too happy to pull the trigger.*

As she looked back out the window, still forcing back the tears she saw the signpost for Fyvie. They turned into the village and followed the road up through the main street, passing the war memorial. The village Christmas tree had been located near to it, the lights switched on but only some of them working. Several bulbs had been broken or removed, probably by local kids up to hijinks.

They followed the road up the hill, passing the primary school and playground, both of which were deserted. They hadn't seen a single person as they drove through the village. The only signs of life were a giant inflatable Santa and snowman in one of the gardens and the outdoor lights decorating the row of council houses.

They were soon out of the village and heading back into the countryside. They drove for about a mile, turning off a couple of times and eventually heading up a farm track to their final destination.

"Scotty was right," said Tony, "this is in the middle of nowhere!"

The cottage was small. An old farmhouse but this was no longer a working farm, the land having been sold off years back and the house now a simple family residence. It was open to the elements, which was probably a good thing if you wanted to keep an eye out for unwanted guests. There was an old steading behind the cottage, but it was in a state of dilapidation. A path led upwards to a hill behind the cottage with a close of trees starting halfway up. A red car was parked to the back of the building. A male and a female got out as they came to a halt.

"My colleagues here will be staying with you," said Adam. "We need to return to Aberdeen tonight, but we'll be back to check on you tomorrow."

The officers from the red car walked over to greet their colleagues. More introductions were made, and they made their way into the cottage with Sandy and Sarah, their new babysitters. The place was freezing, it was probably warmer outside than it was inside. The main door led directly into a farmhouse-style kitchen with wooden units and a large wooden table in the middle of the room.

"Get 'i kettle on then," shouted Sandy to Sarah.

"What did your last slave die of?" she replied.

"I'm awa te get the groceries fae the car so we can hae a fly cup." It was obvious from his accent that Sandy had grown up in the area.

As Sandy went back out to get their food supplies, Sarah took the kettle over to the sink and began to fill it.

"I presume you two will be wanting a cuppa before you head back?"

"Would be rude not to," replied Bob.

"Does a bear shit in the woods?" laughed Adam. "And I hope you brought some biscuits to go with that. Aye, chocolate ones, nae those diet bar things I've seen you eating."

"You might be lucky," she replied as she switched on the kettle.

"But first, go and see if you can get the heating to work, it's like brass monkeys in here."

Adam found the controls and switched on the heating. The boiler roared into life.

"An old house like this, it's going to take a while to warm up. Do you think there is a fireplace in the living room?" asked Sarah.

Tony headed through into the next room which was the living room adjoined by a conservatory looking out over the garden and surrounding countryside. It was mid-afternoon, and the light was already starting to fade. They were in luck, there was a wood burning stove and a supply of logs had been stacked up next to it. Tony opened the door of the stove and put some kindling in the bottom with some newspaper that had been lying in a magazine rack next to an armchair. He struck a match and lit the paper, adding a small log to the top until the fire properly got going. He shut the door, satisfied that the flames were rising and taking hold of the wood.

He looked around. The furniture consisted of an old, brown leather settee and matching armchairs that had seen better days. The leather was cracked and worn. A couple of throws lay over the back of the settee and he took one down and motioned for Danni to come through and get comfortable.

She curled up on the settee with the throw over her and watched the flames in the stove, mesmerised by them.

There was an artificial Christmas tree in the conservatory and Christmas cards were strung up above the fireplace. Tony switched on the tree lights to make the room feel more welcoming.

"Tea or coffee?" shouted Sarah.

"Coffee," they replied in unison.

"Milk and sugar?"

"No, just as it comes, please," replied Danni.

A few moments later, Sarah entered with a tray of mugs and a plate of biscuits. Chocolate ones like Adam had asked for. The others followed her through, grabbing their respective mugs and a biscuit each and taking up position by the fire. Sarah sat on the settee next to Danni, with Tony taking the armchair to the other side of her and Sandy the remaining chair.

"It's all right, we'll stand and grow big," joked Bob.

"Well, it's not like you're staying," replied Sandy.

Bob and Adam took their mugs over to the conservatory and checked out the window.

"You get a good viewpoint from here," said Bob. "You'll have time to see anyone coming in about."

"Not that we need to worry about that," said Sarah, sensing Danni's concern.

"Oh yeah, right. Of course."

Bob and Adam finished up their coffee, laid their mugs down on the tray and said goodbye. Sandy followed them through to the kitchen and locked the door behind them. They were in for the night.

Sarah picked up the tray and went to head through to the kitchen. "I'm just going to sort out the food supplies as I'm sure Sandy won't have thought about that. Any requests for tea?"

"I'll eat anything," replied Tony.

"He's not joking either," laughed Danni.

"Oi!" he said, trying to sound hurt as he grabbed two more biscuits from the tray before Sarah left. He offered one to Danni, but she shook her head.

"Suit yourself," he said as he polished them both off.

Sandy came back through and looked out the window as Bob and Adam's car headed down the drive. "I'm just going to check out the sleeping arrangements," he said as he walked through the door. There was a bathroom at the bottom of the stairs which was in need of some renovation. The window was filled with condensation and there was mould around the window frame from the damp. There was a shower over the bath, but the taps were showing signs of rust and the shower curtain had seen better days. The floor was green linoleum that was warped in places, again probably due to the damp. *Great.* He wondered how long they would be holed up here.

He headed up the stairs; the third and fifth stair creaked as he put his weight on them. Upstairs there was a bedroom at each end of the landing and a toilet in between them with a wash basin. The decor was dated like the rest of the cottage. Flowery patterned wallpaper, and not the sort that was currently in vogue. He reckoned an older couple must live here and his thoughts were confirmed when he looked in the wardrobe and saw the style of clothing. Corduroy trousers and checked shirts in one side and old wifey dresses and cardigans in the other. After checking out both bedrooms he headed back downstairs to the others.

"Well it's nae exactly een o those boutique style hotels, and it winna be getting five stars on TripAdvisor fae me, but it ill dee for noo."

Tony had stoked up the fire and the room was already starting to take on a warm hue.

"It's much warmer in here than up 'i stairs," said Sandy. "I hope 'i heating kicks in soon or ye ah'll be needing a het water bottle."

"Sandy, give me a hand getting the tea on, will you?" said Sarah as she peered around the kitchen door.

"The devil's work is never deen," he said as he followed her through.

Tony had a feeling that she wanted to discuss them rather than actually make the tea, but he wasn't bothered as it meant she had freed up the space next to Danni on the settee. He threw another log on the fire and sat down next to Danni.

"Stop hogging the blanket," he said as he pulled the end of the throw from Danni over his legs.

"Do you think we will be safe here?" asked Danni.

"Of course," he replied, a little too quickly. "Who's going to be looking for us way out here? This must be the end of the world," he joked.

Chapter Thirty-Six

That night they ate a meal of pork chops, mashed potatoes and green beans, which was expertly cooked by Sarah. Then they sat round the fire and played a game of cards with a pack that they found in a sideboard drawer. Tony had won every round so far, but Danni wasn't really concentrating, she had too much going on in her head, thoughts swarming around about what had happened yesterday.

"You must be a ringer," said Sandy as he lost yet another hand to Tony. "Get dealing son, 'cos I need te win at least ae hand afore I retire fir 'i night."

Danni excused herself at this point and walked over to the conservatory window. It was pitch black outside, dark like she had never seen before. There was no streetlight pollution and in the cloudless skies she could clearly see the stars. She couldn't remember the last time she had just gazed up into the universe and beyond. It was humbling and made her feel at peace. The last time she had seen the stars like this had probably been when she was on holiday with Mark. *Agghhh. Mark.* Why was he constantly popping into her head? How could she get rid of him for good? She had enough to get her head around right now without him adding to the complications.

"Honey, come away from the window," said Sarah as she motioned for Danni to return to the party.

"I think I'm done for the night," said Danni as she stifled a yawn. "I'm going to head up to bed."

"Here, let me get you a hot water bottle to take up with you. Sandy found a couple when he was upstairs before. I'm not sure this house is very well insulated, and I don't want you freezing and catching your death while you're here."

Sarah walked through to the kitchen and switched on the kettle.

"I'll come up with you," said Tony.

"No, you stay here and finish your game, you're obviously on a winning streak," replied Danni.

"If you're sure." Tony had already returned his attention back to his hand, and he had a sneaking feeling that it was another winning one.

Sarah returned to the living room with a hot water bottle that was covered in a pink fluffy cover and handed it to Danni.

"Thanks," she said as she hugged it against her stomach and headed upstairs.

"Take 'i room on 'i right," said Sandy. "It's the 'master bedroom', if there is such ae thing here. Think it ill be 'i maist comfortable. The heating is on an''i radiator is working but it's nae geein oot much heat, like."

"I'll be fine with this," replied Danni over her shoulder.

"I'll be up later to heat you up," joked Tony. "I'm like a human hot water bottle, or so I've been told!"

Danni turned right at the top of the stairs and walked into the 'master bedroom'. It was a small room with just enough space for the double bed, two bedside tables and a chest of drawers. There was a built-in wardrobe with sliding doors. She had a look inside but didn't see what she was looking for. She opened a drawer and found some men's T-shirts. She took one out and held it up against her. It was huge and would cover her modesty. That would do to sleep in. She slipped out of her clothes and into the T-shirt and got under the covers. The bed was freezing. Thank goodness for the hot water bottle, as there was no electric blanket to switch on. She lay there, hugging the bottle for a few minutes before she jumped out of the bed, grabbed her socks and put them back on. It may not be the most attractive look, but she didn't care. She needed to feel warm. Anyway, who would see her? The bottle was starting to heat up the bed and she found herself dozing off quite quickly. The past couple of days had definitely taken their toll.

Tony snuck up the stairs a few hours later, having taken Sandy for every penny he had on him. A whole £22.37. Danni was sound asleep when he looked in on her. He was torn as to whether to sleep in the same room or take the bed in the room down the hall. He looked in there, but he could feel the cold air as he opened the door and decided against it. He didn't want to disturb Danni, so he lay down on the bed next to her under a couple of blankets he found in the top of the wardrobe. He too had been given a hot water bottle by Sarah; his one blue in contrast to Danni's pink one. Like Danni, it didn't take him long to fall asleep either.

*

Danni could hear him shouting after her. She was running, running for her life. Up the hill, into the trees. She had to hide. How did he find her here? They said she would be safe! They were supposed to protect her! Why was no-one coming to her rescue? She was on her own out here. Just her and HIM! She made it to the trees and looked back over her shoulder but there was no sign of him… yet. He was playing with her, stalking her like a cat stalks its prey.

"I will find you, and when I do, I'm going to enjoy every second. I've waited a long time for this, Louise, or Danni, or whatever you're calling yourself these days. It will be worth the wait when I see your face and you realise what I'm going to do to you!"

Danni scrambled up the bank, off the path, trying to hide her tracks. She moved from tree to tree trying to find a hiding place. How could they let this happen? She was supposed to be under police protection. Were they all in on this? Had Mark got to them too? Was this all part of the plan so he could get to her?

She was out of breath; she couldn't run any further. She crouched down, her back against a tree trunk. Maybe he would give up. Maybe he wouldn't find her. But how would she be sure to truly escape from him? He had found her despite her best efforts, and allegedly those of Police Scotland. Would she ever be safe? She could hear him nearby; he was getting closer. She closed her eyes and held her breath. Tears began to run down her cheeks. Was this it? Was this the end? She knew he would hurt her, like she had hurt him. How dare she humiliate him like that?

It all went quiet. She couldn't hear him now. Had he wandered away from her? Was she safe after all?

As she dared to open her eyes, a hand reached out and touched her shoulder.

*

Danni screamed and struck out with both fists, punching Tony in the face with one hand and knocking the bedside lamp to the floor with the other.

"AGGHHHH!" screamed Tony, clutching his nose and leaping out of bed. "What the fuck!"

As the bedside lamp smashed on the floor, Sarah came running in, gun drawn and pointing from Tony to Danni and back again. When she was confident there was no-one else in the room, she slotted her gun back in its holster and ran to Danni, who was now cowering on the floor in a ball, arms over her head, sobbing.

"What happened?"

"I only touched her on the shoulder to see if she was still asleep and she punched me in the face!" said Tony through his fingers as he held onto his nose. He removed one hand to reveal blood.

"Fuck, that hurts!" he mumbled as he went through to the bathroom to clean himself up, almost bumping into Sandy who had come running up the stairs to see what the hell was going on. He looked questioningly at Tony.

"Don't ask!" he said as Sandy walked past him and into the bedroom.

Sarah was on the floor, hugging Danni to her chest and rocking back and forth to comfort her.

"Shh, it's OK, it was just a bad dream," she said as she wiped the tears from Danni's cheeks.

"What the hell…" But Sandy didn't get to finish his sentence as he got that look from Sarah that told him to shut the fuck up.

He backed out of the room and headed down to the bathroom to see if Tony was OK. Tony was leaning over the sink, the taps running as droplets of blood fell from his nose, leaving red streaks down the white porcelain sink.

Sandy grabbed a wad of toilet roll and gave it to Tony to clear up the blood and try to stem the bleeding.

"Fit the hell did ye dee te her?"

"I literally just touched her on the shoulder and she lashed out and punched me right on the nose."

"Well ye winna dee at again in a hurry, will ye?"

Tony continued trying to plug his nose with toilet paper, but the bloodstream was too heavy.

"I'll ging an' see if there is awny ice."

Sandy came back a few minutes later with a bag of frozen peas.

"Here, try this," he said as he handed the bag to Tony.

Tony nodded his thanks to him and held the bag, that was wrapped in a tea towel, to his nose.

He headed back through to the bedroom to see how Danni was. Sarah and Danni were sitting on the edge of the bed and Danni seemed to have calmed down.

Sarah looked round as he entered. "It was just a bad dream; she thought she was being chased by Mark. Who's Mark?"

"Long story," he replied.

Sarah looked questioningly at him waiting for a further explanation, but it wasn't forthcoming. Tony just shook his head as though to say, not now.

"I see," said Sarah, as she put her arm around Danni again to comfort her. "Just give us a minute, will you?"

"Sure, I'll be downstairs. I'll see if there is any more ice in the freezer!"

*

When Danni and Sarah appeared downstairs a few minutes later, Tony was sat on the settee and Sandy was in the kitchen making toast and waiting for the kettle to boil.

"Yiv some right hook there, quine," he shouted through as he heard them enter the living room. "Yell be needin some food te build up yer strength. I've pit on 'i toast, but if yer needin oonything maire then ye'll hae to ask Sarah nicely as I'm nae exactly a dab hand in the kitchen."

Danni went over to Tony who was sitting in the settee, the frozen bag of peas pressed firmly to his nose.

"I'm so sorry," she said. "Can you forgive me?" She was wrapped in a long pink dressing gown.

"I guess so," Tony replied, "so long as I don't need plastic surgery to retain my boyish good looks." He laughed and then wished he hadn't, as a ball of red snot dripped from his nose. He wiped up the snot with a wad of toilet paper that was becoming decidedly more red than white.

Sandy came through with a tray of toast, butter, jam and four mugs of coffee. He placed them on the table and told everyone to help themselves. Tony grabbed one of the mugs of coffee and passed it to Danni, taking another for himself.

"Thank you," she said rather sheepishly, still feeling bad for what had happened after being woken from her nightmare.

Sandy and Sarah took their mugs and walked back through to the kitchen to give them a minute to themselves.

"I really thought you were... him," she said, not wanting to utter Mark's name. "That dream was so realistic, I thought he had found me, and he had chased me into the woods out the back of the house. I was petrified."

"It's OK, honestly, I forgive you. This guy must have really scared you."

"Let's not speak about... him. We've got enough to contend with, what with the Russians, and so far, he is only in my dreams – or should I say nightmares – and hopefully that is where he will stay.

Chapter Thirty-Seven

They spent the next week at the cottage with various officers coming and going. Sandy and Sarah spent a lot of time with them but even they needed some days off. When the weather was dry, which wasn't very often, they went outside and climbed up the hill at the back, up through the trees to the top where there were stunning views of the surrounding countryside. They were never really alone though, as there was always one officer within sight of them at all times. The police still only had one of the Russians in custody and, despite their best efforts, they had been unable to track down the others. They still considered the threat to Danni and Tony to be too great to leave them on their own. But soon came some more positive news as there were reports of one more of the Russians being captured and they had tracked down the leader, Boris Petrov. He had fled back to his hometown of Moscow and they were in the process of negotiating his extradition to face murder charges but weren't hopeful for a quick resolution on this, given his Russian connections. They had set up a Major Investigation Team and had had to call in the Serious Crime Squad for their assistance. Officers had been arriving from London and Glasgow to assist with the serious nature of the crime. The deaths of David Gordon, Becky and the oil workers on the South Platform were all being treated as murder, and the Russians would be facing charges on that basis.

Over the past few days, there were reports of seven more survivors and several more bodies that had been pulled from the water. The process of identifying them and informing the relatives was underway. Danni didn't know if it was better to be told your loved one's body had been found so that you could properly start the grieving process, or to remain in denial over whether they had died as their body had yet to be recovered. Specialist floating barges and cranes had been brought in to try to retrieve parts of the platform that was now resting on the seabed in a watery grave of twisted, burnt metal. The accommodation block had been located by the use of ROVs, as it was too dangerous to send divers down, and plans were in place to recover it back to surface sometime in the early new year.

Scotty had been out to visit Danni and Tony on a couple of occasions. He got a lift out with some of his colleagues when they were swapping over babysitting duties, as his right arm was still in plaster and he couldn't yet drive, although he had been told it was healing nicely. The drugs were keeping the pain at bay, but he was still managing to bash his arm off anything and everything. He had been able to bring out Tony's rucksack and some clothes and toiletries from Danni's flat that a female PC had packed for him. The forensic team had finished going over the flat with a fine-tooth comb and, despite their best efforts, unfortunately they had not come up with any concrete evidence that the Russians had been there. However, the investigation team had found images from nearby CCTV cameras showing two individuals entering the building and leaving shortly afterwards. They were wearing long coats, similar to the ones the Russians had worn when they arrived at the offices when the platform had exploded, but they had scarves up over their faces and they never directly faced the cameras, so it would be difficult to identify them.

On New Year's Eve, Scotty had some important news to pass on. "Good news," he said.

Well, it depended how you looked at it, really. It was good news for the police as they were getting ready to bring the Russians to court. It probably wasn't such good news for Danni and Tony as it would mean them having to go to court as witnesses. Danni in particular was not looking forward to the trial. The media would be all over it like a rash. It was all that was being talked about in the news on the TV and the radio. That and the usual top ten of everything that always followed Christmas, and the round-ups of the year. She had managed to keep herself away from prying eyes since the incident, but now she was going to leave herself wide open to being spotted on the TV by Mark. It would be difficult to avoid the cameras although she had been reassured by Scotty that both her and Tony would be ushered in and out of court through the back doors for security reasons. She didn't feel particularly reassured by that! What did he mean by 'security reasons'? Were they still thought of as targets for the Russians? If they were out of the picture, then would the case collapse due to lack of witnesses? She had heard about the Russian mafia before; would they be looking to take out the trash, so to speak? Snipers on the rooftops overlooking the court? She didn't know who she was more scared of, the Russians or Mark? Either one was a scary prospect. But that was going to be a few weeks away yet while the police finished all their investigations and submitted all their evidence.

That night, on New Year's Eve, they were happy to celebrate the end of the year and the start of what would hopefully be a much less eventful one, court case aside! It was still a quiet celebration, in the cottage with Sandy and Sarah, who had returned that day after a few days off. Danni had managed to catch Scotty on his own as he was leaving one day previously and asked if they could collect the bottle of whisky that she had bought as a present for Tony and bring it out to the cottage. Sandy had brought the bottle of single malt – much to Tony's delight – and Sarah had a bottle of champagne. They would be allowed a glass or two to see in the New Year despite being on duty. Well, who would know anyway, apart from Danni and Tony? There was no-one to see them out here! Sarah and Danni fixed a feast of party food for the evening. The typical fare you would have on New Year's Eve. Sausage rolls, cocktail sausages, cheesy bites, there was even some smoked salmon and cream cheese on blinis.

"Wow, Police Scotland are certainly pushing the boat out for their star witnesses," joked Tony as he picked up another sausage roll and stuffed it in his mouth whole, wiping pastry crumbs from his shirt.

"Don't get too excited," replied Sarah. "It all came from the sale aisle at Asda. Everything has a best before date of 1st January, so you better eat up as I don't like waste!"

"There's no need to worry with the human hoover over there," said Danni. "He'll eat anything, whether it's in date or not!"

"Oi, that's a bit harsh," replied Tony.

"Harsh but true," joked Danni.

Spending the last week in the company of Tony, and their minders, she had got to know him a lot better, and what she saw, she liked. They were never left alone, so their conversations had been fairly generic, but she felt safe having him around. They continued to share the same bed, albeit not under the same covers, but she wanted him to be near her, to look after her, protect her. She had also managed not to punch him in the face again, despite having some crazy dreams.

They spent the evening playing board games with the TV on in the background. They stopped their game of Monopoly when Jools Holland's *Hootenanny* came on, which Tony was happy about, because for once he was not winning. They saw in the New Year by raising a glass – Sandy and Tony with whisky, Sarah and Danni with champagne – as they counted down to the bells. At the stroke of midnight, they all shouted, "Happy New Year," then hugged and kissed each other in turn, the men shaking hands. As Danni leaned in to peck Tony on the cheek, he moved at the last second causing her to kiss him on the lips. She drew back, shocked, her cheeks flushing red with embarrassment. Although she was embarrassed, she was secretly glad he had done that as she had been wanting to kiss him for some time now. Ever since the kiss in the flat on Christmas Eve.

They sat next to each other on the settee and watched the firework display live from London. Danni saw the London Eye, the Houses of Parliament and Tower Bridge and started to feel homesick. She picked up the remote control and switched the channel over to STV to watch the Edinburgh celebrations instead.

Tony gave her a funny look as to why she had suddenly changed the channel.

"Sorry, just wanted to keep the celebrations Scottish this year," she said, trying to find an explanation that didn't solicit any further suspicion.

"Nae problem, quine," said Sandy. "They Southerners dinna ken how te celebrate Hogmanay like the Scots onywaie!"

They stayed up till around 2am, drinking and chatting about nothing in particular with the TV turned down in the background. They got onto the subject of holidays. Sarah mentioned she had been allowed to carry over some annual leave due to working over the Christmas period and she was planning to get away to the sun with her husband as soon as the court case was over. Sandy was retiring that year, so he would have all the time in the world to travel around Britain in his motor home with his long-suffering wife. She would prefer to head to the continent, but Sandy was a home bird and wasn't interested in eating all that foreign muck. Danni said she wanted to get far, far away from here, heading west and definitely avoiding Russia as a holiday destination anytime soon! She fancied travelling along Route 66 and Tony's eyes lit up at this as that was something he had always wanted to do too. Maybe they could go together. If they survived the court case, of course!

When the conversation around holidays came to an end, Sandy and Sarah started to tidy up and Danni and Tony headed upstairs to bed. Danni was a little tipsy from the champagne. She had drunk most of the bottle as Sarah had only had one glass to see in the New Year. Tony helped her upstairs, as she was a little unsteady on her feet. She hadn't had anything to drink since Christmas Eve and was still suffering a little from the aftereffects of the morphine.

As they got ready for bed, Tony pulled out the blankets he had been sleeping under from the wardrobe shelf.

"You won't need them," said Danni as she threw back the bed covers and invited him into the bed.

"Are you sure?" asked Tony.

"Yes, but no funny business, because there are two armed officers downstairs," joked Danni.

Danni got into the bed, shivering as the coldness of the sheets touched her skin. She was wearing a nightshirt that had been brought from her flat.

Tony jumped in and snuggled up to Danni, placing his arm around her.

"You're freezing."

"And you're roasting."

"I told you I was a human hot water bottle. See what you've been missing all these days we've been here?"

Danni held his hand and pulled him close to her, pressing her back into his stomach and feeling the warmth of his body against hers. She wasn't going to need her fluffy pink hot water bottle tonight!

Chapter Thirty-Eight

"I can't do this anymore. It was OK before I got to really know her, but not now."

"What do you mean, you can't do this? You owe me big time, pal. Do I need to remind you what happened in Iraq?"

"Look, mate, I know what you did for me out there, but this is just… it's wrong. She's a nice girl, she doesn't deserve this."

"Nice girls don't run off and humiliate their boyfriend. You don't know what she did to me. She made me a laughing stock at the station. She has to pay."

"I'm sorry, mate, but I can't do this. I can't pretend to be her friend, knowing what you have planned."

"You've fallen for her, haven't you? She's sucked you in, like she did to me. She gets under your skin."

"It's not like that. I can't lie to her anymore. I'm out."

"Well you better watch your back then, because what I had planned for her is nothing compared to what will be waiting for you. You know what happens to people who double-cross me. What happened in Iraq will be like playschool. Anyway, I don't need your help anymore. I know where she is now and, thanks to you, I can track her every move. Just make sure you don't get in my way."

Mark hung up and punched the wall, scaring a WPC who was walking down the corridor of the station. He was enraged, absolutely fuming. *That's two people who are going to get what's coming to them.*

Chapter Thirty-Nine

Danni awoke, having had a great night's sleep. She had felt safe knowing that Tony was there with her. But where was he now? She hadn't heard him leave the bedroom. She got up and opened the curtains. Daylight was still coming in, but she could see he was outside on the driveway, on the phone to someone. He looked annoyed, like he was arguing with them. He hung up and thrust his phone back into his pocket and kicked the fence, shouted, "Fuck!" then kicked the fence again. Danni had no idea what that was about. She moved away from the window, so he didn't see her.

By the time she got dressed and went downstairs, he was back inside lighting the fire. Sarah was in the kitchen making breakfast. She didn't know whether to ask Tony about the phone call or just pretend she hadn't seen him. If it was anything important, she was sure he would tell her. *Wouldn't he?* After all, they had become close. This whole sorry situation had thrust them together, more than they had been before it all kicked off. They were partners in crime, for want of a better metaphor! She decided to leave it. Maybe it was to do with his estranged wife and she really didn't want to hear about her.

Sandy walked into the living room. "I've jist bin on 'i blower tae heid office. The folks that bide here are hame 'i morn so we'll hae to move ye te anither safehoose."

Danni was visibly upset at the prospect of moving. She had enjoyed her time at the cottage, well, as much as you could enjoy it when you were on the run from the Russians under police guard!

"Dinna worry yersel, quine, we've anither place nae far awa that we can ging te."

"He's right," said Sarah as she came through from the kitchen carrying a tray of mugs. "There's a safehouse about twenty miles away from here that I've been to before and believe me, it's a lot more mod-con than here. I think you will like it. At least it's got central heating that works, and the bathroom window doesn't have ice on the inside!"

Danni didn't want to leave. She had felt safe here, safer than she had in a long time and that was saying something considering the circumstances.

That afternoon, they packed up what few belongings they had and travelled north to the new safehouse. It was a much more modern-looking house, a steading conversion. Still quaint but not a chocolate box cottage like the first place. Sarah was right, it did have all mod-cons. A boiler that worked and hot water as soon as you turned on the tap. Fully double-glazed and decorated in a modern but boring magnolia throughout. There were no signs of life here, though. No decorations or Christmas cards. No photos on the mantlepiece or pictures on the walls. No-one had actually lived here for a long time. It was a house that was rented long-term by Police Scotland for people who found themselves in similar circumstances to Danni and Tony and needed somewhere safe to stay before fronting up to their demons in court. This was to be their home for the next few weeks, until it was their turn to face their demons. With it being multiple murder charges, they would be heading to the High Court, but thankfully they had got a date in Aberdeen, so they wouldn't have to head down the road to Edinburgh. D-day would be the 4th February, just over four weeks away. Only four weeks to hide from the Russians and try to stay alive!

*

Those four weeks went past faster than Danni had expected. Probably because she wasn't looking forward to having to go to court and face the Russians and recount what they had done. Becky's funeral had been held just after New Year and Sarah had gone to it on behalf of Danni. They said it just wasn't safe for her to attend in person. It wasn't as though she had even liked Becky, in fact the exact opposite was true. Becky had made her life a misery at work, but nobody deserved to die like that and, having been with her when she died, Danni felt a sense of duty to her. The funeral was held at the crematorium in Hazelhead in the West Chapel, the larger of the two chapels. Sarah recounted that it was standing room only and in fact there were people standing outside. Of course, the TV crews had drawn the crowds and every Tom, Dick and Harry had been there, even though they didn't really know Becky. Folks from her childhood turned up. Some people would do anything to get on the TV nowadays. Reality TV really did have something to answer for. People who had allegedly been her best friends from school broke down in fake tears when the cameras pointed their way and were only too happy to give an interview about how wonderful she was and how tragic her death had been, live on TV, of course.

This is what Danni dreaded. If the media frenzy was like this for Becky's funeral, what on earth was it going to be like for the court case? There was no way she was going to be able to keep her face out of the news. The police had told her they would keep her safe, but how would they protect her from one of their own? She knew how devious he could be, how he could charm his way in. Is that not what he had done with her? If she had had any idea what he was really like she would have stayed well clear. But he was a charmer, a smooth talker. That was how he had been with her, before he started to show his true colours. Nobody really knew what he was capable of as she had kept that hidden too. Afraid of what people would think of her. Ashamed. He had made her feel so helpless, so irrelevant, like she couldn't live without him. But she had proved him wrong and this was why she was now so worried. She had kept hidden from him all this time, but what with the circumstances she now found herself in, could she really keep hidden from him any longer?

Since they had moved to the new safehouse, Tony had seemed somewhat distant with her. Nothing she could really put her finger on, it was just a feeling she had. When she confronted him about it, he laughed it off and just said he was worried about going to court, wasn't she? Then he would change the subject. But she knew there was something going on. She didn't know for sure, but she thought it had something to do with that phone call before they left the cottage. He was still sleeping in the same room as her, but he had chosen to sleep on a camp bed rather than in her bed. She wondered what she had done wrong. She thought they had a connection, that they were getting closer, but now it felt like they were drifting further apart. Maybe it was just with the court date getting closer, but her instinct told her there was more to it than that. She didn't push it, though, they were both under enough stress without her causing any more. Mark had always told her she was insecure. Maybe he had been right.

Chapter Forty

On the morning of their first day in court, they got up early and dressed in appropriate attire. Danni wore a black, below-knee dress with capped sleeves that matching suit jacket, and Tony a dark grey suit, white shirt and blue tie. Danni had not been able to eat anything, only just managing to force down a cup of strong black coffee. Tony had eaten half of a plate of porridge but played with the remainder of it until it went cold and congealed. It seemed that even his appetite was stifled today. They were driven to court in separate cars for security reasons, they were told. Both were black Range Rovers with blacked-out windows and they were accompanied by armed guards. They were to take different routes into town and were followed by unmarked police cars, the occupants of which were also armed. They had been told this was just as a precaution, but what they didn't know is that there was intelligence to suggest that an attempt could be made on the lives of the star witnesses.

As they reached the outskirts of Aberdeen, a call came through on the police radio. Change of plan. They were to be redirected to the Sherriff Court. A suspicious package had been found at the High Court, which was being evacuated as they weren't taking any chances.

The Russians would not be expecting them to change location at the last minute, so it would be safer there. Everyone who needed to know would be contacted.

Danni felt sick, physically sick, like she could throw up at any minute, despite her stomach being empty. She could feel the bile starting to build up in her throat. She swallowed hard. The one good thing about the last-minute change of venue meant that the press would probably still be waiting at the High Court, so they would be able to bypass them quite easily today. She should be thankful for small mercies.

They pulled up outside the rear entrance to the Sherriff Court, more normally frequented by Aberdeen's criminal element who were transported over from the holding cells at Queen Street Station. Danni was ushered in quickly. The police cordon was armed and ready for action, observing in every direction, including the roofs above. She looked up at the steep turrets of the court house casting judgement down on the unworthy below.

She was taken through to the witness waiting room. The clean, cold, grey granite facade and the marble-effect floor aided the echoes of the conversations of those already present. Other witnesses, solicitors and police officers. All gathered together awaiting that fateful call to the courtroom, waiting to give evidence in their respective cases. The bright light cascaded down from the glass roof of the atrium, teasing those imprisoned within with visions of blue sky and sunshine, ironically not a day you wanted to be stuck inside in Aberdeen. There were all sorts in that room. Families comforting each other, business-like men and woman constantly glued to their phones and iPads, reading emails and checking their Facebook pages and rueing the day they had come forward as a witness. Others sitting and staring in shock, some of them in tears, the nerves of what they were waiting to encounter clearly visible on their faces. Little did they know the agony that lay in wait for them, sitting on hard chairs and losing precious hours of their lives.

The solicitors, with their piles of brown folders diligently reviewing case notes with highlighters to hand, were all wearing black robes which hung off their shoulders. The robes reminded Danni of a maths teacher from her school who was feared by all his pupils. He had been nicknamed Batman as he was known to belt pupils by having them stand at one end of the maths block while he took a run at them down the corridor, swinging the belt with his black cloak flowing behind him like a superhero cape.

The police officers were reading through their notebooks with the lined yellow pages reminding themselves of the details of a statement they took months before. Their hats were removed, sitting upside down in a circle on the table. Witnesses nervously looked around as people came and went. Were they willing their assailants to plead guilty at the last minute or settle out of court?

The door opened and finally Tony arrived. He walked quickly towards her, sitting down next to her and grabbing hold of her hand.

"Well that was an interesting ride in," he said. "I don't know about your journey, but we were diverted on the way here. I wasn't sure I was going to see you again!"

"I didn't think you would be too worried about that," said Danni as she pulled her hand free from his.

"What do you mean? Of course I want to see you."

"Well you haven't been too bothered about me these past few weeks at the safehouse." Danni knew this was not the time to be having this conversation, but her emotions were taking over and she couldn't hold them back any longer. Everything was boiling to the surface.

"I don't understand, what do you mean?"

Danni turned away from him, giving him the cold shoulder.

"Hey, what's up? If I've done something wrong, then you'll have to tell me what it is."

"You've been cold and distant towards me since we left the cottage. Since you took that phone call."

"What phone call?"

"You know what phone call."

Tony searched his mind, trying to think what she was referring to. It suddenly dawned on him that she must have seen him that morning. But how could she know who he had been talking to? She had no way of knowing that. *Best just to play dumb*, he thought. *Besides, this was not the time nor the place to get into what had really been going on.*

"The morning we left the cottage, I saw you outside. You were on the phone and you were angry. You kicked the fence. You didn't see me at the window. You've been funny with me ever since. Who were you talking to? Your wife?"

"My wife?" he questioned. *Though, wait a minute, that was as good an excuse as any right now.*

"Erm, yes, it was my soon to be ex-wife. She's started divorce proceedings. I didn't want to discuss it because I've got enough going on at the moment without this added complication."

"Oh, right. I'm sorry. I didn't realise." Danni felt a little bit stupid now for being so jealous and so insecure. *That explained why he hadn't been himself, been so reserved.*

She took his hand in hers and stroked it. Now she understood.

Tony hoped she believed him, because the truth was a totally different matter and she was not going to be so understanding when she found that out.

There was an announcement over the PA system.

"Will the witnesses in the cases against Anderson, McDonald, Kowalski and Andronikov please report to reception."

Most of the people in the witness room slowly started to funnel out to the reception desk, leaving only a few others behind.

Sarah arrived, pushing through the crowds and made her way over to them.

"What's going on?" asked Tony.

"They have cancelled all the other cases for today since we have had to move over here. It's a security precaution, both for them and for you. It's easier for us to keep you safe when we can control how many other people are allowed into the building."

"Thanks!" said Tony. "That makes me feel so much better!"

They waited impatiently as the witnesses for the other cases were released from their hell.

Danni looked around nervously, catching the eye of another woman. They smiled and quickly looked away, not wanting to hold eye contact, the woman staring back at her phone as though some very important message that urgently needed her attention had come through. The door to the atrium swung back and fore as everyone apart from those involved in the case against Moskaneft left. Several of them joining those chain-smoking at the front door to the imposing granite building, cigarette ends littering the pavement despite bins being available either side of the door. An advert for

Aberdeen's most wanted, or least wanted, depending on how you looked at it. The great unwashed who had been waiting to be called into trial were set free for another day.

It was now several hours since they had left the safehouse and Danni's belly was starting to rumble. Sarah heard it and offered to get them something from the cafe. She returned with paper cups of coffee stacked in a cardboard carry tray and dropped several brown paper bags on the table in front of them.

"I didn't know what you would like so I got a selection."

"Thanks," said Tony as he reached for the bags and started looking inside them to see what delights had been brought. There were croissants and Danish pastries, but Tony settled on a buttery smothered with butter.

"I still don't know how you could eat those things," said Danni. "It's like a heart attack looking at you."

He just smiled and stuffed a bit more into his mouth.

Danni picked at a dry croissant. Despite her belly rumbling, she wasn't sure she could keep anything down.

Sandy came over to join them. "Ony of these got my name on them?" he asked as he began checking out the bags.

"Oi, they are supposed to be for the witnesses," replied Sarah as she smacked his hand away from them.

"Help yourself," replied Danni. "You can have my share."

"Cheers, quine, I ken't ye wouldna let me doon."

He picked up a custard Danish and bit into it, sending bits of flaky pastry falling all down his suit. He smiled at her as he removed them with a flick of his hand.

Sarah was called over to speak to one of her colleagues. She came back moments later looking a bit serious.

"Nothing to worry about, but they are going to move us to another room. They've assessed the area and this room is not as secure as they would like."

Danni and Tony looked at each other, clearly concerned.

"It's just a precaution," said Sarah, trying to put them at ease.

"Everything seems to be a precaution today," replied Tony, trying not to show his unease.

Chapter Forty-One

Tony and Danni were ushered from the witness waiting room, out the rear exit, up some stairs and into a much smaller waiting room with a well-worn, faded red carpet and had oak panelling on the walls. There were no windows and only one door in and out. Danni felt quite claustrophobic, like the walls were going to close in on her. At least the chairs were more comfortable. Old-style leather seats with a bit more padding than the chairs of torture in the witness room.

"We'll be back shortly, we're away to see if we can find out what is happening and when you will get taken through to the court room," said Sarah. "Some of the other investigating officers might pop in just to check some details with you. Nothing to worry about."

With that she and Sandy walked out and left them alone. It was probably the first time they had really been left alone in a long time.

Danni and Tony sat in silence, glancing at each other and smiling, then dropping eye contact. They felt awkward with each other, not at ease like they had at the cottage or before all this had happened. Danni didn't know what had changed, but she could sense something was different.

Eventually Tony broke the silence.

"Danni, there is something you need to know. I don't know how to tell you this and you have to believe me when I say I never wanted it to work out like this. At the start I thought I was doing the right thing, repaying a debt, but as I got to know you… well, I just can't be part of this any longer."

"What? I don't understand. What are you saying? You don't want to be with me? Is that why you've been so distant recently?" *Here we go*, thought Danni. *I'm about to get the brush off.*

"No, it's not that. It's… well… it's complicated… please, just hear me out. I need to explain, and it's a long story."

He took her by the hand and motioned for her to sit. He sat next to her, still holding her hand and looked into her eyes. How was she ever going to forgive him? He had broken her trust in a way that was unforgiveable.

He couldn't bring himself to tell her, but at the same time he couldn't go on living this lie.

"What is it, Tony? You're starting to scare me now."

He couldn't find the words.

"I, erm, I made a promise to a friend, a friend from way back when I was in the army." He cut off, trying to think of the right words to say. There were no right words.

"And?"

"And…"

The door eased open and they both looked up, expecting Sarah or Sandy to be there, but it was neither of them.

"Hello, Louise, or should I say, Danni? That is what you are calling yourself nowadays, isn't it?"

"MARK!"

Danni jumped from her seat and instinctively stepped backwards, trying to put as much distance between him and her as possible.

"It's been a while. I would say you're looking good, but we both know that's not true." He laughed as he shut the door behind him.

"But how did you…? They said I would be safe…"

Mark looked towards Tony and back at Danni.

"Didn't your new friend tell you? No, of course he didn't. He wanted you for himself. He was trying to back out of our agreement."

Danni stared at Tony; tears were building up in her eyes. She reached for the guardian angel around her neck and held it tight.

"What is he talking about? Tony…?"

Tony couldn't look at her. He sat there, hanging his head.

"What? You didn't actually think that he liked you, did you? Oh, you did! Oh boy, he really did a number on you. How could you think that anyone could fancy someone like you? Someone who is fat, ugly and pathetic."

She continued to clutch the angel, like it would bring her strength. Protect her.

"There's no point counting on that to save you," said Mark, pointing towards the angel. "That is what guided me to you, you stupid bitch. There's a tracker inside it. I've been monitoring your movements since he gave it to you."

"Tony, what is he saying?" Danni backed away from both of them. Her back was against the wood-panelled wall.

Tony finally looked up and faced her. "I'm sorry," he mumbled. "I was trying to tell you… trying to explain. But it's not like he said."

"It's exactly like I said," replied Mark. "He's been working for me. Worming his way in so I could keep track of everything you were doing. Keeping an eye on you until I had the opportunity to see you face to face for myself."

Mark moved towards her. Danni couldn't back up any further, but Tony stood up, placing himself between them. He held out his hand towards Mark.

"Leave her alone."

"You don't tell me what to do." He pushed Tony's arm aside.

"I said, leave her alone." Tony made a move towards Mark and pushed him backwards with both arms.

"You will regret the day you crossed me."

Mark took a swing at him, but Tony ducked and punched Mark hard in the stomach. He fell to the floor on all fours, groaning.

"Quick, Danni, get out of here."

Tony grabbed Danni's arm and tried to pull her towards the door.

Danni stood firm. She was in shock. She pulled her arm away from Tony.

"You were working for him? None of this was real?"

"No, it's not like that, I was trying to explain. It started out that way, but then I got to know you and I told him this had to stop."

"This, you gave me this." Danni ripped the guardian angel from her neck, breaking the chain and throwing it to the floor. "You said this would protect me, but all the time he was tracking me. He knew where I was, and you were helping him. I told you what he did to me."

"And when you did, I understood what he was like. He's a bully. He was blackmailing me. There are things that happened in Iraq that you don't understand – don't want to understand

– but he had me over a barrel. If I didn't help him, then he could make my life a misery."

Danni struggled to take it all in. Her head was spinning with thoughts of her and Tony. Why had she not seen what was happening? Had she been blinded by her infatuation with him? How could she have been so stupid? Of course no-one was going to love her. How could they? She was vile, disgusting. That's what Mark had made her feel, made her believe. Memories of their time together flashed through her head. The laughs, the kiss.

"The tattoo!"

She suddenly had a picture of him when he had come out of the shower. She had glanced the tattoo.

"I knew I had seen it before. You were in Iraq together? Brothers in arms?"

This was starting to make sense. How Tony had known Mark. Why he was helping him.

"Yes, but as I got to know you, I knew you weren't like he described, you were not the bitch he made you out to be. I realised it was him that was the problem, not you."

"Well, I hate to break up the reminiscing, but I came here to do a job and intend to carry it out."

They had been too busy trying to make sense of all this that they hadn't been aware that Mark had got to his feet and was now pointing a gun towards them.

Danni screamed.

"There is no point shouting for help. There is no-one outside, they won't hear you. You see the building is being evacuated, as it seems a suspicious package has been found in the court room. I wonder who could have left that there?" He laughed an evil, dirty laugh. "I told your bodyguards I would get you out to safety, and they believed me! How stupid are these Aberdonians? Mind you, who is going to question one of their own?"

Tony instinctively moved in front of Danni to shield her from the gun.

"Don't think I won't shoot you too, after all, your loyalty is questionable at best. We both know that. You've been useful, but now you are surplus to my requirements. In fact, it will be my pleasure to put your traitor ass out of its misery."

He pointed the gun directly at Tony and pulled the trigger. Danni screamed and closed her eyes, but when she opened them, they were both still standing. The chamber had been empty.

Tony flew at Mark and knocked him off his feet. He lay on him and tried to knock the gun from his hand. They struggled on the floor, Mark's fury powering him on. Danni stood there, frozen to the spot, unable to move, to scream, to do anything. They continued to battle, punches landing left and right. In a whirlwind of arms, legs and coats flying, it was difficult to tell which was which.

BANG!

The gun went off and a bullet ricocheted off the wood panelling behind Danni.

They continued to struggle, the gun appearing and then disappearing again as their bodies entangled.

BANG!

The gun went off a second time. They both slumped to the floor. Neither moved.

"NO!" screamed Danni, still frozen, petrified, legs like lead.

What seemed like an eternity passed, but it was only seconds before the door flew open and Sarah and Sandy ran in, weapons drawn. They reccyed the room, seeing Danni in tears and two bodies lying on the floor, not moving. Sarah ran to Danni and put her arms around her while Sandy kicked the two bodies with his foot, trying to figure out which limbs belonged to which. He pushed the top body over onto the floor.

It was Tony, and there was a large red stain on his chest. But he was conscious.

Danni screamed again. "Is he dead?"

Tony looked at his chest; he moved his hand over the pool of blood and his head slumped back to the floor. Sarah left Danni and bent over Tony, feeling for a pulse.

"He's still breathing." She pulled her police radio from her pocket and called for an ambulance.

Meanwhile, Sandy had removed the gun from Mark's hand and made it safe, emptying the bullets from their chamber. The red stain on Mark's abdomen was growing bigger and the blood was starting to pool on the floor next to him. Sandy felt for a pulse but shook his head.

"He's gone," he said, as he closed Mark's eyelids, the way he had done to many others before. It really was time for him to give this up and retire.

A few minutes later the paramedics arrived. They tried to stop the bleeding from Tony's chest by applying pressure, fitted an oxygen mask and gave him something for the pain before quickly scooping him up on to the trolley and disappearing out of the room to the waiting ambulance. Sandy went with them.

Danni was in shock. She stood there shaking. Tears were trickling down her face. What had just happened? Now there was just her, Sarah and HIM in the room.

Mark.

Her nemesis.

The one she had run from, been hiding from for the past year.

Suddenly he didn't look so menacing. Lying there, in a pool of blood. Not moving.

Was her nightmare over? Was she free? He was gone, but still she could not believe it, even though he was lying there in front of her eyes.

Was she going to wake up and find this had all been a vivid dream? A nightmare? Like the ones she had been having since she left him.

Could this be real, the end? No more hiding?

She wanted to believe it, but the way her luck had been lately, she couldn't bring herself to acknowledge the truth. She closed her eyes and pinched herself. But when she opened her eyes she wasn't lying in her bed, with a soft pillow against her head. She was still there, in the court. And he was still there, slumped on the floor, not moving.

Maybe this wasn't a dream after all.

Danni fainted.

Chapter Forty-Two

The ensuing days were made up of hospital stays and more police interviews. Tony was lucky, the bullet had just grazed him and had not hit any major organs or arteries, so he was patched up and allowed to leave the next day. Danni was checked over and apart from suffering from shock, she was given a clean bill of health.

In all the turmoil at the court house, it transpired that the two Russians in custody had somehow got their hands on some arsenic and had poisoned themselves. A suicide pact, or perhaps it was forced upon them. Nobody would ever really know. They had been taken to Aberdeen Royal Infirmary, but one was already dead on arrival and the other died a few hours later. With no-one to answer to the charges and the ongoing saga of attempting to extradite or even track down the other accomplices, the case against the Russians had been put on hold.

Mark had been declared dead at the court house. Tony would not be facing any charges as it was classed as self-defence. The gun had been identified as Mark's police issue firearm and with Tony and Danni's statements it was clear that Mark had made the first move and Tony had been trying to defend Danni. Danni had told the police the whole story about her escape from Mark, moving to Aberdeen to start a new life and changing her name. She still wasn't sure if she would go back to her original name, Louise, or keep Danni, as she had come to like it. She thought she looked more like a Danni, plus it was Danni that had finally defeated him. Going back to Louise would feel like going backwards, and she had no intention of doing that. Louise had been a victim, but Danni was a survivor.

She had spent some time with Tony, who was currently camping out at Scotty's flat until he found a flat of his own to rent. Things had been a little strained to start with as she struggled to come to terms with what he had done. But, at the end of the day, he had saved her life. Risked his life for her. That must say something about his feelings for her? It hadn't been the best start to a new relationship, but in their short time together they had endured a lot, and survived, so surely they could survive anything? Danni thought he might just be worth the chance.

Danni had been allowed back to her flat, which was no longer a crime scene but still looked like one. The police had done their best to tidy up, but there were still things everywhere and those items that had been tidied up had been put in the wrong place. It would take her a few days to straighten things out. Sarah had come by to see her and asked what her plans were for the future. Would she stay in Aberdeen or move back to London? Danni wasn't totally sure, but she thought she might just have a shot at a future with Tony so was going to hang around for now. Sarah asked what she would do for work and told her of a position they were looking to recruit for at Queen Street. It was a counsellor for people who found themselves in similar circumstances to Danni, those who had suffered or were still suffering from domestic abuse. With all Danni had been through, she certainly had the credentials. She told Sarah she would give it some thought but right now she just wanted to take some time off to get her life back into some sort of order. She had managed to make contact with her mother and that had brought great delight to them both. Her mother was booked on a flight in the next few days and she was looking forward to seeing her after all this time.

Having spent some time on her own again, Danni had had time to think things through and to try to make sense of the chaos of recent events. She didn't really believe that she was a puppet in some great masterplan, but it was strange how things worked out. If it was fate, she was a cruel mistress, playing dangerous games with her human puppets. Danni had escaped from one disaster only to find herself embroiled in another. But Danni realised that she had only truly escaped now that Mark was dead. Even if fate had her dancing to a pretty perilous tune, then she, Danni, was going to go on dancing.